"Did he kiss you good-night?"

"What?" Aghast, Jeannie glanced over her shoulder at the twins.

"That's what a man does at the end of a date. He kisses the girl good-night," Mimi explained.

"Yeah, we seen it in lots of movies," Cindy agreed.

"It was not a date." And no kiss. Jeannie's lips tingled with…regret. "And I'm not intending to date Dr. Jake. I've got you two to take care of, remember?"

"But Dr. Jake likes us," Mimi said.

"Yes, he does. But I'm just his office manager. I work for him. That's *all*. Dr. Jake and I aren't dating. If that changes, I'll let you know." *But it won't change.*

"You'll let us know right away?" Mimi asked.

"Yes, you'll be the first to know. So until then— no comments about Dr. Jake and I kissing and dating. Got that?"

"Got it," they repeated in unison.

Jeannie wished she felt some satisfaction, having succeeded in getting this knotty issue all sorted out. She didn't. Kissing Jake sounded very appealing. *Don't go there. Men don't go for package deals. You found that out the hard way—twice already. Got it?*

LYN COTE

and her husband, her real-life hero, became in-laws recently when their son married his true love. Lyn already loves her daughter-in-law and enjoys this new adventure in family stretching. Lyn and her husband still live on the lake in the north woods, where they watch a bald eagle and its young soar and swoop overhead throughout the year. She wishes the best to all her readers. You may email Lyn at l.cote@juno.com or write her at P.O. Box 864, Woodruff, WI 54548. And drop by her blog, www.strongwomenbravestories.blogspot.com, to read stories of strong women in real life and in true-to-life fiction. "Every woman has a story. Share yours."

Daddy in the Making
Lyn Cote

Love Inspired

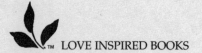 LOVE INSPIRED BOOKS

Recycling programs
for this product may
not exist in your area.

ISBN-13: 978-0-373-87663-1

DADDY IN THE MAKING

www.LoveInspiredBooks.com

Printed in U.S.A.

God made each of us unique and equally valuable to him. We don't earn God's favor. He loves us no matter what, but how wonderful if we accept his love and generously show it to others.
—Ephesians 2:8–10 The Message

Dedicated to my dear friend Eunice
and her "granddog," Ripley, a basset hound
who really likes to ham it up!

Chapter One

Longing for food and then bed, Jake McClure fumed over being forced to delay both. As he jogged through the winter's early darkness toward the church, his basset hound Bummer padded along beside him over the hard-packed snow. Jake slammed the side door behind him, shutting out the below-zero windchill. He paused, his glasses fogged from the temperature change, permitting himself to let the burn of irritation build inside.

Earlier after catching up on voice mails, Jake had felt compelled to come here to find Mike, to see if he'd done harm to himself. Glasses clear, Jake shuffled down the steps, with Bummer trailing behind. The two of them entered the brightly lit church basement, where laughter punctuated cheerful voices of those attending the fundraiser potluck. As he scanned faces for Mike's, several people, many of whom recognized him from his vet practice, greeted him.

Then the door opened behind him, letting in another rush of Arctic wind. Two little girls rushed down the steps.

"We found two kittens!" they shouted. "Out in the snow!"

Jake turned. He saw two little girls so bundled up that little of them showed, except their pink noses and tendrils of blond hair. And in the mittened hands of each little girl, a small golden tabby kitten mewed and shivered. He hurried to them and knelt down on the hard, cold linoleum. "Where did you find these little ones?"

"They were in the snow near where I parked," a tall woman behind the girls replied, her voice low and rich. "Are they okay? It's so cold out and the kittens are so tiny." She dropped to her knees beside him.

"I think their eyes have just opened recently," Jake said. At his elbow, Bummer did something unusual. He licked one kitten and then the other with his big tongue.

"Don't let him bite the kitties!" one of the little girls cried.

Jake held up a hand. "Bummer isn't going to hurt them. Let's see what he does."

Bummer licked the kittens thoroughly. Then with delicate care, he lifted each kitten with his teeth by the scruff of its neck and placed it into Jake's hand, one then the other. The basset hound woofed.

"Do you want me to keep the little ones warm, Bummer?" Jake asked.

Bummer woofed again and licked the top of the kittens' heads. Jake pulled off his gray wool scarf and made it into a tight circle. Then he placed the kittens in the center of the makeshift nest. He cuddled them close, knowing they needed warmth fast.

"Oooh," the little girls sounded their approval. They both petted Bummer, crooning, "Good dog. You're a good dog."

"You're the vet, aren't you?" the young woman kneeling beside him asked.

"Yes." He realized he'd neglected his manners. Sliding the scarf nest to one arm, he offered her his hand. "I'm Jake McClure."

"Jeannie Broussard and these are my girls, Mimi and Cindy."

Jake became aware that Annie, a frequent volunteer at the local animal shelter, had appeared beside him. Middle-aged, Annie wore her usual denim "outdoorsy" attire and hiking boots. He recognized the concern on her face. Would they have to squeeze in two more stray kittens? Another question came to mind. "Mimi and Cindy, did you see a mama cat outside?" Jake asked.

"No," Jeannie replied for them. "I looked around, too. I can't see why kittens so small would be outside in this weather."

A man in the crowd that had gathered around them cleared his throat. "I'm afraid I saw a cat at the side of the street near here. It was a golden tabby, too."

Jake didn't have to ask. The tone of the man's voice and his use of the past tense said loud and clear that the mother cat no longer needed his help. He and Annie exchanged weary glances.

Beside him, Jeannie made a sound of sorrow and regret. "Poor little orphans."

As if understanding their words, Bummer bayed mournfully and licked each kitten again. Jake rose, still cradling them in his scarf. "I'll take these little ones to the animal shelter before I go home tonight," he said.

The two little girls bounced up and down. "Mom, Mom, can't we keep them? Mom, please."

Jake hesitated, certain that the girls were putting Jeannie on the spot.

But Jeannie nodded, a smile lifting her face. "I've been promising you kittens, haven't I? It looks like God has chosen just the ones He wants us to have."

"Thank goodness," Annie breathed.

Again as if understanding, Bummer woofed and grinned. From around her neck, Jeannie untwined her fuzzy red scarf, followed Jake's example and soon the two babies were transferred to it. The gathering around them broke up.

Jake leaned forward. He wanted to make sure she knew how to take care of the babies. "From my observation of their teeth, these kittens should be old enough to eat soft warmed food. I suggest a food specially formulated for kittens so it doesn't upset their delicate systems."

"I was thinking warm milk?" Jeannie lifted one eyebrow.

"No, most kittens are lactose intolerant. You can buy special kitten milk, but canned food and water is sufficient. They'll need to be fed every four hours."

Jeannie looked worried.

"Is that a problem?"

"No," one of the girls piped up. "Our babysitter likes cats. She'll help us when you're at work, Mom."

The woman's pretty face lightened. "Yes. Yes." She beamed at him. "Thank you."

He pulled out his card and handed it to her, slipping into the usual doctor-pet owner relationship. "I'm happy that these two have found a good home. Please bring them by sometime this week and I'll thank you with a free checkup and shots for them."

"Oh, no—" she protested.

He held up a hand. "I insist. I volunteer my services at the local no-kill shelter. You just bypassed that step. I'm glad these two found a good home."

She took his hand and squeezed it. "Thank you."

This impulsive gesture embarrassed him. His usual shyness around women rushed back. He nodded and stepped back.

"No, thank you, Jeannie," Annie said. "We're almost out of room at the shelter. You're a Godsend for these two."

Still smiling shyly, Jeannie began shepherding the girls toward the coatrack along the wall.

Unable to look away however, he followed her with his eyes. Something about her caught and held his attention.

"Well, we dodged another bullet," Annie said in an undertone. "What are we going to do when we reach capacity?" She walked away, not waiting for an answer.

"Hello, Jake," a seductive feminine voice hailed him as he turned.

He glanced over to see a woman who owned a pampered poodle, named *Something Ridiculous in French*. He nodded, not recalling if they had progressed to first-name status. And they likely hadn't because she reminded him too much of Sheila, the only kind of woman he seemed to attract. He kept moving.

A petite, silver-haired woman named Ginny bustled up to him. "He's over there." She pointed to Mike, his man Friday. "He shouldn't be out in this cold after being so sick."

"Tell him that," Jake said, one side of his mouth drawing down as he remembered just why he'd come here tonight.

"I did," she said with a decided nod.

"So did I. A lot of good it did." Jake moved through the crowd. And then confronted Mike, best friend of his late grandfather, who kept house for Jake. "I told you—"

"You're a vet, not a people doc," Mike interrupted, rising from where he sat with his cronies and looking Jake nose to nose. "I covered my face with my muffler, breathed through my nose, and I'm fine." He turned to Ginny, behind Jake. "I wasn't going to miss this potluck. This church has the best food in town, especially your baked macaroni, Ginny."

Ginny flushed at the compliment, got flustered and retreated to the kitchen.

"Don't try that soft-soap macaroni flattery on me," Jake warned.

"Wouldn't dream of it. But that wasn't flattery. It was a sincere compliment."

Mike's cronies, the over-eighty-five group of retired farmers and paper mill workers, chuckled with appreciative grins. Most wore jeans or overalls and plaid flannel shirts.

"I'll come back and take you home after the meal," Jake said.

"No, on both counts," Mike announced, looking for agreement from his cronies. "You're staying to eat. Otherwise, left to your own devices, you'd just eat a granola bar or some other garbage. And after the meal, I'm staying to play pinochle. One of my pals will see me home. And again, you're not my nursemaid. Don't go trying to give me a curfew. I'm too old for that nonsense. We've all been getting cabin fever and this potluck and some pinochle afterward is just what we needed."

Jake looked at the deeply wrinkled but smiling faces all nodding in agreement with Mike. One of them piped up, "You need a good wife, Doc. That's what you need."

I had a wife. Two years post-divorce, Jake still had no desire to repeat that mistake. He shook his head and stifled a yawn, ready to make his departure. However, the fragrances of good homemade food made him reassess his plans to head straight home and early to bed. *Why not stay? I have to eat.*

"Okay. But, Mike, make sure you don't breathe that cold air. It strains your lungs and heart."

"Hey, Jake." The tall, graying pastor of the church came to the table and offered his hand. "Glad you could come. We're trying to raise several thousand dollars tonight for our Jeannie." The pastor motioned toward the woman with the girls and kittens.

She had shed her winter outerwear, revealing a slender figure and waist-length golden brown hair. She wore it loose, gleaming in the light. Jake paused, captured by the sight. "So Jeannie is getting the Habitat for Humanity house?"

"Yes, Jeannie Broussard. We couldn't be happier for her. A hardworking single mom. Her dream has been to have a home of her own. Those are her twin nieces." The pastor lowered his voice. "Jeannie's had custody of the girls since they were babies."

"I see." Jake didn't know what else to say, and watching Jeannie took most of his focus.

The pastor urged Jake to stay and eat. Then the man moved away to greet others.

Alone again, Jake recognized something unusual, unexpected had happened. Till now, he hadn't realized that his faithful shadow Bummer had not accompanied him when he went to talk to Mike. Instead, Bummer had stayed with Jeannie, her little girls and the kittens. Jake stood still, trying to decide if he should go get Bummer or not.

Jeannie waved to him, her face lifting into a welcoming smile. The smile transformed her from merely pretty to lovely.

Jake found himself moving toward her, his mouth suddenly dry. He halted when he reached her but couldn't think of a thing to say that made sense. "You're pretty" would not be appropriate. *This is why I'm good with animals, not people.*

"I was wondering when you'd miss Bummer," she said with an impish gleam in her eyes.

"He's my sidekick all right," Jake managed to say. He stared at Jeannie, taking in her brown eyes. They reminded him of the fur of one of his dogs, a deep warm brown. He loved that rich shade of mahogany.

"Sidekick?" one of the little girls repeated after him.

"It means," Jeannie said, stroking the little girl's white-gold pigtails with obvious affection, "that the dog is his companion, right, Dr. McClure?"

"That's right." Her fingers were long, slender and gentle. Mesmerizing. Bummer woofed and Jake looked down at him and the children.

Both little girls were pretty and blonde but not carbon copies. One wore her hair in pigtails and one in braids. Both were dressed in turtlenecks and worn blue jeans but not matching outfits. He approved of that.

"You're not identical, are you?" he asked, the doctor in him coming out.

"No, we're fraternal, Doctor," the one with the pigtails replied seriously.

Then both girls dropped to their knees again and began petting his basset hound. Bummer yodeled his pleasure and wiggled in welcome. Jeannie swung her head, shifting a few strands of hair that had swung forward.

He watched the very feminine gesture. Long hair didn't always look this good, shiny and full. He tried to think of something to say but—as usual—came up empty.

The sound of mewing caught his attention. Jeannie's fuzzy

red scarf with the two kittens still rested in the crook of her arm. Jake said the first words that came to mind. "Bummer doesn't usually take to kids like this."

She gazed down at the basset hound. "I think it might be the kittens. Your dog seems to have taken an interest in them."

"That does happen." Jake couldn't resist reaching over to stroke the soft kitten fur with one index finger. He imagined that this woman's hair would feel as soft. That froze him in place.

He had stepped out of his comfort zone tonight. He usually just kept to work and home. This social stuff always baffled him. He wanted to walk away, but stayed to watch the interaction of the girls and kittens and his basset hound. When it came to social confidence, Bummer certainly topped him. Jake folded his arms and just watched Bummer charm everyone around him.

The twins continued taking turns petting the kittens and Bummer, who was moaning with pleasure in his low gruff voice. Bummer's unusual affinity for these two kittens and little girls amazed Jake. Yet he couldn't stop himself from concentrating on Jeannie, a beacon in the crowded, noisy room.

The pastor stopped further conversation by raising his hands for silence. The cheerful hubbub in the church basement subsided.

"You all know why we're here. Our Jeannie needs funds to help get the work on her Habitat house moving. This unusually cold winter we've been having has slowed progress."

While the pastor spoke, Jake wondered how the man could speak so easily in front of all these people and ask for donations. If he had the pastor's gift, he could do more than just volunteer at the animal shelter. He could make his life's ambition real.

He caught a glimpse of movement from the corner of his eye. The woman who owned the spoiled-rotten poodle was wending her way toward him. He'd seen that intense, almost predatory expression before. Jake moved closer to Jeannie, hoping this would deter the poodle woman. But he doubted it would.

The pastor was still speaking. "Please be generous and leave your donations for Jeannie's house in the buckets on the buffet tables. Make checks out to the church and mark the memo line with 'Habitat.' Thanks for your support. Let's pray." The pastor said a short grace and then called out, "Now let's eat!"

People applauded and children rushed ahead to line up. Jeannie and her nieces were swept away from him to be the first in the buffet line. Bummer surprised him by loping after the little girls.

Jake's radar picked up the poodle woman. She had almost reached him. Jake started to go back to Mike, then remembered something.

"Girls!" Jake called out. "Don't give Bummer any food! He's good at begging."

They waved to him, but clearly were more impressed by Bummer's preference for them than Jake's caution. And this hesitation had done him in. The poodle woman had come up beside him.

"Be sure to try some of my homemade lasagna." She tossed her shoulder-length dark hair, but it didn't have the same effect on him as Jeannie's. "Some people have told me it's the best they've ever eaten."

"Uh-huh," Jake replied, his gaze following Bummer, the twins and Jeannie, who appeared bashful to be first in line. The poodle woman, who must have bathed in some heavy perfume, edged closer still. He wrinkled his nose.

In the buffet line, Jake managed to break away from the poodle woman. Then he wedged himself safely within the male gathering of Mike and his cronies. Half listening to their stories that he'd heard many times before, Jake tracked Bummer, who had stayed with Jeannie and her girls and the golden tabby kittens. He had seen animals form attachments to abandoned babies even of different species before. But he hadn't expected this from Bummer, a "bachelor" basset hound.

By the time Jake surreptitiously slipped in his donation, dollar bills and checks choked the clear plastic half-gallon ice cream buckets with slits in the covers. He imagined for just a moment this fundraiser had been set up for his dream: a place where unwanted animals and disabled or disadvantaged children could spend time together enjoying each other, healing each other. Someday he would build it. He had the perfect location; he just needed to get it all figured out. But his day-to-day work at his vet practice kept him too busy.

At Jake's elbow, Mike snorted. "Why's that woman over there looking at you like that?"

For a moment Jake thought Mike referred to Jeannie. Then he realized that the poodle woman hovered nearby, casting glances his way. Her manner reminded him of Sheila when they had first met.

"Like what?" Jake asked, acting as if he hadn't noticed.

"Like you're a…" Mike's face twisted as he struggled with the birth of a description.

"Like Jake's a box of chocolates on Valentine's Day?" one old-timer suggested with a sly expression.

"Like a fox eyein' a hen house?" another offered, grinning.

"It's 'cause you're a doc," one more weighed in. "They all think you got the green stuff." The man rubbed his forefingers and thumb together and the whole eighty-five-plus group laughed.

Jake didn't appreciate the humor at his expense. Sheila had been interested in green stuff, all right. And she'd been fooled by his father's affluence and national reputation, thinking that Jake would be just like his dad, not a simple rural vet.

Jake tried to ignore the poodle woman without success. Maybe the men were right. Perhaps the title "Dr." attracted a certain kind of attention. But that didn't mean Jake had to like it. He tried to hide the steam rising inside.

One thing he did know—he'd stay at this table until she left. He wanted no chance of her getting him alone to issue an invitation for any kind of date. So he played a few hands of pinochle. When she finally gave up and exited in a bit of a huff, he breathed easier. He didn't want to fend off any more enticing glances and practiced mannerisms like the hair tossing intended to attract a man.

He rose and scanned the faces for Jeannie in order to find Bummer. He found her looking for him. Their gazes connected and she smiled so differently from the woman who'd just left. Jeannie gave him an honest, not-asking-for-anything smile.

As more of the party started breaking up around him, Jake joined Jeannie in the cheerful crowd moving to the coatrack to bundle up for the winter night.

"Be sure to call my clinic for that appointment," Jake said at Jeannie's elbow.

"Thank you. I…we will." She beamed at him.

He felt soaked in the warmth from her smile. Embarrassed, he turned his attention to the girls, who were still taking turns petting Bummer while they pulled on their jackets, mittens and boots.

People began climbing the stairs to the doors. When one man opened the door, he called out, "Snow!" A mixture of positive and negative comments greeted this announcement. But the people braced themselves and started venturing outside.

Jake pushed open the church door for Jeannie, her girls and the kittens. And Bummer. The strong wind tried to wrench the door from Jake's grip and slam it shut. He used both hands to hold it open to let Jeannie's group safely outside.

Another man appeared and took control of the door. Jake hurried after Jeannie. Bummer's legs churned as they fought the wind and light snow to the pickup. Jeannie held the scarf-wrapped kittens close to her, shielding the little ones from the wind. Jake opened his pickup door and Bummer jumped inside to the space behind Jake's driver's seat where his basket and blanket were wedged.

A feminine voice called out, "I need a jump! Anybody got jumper cables?"

At the plea, Jake looked out. Jeannie, parked right beside him, waved. Opening his door, he shouted, "I've got them in the back." He spent the next few minutes under his hood and the hood of Jeannie's ancient minivan. After watching him connect the cables, she hurried back into the van. Her engine whimpered to life.

Jake quickly unhooked the cables, waving away her thanks and hustled into his pickup. He waited till she drove away. Why hadn't some man volunteered to help a pretty, obviously kind-hearted woman raise those two great kids? Well, he'd been blind to Sheila's motives for marrying him, Mr. Shy Guy. So did he have a right to criticize anybody else?

Shaking off these depressing thoughts, he drove through town on the road toward home. Finally, he bumped over the rutted path to his late grandparents' two-story farmhouse. The yard light illumined the property. A light gleamed through the frosted kitchen window.

Once inside the garage, he folded his driver's seat forward so his basset hound could get down.

"Come on, Bummer!"

But no Bummer.

Jake bent farther inside, thinking that Bummer might have gone toward the far side of the cab or huddled under the seat. How could Bummer be comfortable squeezed in tight like that?

"Bummer!" he shouted. No Bummer.

For a moment Jake doubted his senses. Bummer rarely left his side day or night. The faithful basset hound always rode safely behind Jake's driver's seat. But Bummer's large oval basket with its comfy blanket sat empty under the cab light. Jake stared at it, dumbfounded.

Chapter Two

The cutting wind gusted against Jake, penetrating to the skin. He slammed the cab door and sprinted over the shoveled track through the two-feet-plus of snow. A few of his "outside" dogs came out of their heated doghouse and barked in greeting. The wind lashed his exposed cheeks. Jake ducked inside the house and shoved the door closed, stomping the snow off his boots on the thick mat. He headed into his kitchen to the window over the sink. He didn't take off his jacket, and the cold lingered around him. He gripped the countertop. What could have happened? Jake looked out into the night, lit by the tall yard light, which reflected on the snow. That he'd been out very late last night on an emergency didn't help his concentration. Fatigue clung to his eyes, making him want to shut them.

"Bummer, how did you get out of the truck? And why?" Speaking out loud made the far-fetched situation feel less surreal and kept him more alert. The wind whistled around the old farmhouse, not a night for Bummer to be outside.

He slid onto a chair and said in the silence, "Start at the last time you remember seeing him tonight. When I left church, Bummer was with me." Jake pictured Bummer at his heels, hoofing it over the packed snow toward the pickup. "I opened the cab door for Bummer. Jeannie needed a jump-start so I hooked up the cables. I was busy getting her car running. Then I unhooked everything, slammed the hoods. I got in and drove away."

Jake went over the scene in his mind once more. *Before I drove off, I didn't check to see if Bummer was in his basket.*

"Bummer wouldn't have gotten out of the truck and back into the cold. It's less than ten below out there." But the idea that somebody must have taken him out of his truck... *Ridiculous.*

Jake's cell phone vibrated in his pocket. It startled him. Bummer's disappearance had his nerves on edge. He lifted the phone to his ear and said, "Dr. McClure."

"Oh, I'm so sorry to have to bother you. I was frantic, then I remembered your business card in my purse. I'm so sorry," she repeated, sounding distressed.

He thought the woman's voice sounded familiar. "How may I help you?"

"I didn't know that the girls had gotten into mischief."

The thoughts in his head ricocheted like pinballs. "Pardon?"

"Bummer's here. While we were busy with the car batteries, my girls coaxed him into my van."

Bummer? Girls? Van? The light finally went on in his dim bulb. The chain of events clicked into place. "Jeannie."

"Yes, Jeannie Broussard."

"Jeannie, you've got Bummer?" The absurdity of this development still kept him off-kilter.

"Yes, if you give me your address, I'll bring him to you. I'm just about to leave for my job at Hope Nursing Home."

Jake thought of Jeannie's battered decade-old van and its temperamental battery. "No, I'll come and get him."

"Dr. McClure, I'm so sorry—"

"Don't be. Kids and animals are always unpredictable." *And always at the worst possible moment. All I want to do is go to bed.* Yet the thought of seeing her again warmed him. "Where do you live?"

She gave him quick directions. Within minutes he was driving down the back roads to the old mobile home court outside of town. He turned in at the Shady Prairie sign and drove over the speed bumps till he saw number thirty-four, surrounded by mounds of snow. In the midst of shiny new double-wides, number thirty-four looked downtrodden. Jeannie waited at the window, waving. Jake parked and hurried through the door.

After wiping his fogged glasses, he saw Jeannie in front of him, wringing her hands.

"I'm so sorry to cause you this trouble."

Her obvious distress curbed his simmering irritation. He wished his dog hadn't helped cause this frustrating situation. "It's okay. Kids and dogs." He lifted his hands in a gesture of surrender. "They do the craziest things." To keep from staring at Jeannie, he glanced around, looking for Bummer.

"Girls, bring Bummer here, please," Jeannie scolded in a tone that reminded him of his mother. She turned to him. "I'm due at work soon. I don't want to be late."

The little blonde girls inched from the narrow hall into the living-room/kitchen area. Though scrupulously clean and neat, the interior of the trailer retained a 1980s decor. The girls kept their eyes lowered. The sound of the mewing kittens came from the hallway, too. Still, Jake didn't see his dog.

"I asked you to bring Bummer out with you," Jeannie prompted with her mother voice.

"He wouldn't come," one of them said.

"What do you have to say to Dr. McClure?" Jeannie used the mom tone again.

The two girls gave him innocent expressions of remorse. "We're sorry, but Bummer kept jumping up so he could see me and Cindy through the window," Mimi, the one with pigtails, said.

"So we got out just to pet him again and he kinda followed us back to our van," Cindy, the one with braids, said, looking down.

"What do you have to say to Dr. McClure?" Jeannie repeated.

"We won't do it again," the two chorused.

Jake murmured, "That's okay."

Jeannie looked disgruntled. However, as she went past the girls, she patted their shoulders.

"Come on, Bummer," she ordered in the hall. "Come here."

Jake waited, looking at the girls, already in their faded pajamas and wool socks. They avoided his gaze, staring at the worn rose-colored rug. Fatigue made him feel like a scarecrow propped up against the door. Then he heard Bummer's yodeling moan.

Jeannie appeared in the main room. "He won't come out. He's lying right beside the box I made up as a bed for the kittens. When I took his collar to get him moving, he…growled."

Jake's aggravation zoomed like hot air up a flue. "Let me."

He moved past the girls and their mom. The first door off the narrow hall obviously led into the girl's room with its pink walls and bunk beds. Bummer lay sprawled on the pink oval throw rug on the floor beside a small box. The two kittens gripped the top of the box with their little paws, peeping out. "Come on, Bummer. Time to go home." Jake snapped his fingers. "Come on, boy."

Bummer looked up at him with his big, brown, mellow eyes. His big, brown, mellow, *stubborn* eyes.

Jake's patience snapped. Bummer was causing this woman trouble and she didn't need it. He barged into the room, picked up the heavy dog and headed for the front door. Bummer opened his mouth and bayed loud and long. In between blasts of this, the sound of the kittens' mewing objections came through.

"I'm so sorry!" Jeannie called over Bummer's protests as she opened the door.

"Not your fault. I'm sorry." Buffeted by the wind, he rushed to his pickup. He deposited Bummer in his basket, then looked up. Jeannie stood, framed by the window again. He waved, trying to reassure her. Bummer had caused this fuss. She lifted a hand in reply.

He drove down the road toward home—with Bummer still

yodeling mournfully. What was with this crazy dog? And why had seeing that sweet woman in that shabby mobile home bothered Jake?

Jeannie stood in her trailer, still stunned by what had just taken place. And charmed by the way Dr. McClure had paused in the cold wind to wave to her. *What a good man.* He could have been so cross with her girls, yet he hadn't been. She quelled the urge to linger on thoughts of the vet. He probably never sat home alone on Saturday night. Then again, neither did she. The girls were always with her. A glance at the stove clock warned her—time to hustle.

"Mom," Mimi said, pouting, "Bummer wanted to stay with us."

"Yeah," Cindy agreed, twisting a braid. "He was crying."

Jeannie sighed and checked her watch out of habit. "Bummer is not our dog. And I would think that after I let you keep the kittens tonight, you two would try to behave." Jeannie sighed loudly. "Time to go to Aunt Ginny's. Get your jackets on. We've got to hurry."

Still grumbling, the girls pulled on their coats and boots for the trek next door. They got the box from the bedroom and put a towel over it. Jeannie grabbed their lunches for tomorrow from the fridge and got dressed to face the cold herself. The three trooped over the well-worn path of packed snow to next door. In her worn blue robe and slippers, the twins' honorary "Aunt" Ginny opened the door wide and welcomed them all inside with her sweet voice.

While the twins hung their winter wear on low pegs by the door, Jeannie handed Aunt Ginny the two brown-bag lunches, then showed her the box of kittens in case she hadn't seen them at church.

"They will need to be fed warmed food at least once tonight. I picked up a can at the convenience store on the way home. I'm so sorry to ask you. But—" Jeannie lowered her voice "—since the mother cat was run over in the street and I couldn't deny the girls—"

"Of course not. I did see what happened at the church, and I already fixed up a box with some shredded newspaper for their litter box till you get a regular one." Ginny lifted the kittens out, one in each hand. "Hello, you little sweeties. What are you girls going to name these kittens?"

The girls patted the kittens. "We can't decide."

"Well, sometimes people name kittens for what they look like," Ginny suggested.

Each twin looked at the kitten they held. Then a smile split Mimi's face. "Mine's the color of a Twinkie and that's the best treat for lunch! Hi, Twinkie." She kissed her mewing kitten's head.

"And mine is goldy like peanut butter, so mine's Peanutbutter! My favorite!" Cindy rubbed her cheek against her kitten.

Ginny chuckled. "And for short we can call her Peanut sometimes."

Happy for her girls, Jeannie kissed the girls and told them to go to right to sleep. "And don't give Aunt Ginny any trouble, okay?"

"We won't," the twins chorused and headed for the sofa bed where they slept the five nights that Jeannie worked each week.

Jeannie handed Ginny an envelope with her check for watching the girls for the week. God had provided Ginny, who had taken on the girls as babies soon after Jeannie had moved here from Milwaukee. "Thanks, Aunt Ginny."

"No problem, Jeannie. Happy to have the company." The woman turned, and in her sweet voice asked the girls which bedtime video they wanted to watch before lights out. Then she sat down, still cooing over the kittens.

Jeannie waved and hurried out to her van. She had left it running so she knew she'd be able to get to work. Evidently the frigid temperatures were finishing off another battery. She looked forward to the new house with its garage that she'd be living in come spring. *A garage. Wonderful.*

As she drove away a bit faster than usual, she glanced into Aunt Ginny's window. The light from the TV set flickered. A true Godsend, Ginny usually read to the girls at bedtime, but the fundraiser potluck must have tired her out. Jeannie reached the county road and sped up. If she didn't, she'd be late for sure. Jake's face bobbed up in her mind. She sighed and pushed it away. Doing this would have been easier—if he hadn't been such a nice guy.

Jake rolled over in his bed. He had wrapped his pillow around his head, but Bummer's mournful yodeling penetrated the feathered down. Jake sat up and slammed his pillow to the floor. A glance at the bedside clock told him that this had gone on almost two hours. Not even Jake's lack of sleep dulled the uproar. Earlier he'd looked Bummer over to see if something physical was bothering him. No dice.

"I can't take it anymore." He got up and pulled his clothing over his pajamas and headed down the steps to Bummer, who had refused to move from the vicinity of the back door.

As Jake passed through the kitchen, the wall phone rang. He picked up.

"What is wrong with that dog?" Mike barked. "I can hear him the quarter mile over to my place."

"Sorry. I'll take care of it."

"Do that." Mike slammed the receiver in Jake's ear.

Jake shoved his hair back from his face, trying to think of what he could do, what he should do. Jeannie Broussard's face came to mind. Did he have a choice?

Driving down the darkened highway, Jake questioned his plan. But he didn't know what else to do. Jeannie Broussard had impressed him as a woman who knew kids as well as he knew animals. Maybe they could figure out why this had happened and how to handle it.

In the basket behind him, Bummer still bayed mournfully. Jake could feel a scowl controlling his face. *I can't believe I'm doing this.* This midnight ride only showed how desperate a tired man could get.

He saw the lighted sign ahead for the nursing home where Jeannie said she worked. He lurched to a stop at the back entrance, where he figured he could get to Jeannie easier. He pressed the button by the door and braced himself against the icy wind. Shivering, he waited with Bummer under his arm. The door opened and he charged inside out of the blistering cold.

Jeannie gawked at him. "Dr. McClure, what are you doing here?"

Before Jake could reply, Bummer stopped moaning and woofed at Jeannie, struggling to get down. Jake released the hound. Bummer frisked around her feet, woofing softly with joy—as if he sensed he needed to be quiet in this place. Jeannie stooped to pet him.

Jake stooped beside her, bracing his elbows on his knees. The constant baying had shaved his patience down to a fine, taut line. Jake buried his face in his hands. The emergency call to a large dairy farm last night and Bummer's antics tonight meant he'd hardly had any sleep for two nights now. *I can't believe I'm here. How can I expect this woman to just know what to do?* But he hoped his hunch would pay off.

"Why are you here?" Jeannie asked in a low voice. She glanced behind her as if she expected someone to come and shoo him outside.

"I know I shouldn't have come. And brought a dog here to boot."

"That's all right. We have two dogs who live here as pets for the patients. Bummer is allowed."

At her kind words, he raised his head and gazed at her. She'd pulled her beautiful hair back into a ponytail, giving her a severe look that didn't suit her.

"I'm glad to hear that this nursing home recognizes the healing power of interaction with animals."

Jeannie nodded and looked at him expectantly as if repeating, *Why are you here?*

He hoped he didn't sound ridiculous. "Since I drove away from your house," he said in careful, measured tones at odds with his inner uproar, "Bummer has bayed, moaned and howled. One of my neighbors a quarter mile away even complained."

Jeannie gasped. "I'm so sorry. How can I help?"

Riddled by fatigue, he leaned his face into his hands again. His reserve around young women began reasserting itself. He didn't know what more to say. Silence reigned.

Jeannie cleared her throat. "Why don't you come to the employee lounge for a cup of decaf coffee?" She glanced at her wristwatch. "I can take a brief break now."

Jake straightened up. "You don't have to—"

"My pleasure. Please." She led him down the hall and into a brightly lit room. Her face revealed a kind of bewildered concern. She gestured him to the saggy plaid sofa while she went to the snack area.

Again he regretted having to bother this woman. Yet, too tired to argue or just leave, Jake obeyed and sank onto the sofa. Bummer watched Jeannie pour two mugs of coffee and bring one to Jake. When she sat down in a chair across from Jake, Bummer flopped on the floor with a satisfied sigh. At this, Jeannie looked…flummoxed, a word he hadn't ever used that he could recall.

"I'm really sorry about this," Jeannie said, cupping her white and green Hope Nursing mug between her hands. "But are you sure this is about me and the girls? I noticed that Bummer was very protective of the kittens."

Even in the glare of the fluorescent lighting, the young woman across from him looked somehow ethereal. Wearing a faded blue scrubs uniform, she didn't fit this run-down setting. Why did employee lounges always have to look like thrift stores?

Bringing his mind back to the problem, Jake stirred his coffee and then gestured toward the dog on the floor beside her. "I've had Bummer since he was a pup when I had just finished vet school." Jake couldn't stop the rush of words—something that was out of character for him. "He's been my shadow for almost ten years. He's never done anything like this before."

After glancing down at Bummer, Jeannie asked, "Do you mean his coming home with my girls? I scolded them about helping him into the van. I've warned them if they do anything like that again, they'll lose TV privileges for a weekend."

He stirred his coffee, watching the swirls of cream blend in, nearly hypnotized. "I tried ignoring his baying." He glanced at his watch. "He kept it up for nearly two hours till he saw you here." He shrugged, not even knowing clearly what he wanted to ask her.

Jeannie sipped from her cup, her pale pink lips catching his attention. "You think he prefers to be with my girls and the kittens? But how can that be? Except for tonight my girls never had contact with him before."

"Dogs have personalities just like people." He blew across the top of his steaming cup of coffee. Talking about animals—now he could do that. "Some relate to their early experiences with people and other animals. Some just follow the instincts of their breed. Basset hounds can be very determined and independent."

"So if he's taken a notion to prefer my girls or protect the kittens, he'll just be stubborn about it?" Her sincere brown eyes gazed into his.

"Exactly." He tried not to be rude and just stare at her. "It's been said that basset hounds can be taught anything, as long as they want to learn that *particular* anything." A grin slid sideways onto his face—for her, not the situation.

The young single mom gazed around the lounge. "I can't stay much longer. I don't want to lose this job. After I was downsized from receptionist at the hospital emergency room last fall, it took me a while to find another position."

"I'm sorry. Here you are at work and I'm bothering you with my problems." He rose.

She put out a hand. "Wait. You look really tired." She touched his sleeve for only a moment. Her fleeting touch sent sparks zipping up his arm.

"Understatement," he admitted simply. Why deny it?

"We really haven't solved your problem."

He took a step back. Of course they hadn't. *I shouldn't have bothered her.* "I'll just have to work through it."

His cell phone sounded loud in the quiet place. He excused himself to take the call, returning a few moments later. "I have to go. Another emergency at a different dairy farm." Jake bent to pick up Bummer.

The basset hound dashed away and ducked behind the sofa. Jake had never seen him move so fast. Heat enveloped Jake's face. *I don't have time for this.*

"On the way to your emergency," Jeannie said, as if feeling for each word, "maybe you should stop and leave Bummer with the girls at my next-door neighbor's. Ginny loves animals."

"I shouldn't give in to him like this—"

"You look dead on your feet, and now you have another call. You can't take him with you, baying like that. I'll call her." She pulled out her cell phone and hit speed dial.

"No, I shouldn't—"

She held up a hand and said into the phone, "Ginny, there's sort of an emergency tonight."

Jake listened as she explained the situation to the neighbor. Embarrassment and the urgency of the emergency call ASAP needled him.

She shut the phone. "Ginny says to bring Bummer over. She said she knows you."

"Ginny?" He tried to bring up a face and then shrugged.

"I usually remember the animals more than their owners," he admitted. "Oh, wait—is that Ginny Flatlander?"

"Yes, the one famous for her baked mac and cheese." Jeannie chuckled. "The girls call her Aunt Ginny and she owns the white and brown trailer next to mine. She's waiting for you."

Another unbidden grin slid onto his face. "Thanks."

She smiled in return and pushed him toward the door. "Go."

He wanted to stay. But couldn't.

Seven o'clock in the morning finally came. Jeannie punched out and drove home, her battery reluctant but still alive. Through the bright sun glinting on the fresh snow she walked to Aunt Ginny's. She said goodbye to the girls, who were on their way to catch the school bus, and went inside to get the kittens. Bummer greeted her from the floor by the heat register. The two kittens were crawling over him, playing, pulling at his long ears. "Dr. McClure hasn't come yet?"

"No. But Bummer has been good, and he's been taking care of those kittens." Ginny beamed at the dog and kittens. "It's unusual to see a male so interested in little ones. But I have heard of stranger things."

"Do you think Dr. McClure's emergency call lasted into the morning?" Jeannie swallowed a yawn.

"Maybe. Or he overslept?"

Dr. McClure hadn't seemed irresponsible—much the opposite. She hoped nothing bad had happened to him or his patients. Though Jeannie ached with fatigue, she had no choice. She turned to Aunt Ginny. "Thanks. I'll take the menagerie home with me. If Dr. McClure comes, tell him I've got Bummer, okay?"

"Well," Aunt Ginny teased in a knowing tone, "this is a new one on me. Stealing a man's dog to get his attention—"

"Aunt Ginny," Jeannie scolded, blushing and wondering why. "Don't go there." She suffered the woman's laughter as she walked outside, carrying the box of kittens. Bummer trotted at her side.

At home, Jeannie waited while Bummer did his business beside a tree. Then inside, she warmed food for the kittens and gave Bummer a cold hot dog for lack of anything else. She staggered to her bedroom, stepped out of her shoes and collapsed onto the bed. With the kittens trailing him, Bummer waddled in after her and lay down on the rug beside her bed. Jeannie fell asleep, gazing into the hound's deep brown mournful eyes. And thinking of another pair of kind eyes.

Jeannie swam up from sleep to the sound of insistent knocking. She padded in her stocking feet to the front door. Dr. McClure stood outside. "Ginny said I just missed you."

Jeannie swallowed a yawn. "Come in. Would you like some coffee?"

"No, thanks. I've been out all night and I'm dirty from working in a cattle barn. I'll just take Bummer. I've got to get to my clinic."

Closing the door, Jeannie turned and went to get Bummer. She'd left him lying on the rug. She went from room to room. No dog. On a hunch, she went back to her room and got down on her knees. Bummer had crawled under her bed and all the way back to the far corner. The kittens hovered beside him.

Exhausted, she wanted to lie down and cry. "Bummer, you fit your name. Shame on you." On her stomach, she crawled under the bed.

Bummer growled at her.

She crawled back out. To the door. She opened it. "You'll have to get him. He's under my bed." She sank onto a kitchen chair, too tired to stand.

The vet stalked down the hall. Soon the sound of Bummer growling and Dr. McClure grunting came to her. The vet finally appeared with the large struggling dog in his arms. "Thank you."

The vet hustled out, letting the door slam behind him. Jeannie didn't take it personally. If she hadn't been so tired, she would have felt sorry for him. At least the dog wouldn't be here when the girls got off the school bus at three. She lay down on the couch and fell sound asleep, again thinking of a pair of blue eyes.

Aching for sleep, Jake drove to his clinic to do his small-animal office hours. Bummer bayed on and on as if he were being tortured. If Jake's morning hadn't already been packed with appointments, he would have gone home and slept. He parked behind his clinic and then opened the door, urging Bummer to get down.

Bummer refused.

Jake picked him up and carried him inside the rear staff entrance. He stomped with each step, trying to release some of his irritation and wake himself up. Bummer yodeled his displeasure. This made all the animals in the kennel in the rear of the clinic bark, yip and woof in sympathy. They didn't want to be there either!

Jake carried Bummer to his office, hung up his coat and shut the door on the still-baying hound. He hurried forward to the reception counter. His office manager, a very pregnant Kelsey Witt, looked up at him quizzically.

"Don't ask," he said under his breath. His first two appointments were waiting for him. He asked the woman with the puppy in need of a booster shot to come back with him. In the background behind their voices, Bummer's trumpeting bass could be heard. The sound brought thoughts of Jeannie. He hoped she would get some sleep. He hated that Bummer was causing her trouble, too. She obviously didn't need any more burdens. Then Jake tried to ignore Bummer's baying and concentrate on the patient. He tried to look on the sunny side. At least Bummer's ruckus would keep him awake.

Jake looked into the puppy owner's eyes and saw there the obvious question: What's with the dog? He didn't try to answer it. As he continued the examination against the background of Bummer's baying, he thought about all the animals crowded into the animal shelter who wanted a home. Bummer didn't know how good he had it.

An hour later, Kelsey closed the door to the treatment room where Jake had just finished treating a cat with ear mites. She glared at him. "If Bummer stays, I'm taking the rest of the day off." She folded her arms and rested them on her bountiful abdomen, showing just how near the end of her last trimester loomed.

Jake didn't blame her for being irritated. He was *more* than irritated. "I'll go now, take him home, and leave him with the outside dogs."

"Good, that should only take a few minutes and save you hiring a new office manager earlier than expected." She reached for the doorknob. "I'll explain to the next appointment that you've been delayed briefly by an emergency."

Jake watched her go. He was tired. He was hungry. He wanted Bummer to shut up. He marched to the rear and collected his dog.

He drove home, carrying Bummer over the snow to the large dog run beside his garage. He opened the gate and set Bummer inside. The other outside dogs greeted him with friendly overtures.

Jake shook his finger at Bummer. "If you don't stop this, you're going to end up living out here." Not a harsh threat. Jake's outside dogs were the ones that ended up with him because no one else wanted them. Like the dalmatian who'd lost a leg in an accident. Besides the large run, the dogs had a heated dog house.

And when he was home, Jake let them run in his fenced wooded pasture.

Bummer grimaced at him, turned his back and bayed loud and long. Hoping a day of barking outside without a human audience would scotch this mutiny, Jake hurried to his truck and headed back to the clinic. *Get over it, Bummer. Fast. I mean it.*

Chapter Three

Saturday morning at 7:47, Jake groaned silently when he saw the parking lot outside his clinic. Surrounded by mounds of plowed snow, cars were packed tight together. He wouldn't be closing up early this Saturday. He parked by the rear entrance, got out and motioned Bummer to get down. The dog gave him a look of pining misery and obeyed dejectedly.

Since ending his baying fest, Bummer gave his owner the silent treatment, interlaced with recriminating stares. Jake wondered how long this phase would last. How long would it take for Bummer to forget the kittens and little girls he'd latched on to as his responsibility?

Jake's cell phone rang. He glimpsed the caller's number; his low mood dropped to the soles of his feet.

To get out of the piercing cold, he hurried through the rear door to the clinic. "Hello, Dad."

"Jacob, I'm flying in Wednesday afternoon. Can you pick me up?" His father spoke as usual in clipped sentences and without any preliminary conversation.

"What time?" Jake watched Bummer pad listlessly down the hallway past the office door, toward Kelsey's station at the front.

"Around four o'clock. My flight number is 5672 from Chicago on United. Check on it before you start out in case of delay."

"Will do." Jake sank figuratively under this new weight that had just been dropped on him. What next?

"Thanks. See you then." His father hung up. One would have thought their conversation cost him per word like an old-fashioned telegram. Jake scrubbed his face with his hands, trying to figure out how he felt through the haze from an over-busy week. He came up with just "not good."

Hand on her hip, Kelsey appeared at the front end of the hallway outside the treatment rooms. "I was wondering if you were going to show up or leave me with all these people and pets."

Jake didn't reply. He tossed his coat into his office and headed back to the reception desk. "How many patients?"

Kelsey's good nature had been seriously compromised during the last month. Jake knew it probably stemmed from her obvious physical discomfort and lack of sleep. He'd been trying to find a replacement for her by word of mouth, but so far there'd been no takers.

"Let's just say that the word for today is booked."

"Okay, let's get started." His vet assistant, Sandy, in her thirties and known for flannel, not "frilly," came in the rear door and shed her down jacket. After greeting her, he took the first file from Kelsey, ready to invite the first patient and owner into Exam Room One.

The phone rang as he began escorting the patient.

"Dr. McClure!" Kelsey said. Sandy led the patient and owner to the examining room. Jake took the phone from Kelsey. "Dr. McClure."

"Hi, Jake, it's Annie. Just wanted you to know we hit capacity at the shelter this morning. We don't have room for even a canary now."

The news triggered a low fire in Jake's stomach.

"What's plan B?" Annie asked.

"I don't know. I guess we'll have to start boarding strays with host families. You started the list, right?"

Annie sighed loud and long. "Yes, I have the list, but I hate this. I can't understand why people aren't adopting animals this winter."

Like in a cartoon, Kelsey sent Jake looks that resembled firecracker streaks. She mouthed, *We have patients waiting.*

"I can't talk right now, Annie. Start calling people on the list and confirming they will foster strays."

"Okay." Annie cut the connection.

Jake shrugged off the call as best he could. He had enough to worry about with Bummer acting up and his dad coming on Wednesday. Jake didn't want to hear what his dad would say about Bummer. And what could he do to encourage people to adopt animals? Why couldn't everyone be like Jeannie and her girls? He recalled how she had cradled the tiny kittens in her arms and how she'd cooed over and patted Bummer. The world needed more Jeannies.

Jeannie and her girls drove up to the McClure Veterinarian Clinic for the kittens' nine o'clock appointment. She noticed the crowded parking lot. Glad she'd brought snacks for the girls and food for the kittens, she hurried her crew inside.

The chairs around the room were filled, so Jeannie hung up their coats on the jammed coatrack and motioned for the girls to sit on the area rug with the kittens. Her outgoing girls immediately began talking to the waiting patients and showing off Twinkie and Peanutbutter.

Jeannie walked to the counter to give her name to the receptionist. The young pregnant woman looked as if she was in pain or at least in severe discomfort. "Hi, I'm Jeannie Broussard. We have a nine o'clock—"

The rest of her words were drowned out by a dog baying loudly from farther inside the clinic.

Her girls called out, "Bummer!"

Chaos commenced. The basset hound pushed through the door beside the counter and reunited with Mimi and Cindy and the kittens with joy-filled barking. The other dogs and cats in the waiting room erupted, joining in the reunion, barking, meowing and trying to get free of their owners.

Dr. McClure burst through the doorway into the waiting area. When he saw the cause of the commotion, he stopped in his tracks.

"Bummer!" he scolded, sounding exasperated.

Jeannie worried her lower lip. "Cindy and Mimi, get Bummer settled down!"

Her words calmed the storm. Bummer licked the faces of both the twins and the kittens and then flopped down beside them on the rug. The other animals came back under control except for one dog who continued barking.

Jeannie looked into the doctor's blue eyes and gave him an apologetic shrug. "I didn't think he'd be here or remember them. Sor—"

"Oh!" a voice called out. "Oh!"

Both Dr. McClure and Jeannie turned to the panicking receptionist.

"Dr. McClure! I think I'm in labor!"

Jeannie hurried forward and few of the other women from the waiting room joined her behind the counter. A middle-aged woman took charge. "Kelsey, are the contractions starting at the bottom or the top of your abdomen?"

"The bottom," Kelsey gasped, her hands on her stomach and her eyes wide.

"You're in labor," the middle-aged woman said. "When's your due date?"

"In five weeks."

"Call your doctor. *Now*," the woman ordered. "You need to be looked at right away."

Jeannie stepped to one side. Even though she was a Certified

Nursing Assistant, she'd never given birth, so she thought the other women more capable of giving good advice. She did recall the day her younger sister had gone into labor with the twins. And she knew that premature labor required immediate attention.

The middle-aged woman and Dr. McClure handled everything with a few quick phone calls. They helped the young mother-to-be out of the office and down the hallway toward the rear door. Her husband was on his way to take her to the emergency room on doctor's orders.

The office phone shrilled loudly—once, twice, three times. *It might be an emergency.* When no one else moved to answer it, Jeannie lifted the receiver. "McClure Veterinarian Clinic," she said, moving to look at the appointment book lying open on the desk.

"I need an appointment on Monday afternoon."

Jeannie only hesitated a moment. Almost seven years of working as a receptionist at the E.R. probably explained why she'd felt compelled to answer the phone and why it felt so natural to do so. She flipped the book to Monday and saw the notation, *No office hours.* "Could you come in—" she flipped another page "—on Tuesday afternoon? The doctor has office hours then."

"That's fine. What time?"

Jeannie studied the page, sitting down behind the desk. "I see he has an opening at two-thirty. Please give me your name and number in case we have to make any changes." After jotting the information in the appointment book, Jeannie wished the caller goodbye.

A cheerful-looking woman in jeans and a white lab coat came to the reception area. "Kelsey's husband just drove up. I'm Sandy. Who are you?"

Jeannie jumped up. "I took a call, but I'm just here with my kittens to get their shots."

Dr. McClure appeared beside the young woman. "Jeannie, did I hear that you just took a call?"

She nodded. "I hope that was all right. I took down the name and number in case there's a problem with the appointment." She distanced herself from the desk, feeling as if she'd been caught in wrongdoing. "I've worked as a receptionist before and—"

"Could you handle the desk today? I really need help." He waved toward the crowded waiting area. "You'd just take calls and hand us the files." He motioned toward a stand-up file holder on the desk. "Kelsey already had several ready to go."

What could she say? He was a good man and he needed her help. Jeannie nodded. "If you think I can handle it."

Dr. McClure gave her a smile to die for.

Just after 5:00 p.m. Jeannie finally locked the door after the final patient had left. She could only be thankful that she didn't have to work till Monday night. The girls were napping on the area rug. Jeannie gazed at them. Each had a kitten sleeping beside her, and Bummer had stretched out full length in between them. An image worthy of being on any kid-and-pet calendar in the country. She smiled and rotated her tight back and neck muscles.

"Well, we did it," Sandy said, looking toward the girls also. "Now that's a real lesson in love between the species," she teased. "A dog, two kittens and twins. Sweet."

Jeannie beamed with pride.

"And so much for my plan that Bummer would forget them," Dr. McClure said, coming into the reception area.

Jeannie didn't know what to say to this. Sandy excused herself to feed and care for the animals staying overnight in the kennel. Still uneasy, Jeannie said, "I hope I did everything right."

"You did great. Kelsey called when she got home from the hospital. She'll be on bed rest for the rest of her pregnancy and she's given notice." He sucked in air, sounding worried. Then he smiled at her. "You really did a wonderful job pitching in today. Thanks." He leaned against the doorjamb.

Jeannie swallowed with difficulty. The sight of him—so long

and lean—made her heart skip and jump. "It was just like being back at the E.R. I just answered the phone, pulled folders and then returned them to their proper files." Jeannie couldn't stop the urge to draw closer to Jake. She took a tentative step toward him and then stopped. "No problem."

No problem. Wonderful, welcome words. After weeks of Kelsey's unusual and increasingly contentious attitude added to Bummer's *loud* cold shoulder, Jake reveled in hearing someone speak with kindness. Suddenly it all became clear to him. "Would you be interested in taking over as office manager?"

Jeannie looked shocked. A moment of stunned silence and then she rushed forward and hugged him.

No one had hugged him for a long time. In his astonishment he didn't react—in time. Before he could return the hug, Jeannie pulled back.

"Oh, I'm so sorry," she said, wiping tears from her eyes. "It's just that ever since the girls started all-day school last fall, I've been applying for day jobs. But I haven't found anything but nights at the nursing home."

He wanted to reply that he didn't mind her hugging him. In fact, he had liked it very much. But he'd just hired this woman and didn't want to be the kind of boss who...well, he wasn't that kind of boss. He forced a smile.

She frowned, worry flashing over her features. "But won't Kelsey want her job back after she's had the baby?"

"No, she and her husband plan to have a large family. She already gave me notice that she wouldn't be coming back after the baby's birth."

Jeannie looked relieved. "Oh, then that works out fine. I couldn't give up my secure job for a temporary one." She glanced toward the girls and smiled.

"Great. When can you start?"

"Right away. A new batch of CNAs has just applied at the nursing home." Jeannie beamed at him.

"Fantastic. Then you can start Tuesday." He went over the salary, the days and hours and the office billing system. "Any questions?"

"I've done everything except billing patients before. But I've taken classes in bookkeeping and spreadsheets, so I don't think that will be a problem."

"Great." He turned upon hearing Bummer give a big yawn as he woke up. The girls were stirring and the kittens, too. Jake's completely empty stomach growled.

Sandy came over. "I was thinking you should take this lady and her girls out for supper to thank her. Also to celebrate finding someone competent so easily."

The sudden suggestion electrified him. "Good idea. Are you as hungry as I am? How about I treat us all to a pizza—to celebrate your coming to work for me?"

At the sound of the word "pizza" the suddenly wide-awake girls sprang up with joyful excitement. "Pizza! Yay!"

Jeannie looked hesitant.

"Oh, I'm sorry." Jake hit his forehead lightly. "Did you have other plans?" He offered her a way out.

"No—"

The girls started bouncing on their toes. "Please, Mom, please!"

Jake turned to Sandy. "You'll come, too, right?"

"As it happens," Sandy said with a smile, "I have plans. You four go."

So that's how it happened that within a very few minutes, he shepherded Jeannie and the girls into the Pizza Barn just a couple miles from the clinic. Bummer and the kittens had stayed behind at the clinic, enjoying a meal of warmed kitty food and doggie chow.

Though too early for the dating couples to arrive, a few voices hummed in the dimly lit restaurant. Jake and Jeannie and the girls blended right in with the other young couples with children eating out early.

Jake noted the interest his being with Jeannie elicited. But he figured soon everyone would hear that he had taken her out to celebrate her taking over as office manager. The four of them slipped into a booth, and ordered a large family-size pizza. The twins busied themselves with coloring pages and the crayons provided.

Jake relaxed for the first time that day or, for that matter, for the first time since Bummer had started his antics. He thought, *I should get out more.* And grinned. For over two years now Mike had been telling him to stop living like a hermit. Not even the flickering memory of Sheila—the woman who had driven him to be a recluse—could spoil this rare moment. A rare moment when he didn't feel alone.

He looked across the table. The pretty woman gazed at her little girls with obvious affection. He had once hoped for children. "You're really lucky," he murmured.

She smiled a fuzzy warm smile. "I am."

He groped for a non-animal topic. "How long have you been on your own?"

"Always," she said. She sounded as if she knew what that meant deep in her heart.

His cell phone vibrated in his pocket. He lifted it out and glanced at who was calling him. Annie. "Jeannie, do you mind if I take this call?" He gestured with the phone. "I'll make it quick. It's about the animal shelter."

"Go right ahead."

Jake flipped it open. "Hi—"

"I've lined up two foster families out of a list of thirteen." Annie did not sound happy.

"Then we have at least two."

"Very glass half full of you to say. What happens if we get more than two needy animals in the next few days?"

"We'll cross that bridge when we come to it. I can't talk now. I'm at the Pizza Barn with a lady."

"A date? You're on a date?"

Jake didn't appreciate Annie's incredulous tone, but he didn't let this leak into his voice. "It's Jeannie, the one who adopted the two golden tabby kittens."

"Oh, ask her if she'll be a prospective foster home for a stray."

"Right." Jake wished her good-night and hung up. Annie knew he found it nearly impossible to ask people to volunteer or give. He turned to Jeannie. "The animal shelter hit capacity this morning. That was Annie, who organizes most of what happens at the shelter. She's getting together a list of foster homes for strays." As close to a request as he could make himself come.

"I'm sorry to hear that. I wish I could offer to help, but I can't with a new job—" she smiled with mega-watt voltage "—and taking care of the girls and kittens, I'm too busy. I wouldn't want to take in a stray and then neglect it. I didn't realize the situation at the shelter had gotten so serious. Do you have any ideas for encouraging adoption?"

"I'm just a vet." He shrugged. "I'm not into PR or fundraising." He couldn't bring himself to ask for money.

One of the little girls, he thought Mimi, looked up at him and asked, "Do you got any kids? I mean, are you anybody's daddy?"

Chapter Four

Jeannie wished she had her jacket on so she could pull the hood over her head and then down over her red-hot face. Art Linkletter was right—kids did say the darndest things. "Mimi," she groaned under her breath.

"No, Mimi," Dr. McClure replied, "I'm nobody's daddy. I like kids though. Especially kids who take care of their pets like you and Cindy."

The perfect answer. Jeannie grinned at him. Then hoped he wouldn't think that she'd put the girls up to asking *the embarrassing question of the evening.* "Kids." She shrugged.

"Well, well, well," someone said, pausing beside the booth. "Look who got himself a date. At last. I'd given up hope."

Jeannie looked at the older man she'd seen with Ginny a few times. He grinned at her boss, no doubt trying to tease him.

"Mike, I'm not…we're not on a date," Dr. McClure said, looking flustered.

Jeannie didn't take his denial the wrong way. Why did people do this? Ask arch questions just because two people of the opposite sex were together? To diffuse the situation, she stuck out her hand. "I'm Jeannie Broussard. Dr. McClure's new office manager. Dr. McClure is buying us a pizza to celebrate."

The older gentleman shook her hand with his leathery one.

"Mike Heinrich. Old friend of Jake's family. I work for him, too. I'm his chief cook, floor-mopper and dishwasher. And I know your girls. I've seen them at Ginny's a few times. And what's with this 'Dr. McClure' stuff? For Pete's sake, Jake, you'll never get a second date if you don't let her call you by your first name."

Mike greeted the girls, then drifted away to a table of older men toward the back.

"Sorry about that," Dr. McClure muttered, stirring his drink with his straw. "He thinks he's my caretaker. Although…" He cleared his throat. "He has a good point, Jeannie. Please, stop calling me Dr. McClure. I'd feel much better if you'd call me Jake."

Jeannie nodded and smiled. "Sure, Jake, I'd like that."

Mimi paused with a red crayon poised in her hand. "Why don't you got any kids?"

As usual, not easily deterred or distracted, Mimi made Jeannie cringe again. But she couldn't think of any way to change the subject gracefully.

"Maybe he doesn't got a wife," Cindy pointed out. "You should ask him that first."

When Mimi opened her mouth to ask this even more embarrassing question, Jeannie held up a hand. "No more personal questions. It's not polite." And then their pizza was delivered. Saved by melted mozzarella!

When the four of them, filled with pizza contentment, returned to the quiet clinic, Bummer ran to greet them, barking. Jeannie wanted to make a quick getaway. She sensed Jake's discomfort about her transformation from an acquaintance into the new role of employee. Her girls and Mike hadn't helped the situation. Now Bummer and the girls deserted Jake and Jeannie, leaving them to stand side by side, mute.

Jeannie's own awkward awareness of the new situation made her wobbly, off-kilter. At the beginning of this new venture, she knew that striking the right balance of friendship between a single man and a single woman within a working relationship might prove to be a challenge. Yet one worth forging. Now she had a job she wanted and the home she wanted would be built by spring. *Thank You, Lord. You are always faithful.*

Bummer joined the girls and kittens rolling on the floor, behaving as if they had been separated for weeks, not just shy of two hours. Jeannie couldn't help gazing with pleasure at the sight of her girls so joyful. Then she started lining up words for a friendly but purely platonic farewell.

"If only all dogs and cats could find their own kids, the ones who would love them, and be this happy," Jake murmured.

The simple words revealed Jake's heart. She turned to him, searching his face in the low light. The compassionate expression on his face slipped into her heart, moving her, drawing her to him. A thought came to her. She cleared her throat. "I agree. I was wondering…" She paused, undecided about whether she should broach this. Was it her place?

"What?"

"When I lived in Milwaukee, once in a while someone from an animal shelter would bring pets in need of being adopted on a local TV station. Have they tried that here? It might help nudge a few people to come in and adopt."

"We did that a few years back. But the woman who took charge of that moved away." Jake gazed at her, his expression so authentic, so caring, yet somehow boyishly uncertain.

He drew her—physically, as if they were connected by an invisible thread. *What a kind man.*

But he's not for me. He's my boss. She became brisk. "Okay, girls, time for us to go home. Tell Bummer we'll see him soon."

"Mom, couldn't we take Bummer home with us?" Mimi said, hopping up.

"No," Jeannie said firmly. "We will see him soon."

"When?" Cindy asked, joining her sister in staring at the two adults. And then Bummer turned his gaze on them, too, as if silently asking the same question.

If Jeannie had been in the mood to be amused, she would have been. However, not now. She didn't want to start Bummer creating problems for Jake again.

"You'll see Bummer all the time," Jake said. "Your mom is going to be working here. Sometimes she can bring you with her, like today. You were no trouble at all. In fact, Sandy told me that you did a lot of good calming my more nervous patients while they were waiting out here."

Jeannie looked up at him, speechless at this offer. "Do you mean I can bring the girls with me on Saturdays?" An unexpected boon.

"Sure. As long as they behave as they did today. I told you, I believe in the benefits of humans being with animals. In the past, people and domesticated animals spent their lives side by side. We've lost that, lost something both humans and some animals need." He grimaced. "Sorry. I don't mean to lecture. I've always wanted to—"

"Can girls be vets, too?" Cindy interrupted, tilting her head back to look up at Jake.

"Yes, girls…women can be vets." Jake stooped to be at eye level with the twins. "Girls and boys who want to be vets must study hard at school, especially in science."

"Okay!" Mimi and Cindy hugged him. "We will!"

He clumsily patted both small backs. The sight cuddled Jeannie's heart. She wanted to throw her arms around him, too. She held herself still, yet wondered what he'd been about to say before the girls interrupted him. *I've always wanted to…what?*

When the twins released him, Jeannie cleared the croaking frog in her throat. "Say good-night to Bummer, girls. And pick up the kittens and head for the van." They all moved toward the doorway. The girls obediently scooped up the kittens and ran ahead.

Jake walked beside her and then reached to turn off the lights, accidentally throwing Jeannie off balance. She stumbled into his arms. "Oof!" she gasped. She knew she should pull away. She found she couldn't. She fit into his arms perfectly.

Jake held her close a moment. His wool scarf tickled her nose. His breath warmed her cheek. "Sorry about that. Are you okay?"

"Yes." Forcing herself, she pushed away from him. "I must have tripped." She looked down. Bummer grinned up at her— did he plan that maneuver? *Oh, boy, my imagination is running away with me.* She offered Jake her hand. "Thanks for the job. I'll do my best for you and the clinic."

Jake cleared his throat. "I'm sure you will. See you Tuesday morning at eight o'clock."

"Right." She stumbled toward the door and fled into the cold night, her face flaming. She got into the van and slammed the door.

"Did he kiss you good-night?" Mimi piped up.

"What?" Aghast, Jeannie glanced over her shoulder at the twins.

"That's what a man does at the end of a date. He kisses the girl good-night," Mimi explained.

"Yeah, we seen it in lots of movies," Cindy agreed. "And Aunt Ginny says that's what happens."

Jeannie started her engine and backed out to the road, fleeing toward home. "It was not a date." And no kiss. Her lips tingled with…regret. "Dr. Jake just took us out for pizza to celebrate hiring me to work at the clinic. It was not a date," she repeated. Who was she trying to convince? "And I'm not intending to date Dr. Jake. I've got you two to take care of, remember?"

"But Dr. Jake likes us," Mimi said.

"Yes, he does. But liking us is not the same as dating." *Is never the same.* At this thought, her lungs hitched, making it hard to breathe.

"But he could date you—"

"*Mimi,* Dr. Jake is a good man, but I'm just his office manager.

I work for him. That's *all*. Dr. Jake and I aren't dating. If that changes, I'll let you know." *But it won't change.*

"You'll let us know right away?" Mimi asked, making sure.

"Yes, you'll be the first to know. So until then—no comments about Dr. Jake and I kissing and dating. Got that?" She tilted her head to see the girls in the rearview mirror.

"Got it," they repeated in unison.

Jeannie wished she felt some satisfaction, having succeeded in getting this knotty issue all sorted out. She didn't. Kissing Jake sounded very appealing. *Don't go there. Men don't go for package deals. You found that out the hard way—twice already. Got it?*

Got it, she replied glumly.

On Wednesday afternoon, Jake—finally well rested but tense—drove southwest through strong winds toward the airport in Mosinee to pick up his father. Why did some fathers and sons rub each other the wrong way? Somehow his dad knew unfailingly which of Jake's hot buttons to poke to get maximum reaction. Time for this to change, for Jake to change.

He drew in a deep breath. *Even if he's as critical as always, I will not react negatively to my father.*

The strife between them had started years ago when his mom and his brother Tommy had died. That event set this edgy pattern in motion. Would he ever be able to give up the grudge he carried? *Help me, God.*

Jeannie's face suddenly came to mind, as it often had over the past week. No woman had caught his attention like this for a very long time. He imagined her long golden brown hair soft between his fingertips. *Stop. My life's just too busy. And besides, she works for me now.*

After the havoc Sheila had caused him, he felt a sharp twinge of caution. Though he tried to put the destructive past out of his heart and mind, his ex-wife had left her poisonous claws lodged within him.

Stretching his tight neck muscles, Jake tried to release his tension over the past, over his dad's visit. He turned off the interstate at the Central Wisconsin Airport exit. Soon he pulled up to "Arrivals" and glimpsed his dad, waiting with a brown leather overnight bag and a matching suitcase by his side. Jake pulled in front of him at the curb.

His grim-faced father threw his bags in the back of the pickup before Jake could even get out to help. As Dan McClure got in, they exchanged gruff hellos and polite "How was your flight?" chatter. This ended too quickly. Jake headed back onto the interstate. A heavy silence hung in the truck cab till his dad craned his neck around as if searching for something. "Where's Bummer?"

The question itself wasn't what twisted Jake's insides. His dad hadn't asked a rude or intrusive question. Jake's hypersensitivity was the culprit, and Bummer's recent shenanigans sharpened this. *There's no call for me to respond negatively.* He made his voice light and neutral. "Bummer decided to stay at the clinic while I came to get you."

"What's at the clinic that's so attractive?"

Jeannie. Over the past few days Bummer had showed he was as attracted to her as much as he was to the twins. Jake couldn't blame Bummer. Her soft musical voice drew him also, made him want to sit and talk to her. Hold her hand.

Jake wrenched his mind back to the present, his pulse still skipping. "Bummer's taken a liking to my new office manager."

Dan made an almost approving noise. "A nice woman?"

"Nice enough." Jake passed off the question. He didn't want to set off any questions about Jeannie. He couldn't handle them right now. Especially since his dad had approved of Sheila and blamed Jake for their divorce. That still cinched his gut.

"How long will you be staying?" Jake asked.

"A few weeks. I needed a break."

Jake had not expected his father to come for an extended stay. He usually just came for three-day weekends, either between teaching at medical conferences and schools, or time spent in the mountains at his cabin near Aspen. "Well, don't expect much in the way of outdoor time. This winter has been cold and snowy, unusually so." Jake tried but failed to keep his voice colorless.

"Don't worry. I won't get in your way." Now his dad sounded annoyed.

Jake relented. He hadn't meant to sound unwelcoming. Maybe his dad's hypersensitivity matched Jake's toward him. "It's not that. You know the house is big enough for the two of us and I'll be busy working. It's just been a very severe winter."

"How's Old Mike doing?" his dad asked, changing topics to a safe one. "Still keeping house for you?"

"After Christmas, he had a bad bout of bronchitis. Otherwise he's doing fine."

The two of them lapsed into silence till they both got out at the farmhouse. His father paused, looking around. "It's good to be home."

"You should try it more often." Jake instantly regretted saying this. *What can't we just be father and son, not adversaries?* "I'm sorry. I shouldn't have said—"

"I'm going to be around home more." His dad turned to look at him. "I may be retiring this year."

Jake gazed at his father. "Retiring? You've never mentioned that before. I didn't think you'd ever retire." He shut the garage door.

The two of them hustled toward the house. Inside, they shed their outerwear and hurried into the warm kitchen. Something with cinnamon smelled good. Mike greeted them and shook Jake's father's hand. "I made your favorite apple bran muffins, Dan."

His dad grinned. "Thanks. Nothing to eat on the plane. Not even a bag of peanuts." He sat down and let Mike serve him a buttered muffin and hot coffee.

Jake slid into a chair, too. "So when did you decide to retire?"

"Haven't decided really. Just thinking about it. I figured I'd come for a visit and look around, see old friends. Decide whether to retire here or Colorado. I'm going to visit my old friend Lewis in Madison for a few days later this week. Catch up with a few of my other friends who teach or practice at the university hospital with him."

He began asking Mike about old friends. But Jake thought his dad's attitude has altered a bit. Some of the frost had gone out of him. Jake gripped the handle of his heavy coffee mug, wondering what exactly had prompted his dad to come home in the midst of a hard winter *just to visit old friends.* Why not in summer when they could go golfing and such? What wasn't his dad telling Mike and him about this visit?

"Did Jake tell you he hired a good-looking single mom with pretty twin girls to run his office?" Mike asked.

Jake would have gladly strangled Mike, who grinned at him, chuckling silently.

"He mentioned that Bummer likes her," Dan said, assessing his son.

"Smart hound," Mike said. "Jeannie's pretty and sweet, too. I can't see why some guy hasn't snapped her up. But then, a lot of guys are blind in one eye and can't see out of the other." Mike had the nerve to wink.

His father gave Jake a searching look, not a cheery one.

Jake sipped his coffee. *You'll pay for this, Mike.*

On a cold and clear Sunday afternoon, Jake drove up to Jeannie's half-finished house on New Friends Street. He hadn't dreamed his dad would volunteer to come along today. A new house sat on the corner beside the site of Jeannie's house. And an empty lot sat on its other side for the final of the three being built in town. A few snow-flocked fir trees dotted Jeannie's lot.

Several familiar cars were already parked along the street. Jake hesitated. How would his dad take to Jeannie? Dan could be dismissive of those he considered less important than surgeons. *I don't want her feelings hurt.*

"Are you sure you want to help?" Jake asked his dad. "You could just come in, look around and then pick me up later."

"I don't know how to do much, but what I can do, I will." Dan pulled his scarf up and climbed out of the car. Jake dragged out his bag of carpentry tools and jogged after his dad. Had he tagged along just to get a look at Jeannie? Dan could be condescending when someone didn't measure up to his standards.

Amid the drifts of snow, Jeannie's house consisted of only a shell at present. But last week the doors and windows had been added, so at least it could be heated now.

Over the packed-down path through the snow, they hurried inside and shut the door behind them. Half a dozen people already milled around the large living room/dining/kitchen area. While searching for Jeannie, Jake recognized Eleanor Washburn, who headed up these three Habitat projects.

She saw him and nodded. "Well, we're all here now. Let's get started. We're putting in the plumbing today and starting to insulate. Bosses, hold up your hands. Workers, attach yourself to a boss and let them tell you what to do."

People moved around, getting into small groups. Then Jake saw Jeannie. In fact, the crush of people pushed them up against each other. Jake caught her by the shoulders and the light floral scent from her hair drifted to him. "Great to see so many out to help with your house." He hoped his words hid his pleasure at having her so near. Didn't want his dad to pick up on that.

"You didn't need to come," she said, blushing.

Mimi and Cindy popped up, one on each side of them. "Hi, Dr. Jake!" they chorused. "Where's Bummer?"

He couldn't stop the grin their friendliness sparked. "I didn't tell Bummer where I was going. No animals needed here. They might get stepped on."

"Our kitties are home, too," Cindy said.

"Mom just let us come for a few minutes," Mimi explained. "Aunt Ginny—" Mimi pointed at the familiar older woman standing by the door "—is going to take us home. But Mom said we could see the inside of our new house."

"We'll like it better when it's got walls inside," Cindy said.

"This must be Jeannie." Jake's dad appeared at Jeannie's side. "Mike said Jake's new office manager had twin girls—pretty ones."

Jake's blood slowed with dread. What would his dad say?

The twins looked up at his father, brimming with curiosity. "I'm Mimi," she said, her pigtails bouncing with her.

"I'm Cindy."

"Since you call Jake Dr. Jake, you can call me Dr. Dan." He patted each girl on the head. As if they were stray puppies or something.

"Jeannie, this is my dad, Dr. Dan McClure." Jake nodded toward Dan. "He's home for a few weeks."

Jeannie gave that shy smile that did things to the back of Jake's neck. "Dr. McClure, so glad to meet you. You have a great son." Then she colored. "He's really a great vet and a great boss."

Dan studied her, but not with any evident approval. "I'm sure you're correct." His voice was cool. "Jake, perhaps we should get started working."

"Dr. Jake," Mimi said, suddenly gripping Jake's lower arm, "will you come to church Saturday night? It's Winter Carnival. There'll be a games and hot dogs and cake."

Jake noted the disapproval in his dad's eyes. No, winter carnivals at church wouldn't suit Dr. Dan, internationally lauded surgeon.

"Yes!" Cindy agreed. "Please come! It's to help little children around the world that don't got enough food." Cindy's voice pleaded.

"You come, too, Dr. Dan, okay?" Mimi looked up at him.

Jeannie tried to shush the children.

"That sounds like a worthy cause. We'll try to make it," his father replied dismissively, urging Jake toward two men who had motioned them to come join their twosome.

Glancing over his shoulder, Jake watched Jeannie take the girls to Ginny. He knew when the three left because cold air rushed in. Jake tried to focus on the boss of their quartet—he'd never done plumbing. But he found himself keeping track of Jeannie, speaking to Eleanor in the future kitchen area.

Jake and his dad, with some others, trooped down to the basement. They stood gazing up at the floor joists for a quick lesson in how to glue together plastic pipes, which would weave between and under the joists. Jake began to relax. Dan meeting Jeannie had gone better than he'd expected. Not good, but not bad, either.

The plumber now explained water pressure and the different shutoff valves where water came into the house from the city system.

Jake and his father were standing very close.

"I didn't realize that Jeannie was *so* pretty," Dan muttered into Jake's ear.

Jake steeled himself for what might be coming as he focused on the explanation of pipe compound and the advantages of plastic PVC versus old lead pipes.

"She has a lot of baggage," Dan continued, under his breath. "The girls look like she's done a good job with them, but you don't need to get involved with a single mom of two."

The uncaring words gripped Jake, twisting, tightening his nerves like a wrench. With a sinking sensation, Jake glimpsed movement from the corner of his eye. Jeannie. He hadn't realized that she'd followed them down into the basement. Had she heard what his dad had said?

"That just brings a whole lot of problems you shouldn't have to deal with," his dad concluded. Jake pressed his lips together to hold back the stream of angry words he wanted to spout. He heard footsteps and saw Jeannie hurrying up the open stairs.

He took a deep breath and said into his father's ear in a scorching tone, "She's a wonderful, caring woman, but she's my office manager. I'm not the kind of boss who hits on his female employees."

His dad looked startled. "Of course you're not."

Then blessedly they had to devote themselves to moving to the section of pipe they would be assembling. Still burning with indignation, Jake wondered if he should say something to Jeannie, excuse his father for insensitivity. The twins weren't "baggage." They just showed what a great mom Jeannie was.

On Tuesday morning, Jeannie had, for the very first time, dreaded coming to work at the clinic. The few words she'd overheard between Jake and his dad at her Habitat house on Sunday kept replaying in her mind—over and over.

So much baggage.... Don't get involved with a single mom.... That brings a whole lot of problems you shouldn't have to deal with.

She chewed her lower lip. *I don't know why it should bother me. Lots of people—most people—think like Jake's dad.* She'd better keep that in mind. Jake occupied the position of her boss, not a potential date. A good thing, a very good thing in light of her past failed relationships.

The waiting room filled up with the vet clinic's small-animal clients. Kittens, puppies, canaries, hamsters. The assorted sounds and antics distracted Jeannie. She found herself smiling and focusing on the lively waiting room. *Thank You, Lord, for this great job.*

Sandy came to the front, lifted the first file from the counter, and called the patient's name—Sir Squiggly, the hamster. Jeannie chuckled and answered the phone.

The morning progressed till the final appointment before lunch. A well-dressed brunette who looked familiar came in and approached the counter. She carried a prissy white miniature French poodle. "I'm Brooke Hyde."

The woman then introduced her pet, but Jeannie couldn't understand what the woman had said. "Could you spell that for me, please?"

Brooke Hyde gave her a disdainful glance. "It's French." The woman's tone added *"you're obviously too ignorant to know that."* "*D-o-u-x C-h-a-r-m-e-u-r P-e-u,*" she spelled each word out letter by letter.

"What does it mean?" Jeannie asked, bending to get the patient file. She grinned to herself because the final word sounded like "Poo."

"It means 'sweet little charmer,' and that's what you are, aren't you, Charmeur?" she crooned to the poodle.

Jeannie thought, *Gag me with a spoon. Poor embarrassed dog.*

Jake appeared at the counter.

"Jake, hello," Brooke said in a flirtatious tone.

Jeannie couldn't believe it. The woman actually batted her eyelashes at him, just like in a Daisy Duck cartoon. Jeannie clamped her quivering lips shut so she wouldn't start laughing.

"Oh, hi," he said. "I'll be with you in a moment."

Brooke pouted and turned to take a seat—far away from the remaining pet owners and pets. Obviously she thought she and "Poo" were too good for the hoi polloi, the common herd. As Jeannie reached to answer yet another call, she reflected that Jake's dad would probably approve of little "Poo's" owner for his son. Suddenly Jeannie didn't feel like laughing. She concentrated on the phone call.

The final hour before lunch passed quickly. The vet clinic always buzzed and Jeannie liked that. She focused her mind on filing and phone calls, not Dan McClure's low opinion of her. Or the woman with the poodle who looked like she wanted to gobble up Jake with a soup spoon.

After the poodle had been examined, Brooke, with "Poo" in

her arms, walked with Jake back to the counter. As she wrote the check, Jake turned to go.

"Oh, Jake," Brooke purred, "I have some leftover lasagna at my place. Why don't you follow me home and I'll give you lunch?"

In the nearly empty waiting room, there came one of those awkward, embarrassing silences.

The phone rang. Jeannie picked it up, trying to ignore the uncomfortable atmosphere expanding around her. "Hello, McClure Vet Clinic—"

"I need someone to come and pick up some kittens." The woman's agitated voice instantly caught Jeannie's attention. Something was wrong.

"What kittens? Is this an emergency?" Jeannie asked.

"Yes," the woman said. "I'd intended to drive the kittens to the shelter, but my car won't start. I need to get the kittens out of the house. And the shelter isn't answering its phone. Will Dr. McClure come get the kittens? Please."

"Are the kittens ill?" Jeannie asked, eyeing Brooke, whose embarrassed face had turned pink. Jeannie almost felt sorry for her.

"No," the woman on the phone replied, "but my husband says if they're still here when he gets home, he'll drown them. Please. The children would be so upset."

The words chilled Jeannie's blood. "Doctor," she said, "we have an emergency."

Within minutes, Brooke and her poodle had left in a huff. After taking down the woman's address, Jeannie told Jake about the kittens' plight. "I'll drive over and get them," she said, rising. "Then I'll take them to the shelter."

"No, the shelter's closed today. That's why they're not answering. Besides, it's full, remember? I'll have to get hold of Annie so she can call a foster home. Let's go. I'll take you. The kittens may need medical attention. At the very least, they'll need distemper shots."

Jeannie tried to deter him from accompanying her, tried to keep her distance. However, before she knew it, they were in his pickup, rolling out into the county. Watching for the road signs, Jeannie sat as far as she could from Jake. A snowy sky, a thick white blanket, hovered over them. Snow flurries swirled around the windshield.

Jeannie's thoughts and emotions imitated the snowflakes. Swirling in her mind were the woman who'd called and sounded so distressed, the scene with Brooke Hyde and the poodle and Dan's warnings to Jake about keeping his distance. She shook these upsetting thoughts off. "Is it legal to drown kittens?"

"No, but that doesn't mean people don't still do it," Jake said, sounding aggravated. "Farmers need cats to keep the vermin down. Most are fond of barn cats and would never hurt them. But in every population there are a few...total jerks."

Jeannie sighed, giving sound to her sorrow at this truth. "Have you asked about trying to connect with the local TV station to do a spot about the need for adoptions at the shelter?"

"I'm not good with that sort of thing. I mentioned it to Annie, but she hasn't let me know how she's doing with it."

"You need to call her about this litter, don't you?"

He nodded.

"Do you have her cell number? Why don't we call her about these now and then ask her?"

He lifted his cell from his pocket, pressed a few buttons, and handed it to her. "It's ringing."

Voice mail picked up, so Jeannie left a message and handed the phone back to Jake. She glanced at her scribbled directions. "Here's the road. We turn right."

They drove up to a battered, peeling house with an assortment of half-dismantled cars and machine parts protruding from the mounds of snow. A woman came to the door and waved them toward an ancient barn, which listed to the south on its original stone foundation.

Jake and Jeannie hurried through the cold into the relative

shelter of the old barn, obviously being used just as storage or a dump for castoffs. The woman, who wore torn jeans and an old hoodie sweatshirt under a man's tattered jacket, led them to a cardboard box covered with a threadbare blanket. The pitiful sound of mewing kittens came from it.

Standing close to Jake, Jeannie looked down in the dim light. The little black-and-white kittens were so young they still had their eyes closed.

"Here they are," the woman said with a gentle voice. "Their mom was my best mouser, but she got hit on the road yesterday." The woman paused as if swallowing tears.

The woman's sadness caught Jeannie. She looked into her red-rimmed eyes and the separation between the two was swept away. With her heart, Jeannie glimpsed the woman's lonely, work-filled hours and a black-and-white cat rubbing against her leg and purring. *She's weeping over losing her mama cat, her friend.* Warm sympathy rushed through Jeannie. She blinked back tears, coming back to the woman's voice.

"So I started feeding them with a baby bottle last night. My husband said they aren't worth all that work." The woman bit her lower lip. "I don't think he would really drown them. But I didn't want him to upset the kids."

Jerk. Jeannie patted the woman's shoulder.

Jake knelt down and raised one of the little kittens. "Did you feed them cow's milk?"

"No, I had some powdered soy formula left from my last baby. I mixed that up and warmed it for them."

Jeannie observed the woman, who was loving the kittens with her tender gaze.

Jake rose. "You did fine. We'll take the litter to my clinic. I'll look them over and then get them to the shelter. Or a foster home."

"Thanks. That's such a relief," the woman said, wiping her moist eyes with the back her hand. "I've got something for you." She pulled a jar from each of her two pockets. "Here's some of my homemade strawberry jam." She offered it to Jeannie but kept her face lowered. "For your trouble. I really appreciate you both coming out like this." Her voice trembled. "I was just at my wit's end."

The woman's stark tone pierced Jeannie. How many times had her own voice trembled with the same anguish in her heart?

Jake rose, lifting the blanketed box of kittens. "Thanks, ma'am. That's very nice of you."

"Yes, thank you," Jeannie said, taking the woman's offering. "It wasn't necessary, but thanks."

Her face twisted as if in pain, the woman reached a finger under the blanket and stroked one of the kitten's heads. "You kittens, be good now." The woman's voice sounded thick. A trace of a sob welled up from deep inside her. She nodded and then ran from the barn, her shoulders shaking.

Jeannie thought about her two little kittens and two little girls at home. Suddenly her throat thickened and tears stung her eyes. All the poor orphans in this world, furry ones and little children like hers. Like her.

Heading back to the pickup, Jake forged a path for them through the debris. Jeannie trudged after him, buffeted by the harsh wind as well as a current of sorrow. He opened the door and waited for her to get in. When she sat on the high seat, Jake handed her the box. Soon they were on the road again.

Jeannie crooned to the kittens, stroked them, and held in her tears. *Poor woman. Poor mama cat. Poor orphaned kittens.* The old, never-healed wound from losing Carrie opened. Its deep shaft of pain forced her to take a sharp breath.

When they arrived at the clinic, the parking lot had cleared of cars. No clinic patients had been scheduled this afternoon and Sandy must still be gone for lunch. Relief sighed through Jeannie—no one to face.

Inside, she stood across from Jake, with the high examining table between them. One by one, he gently lifted out the kittens. Murmuring to them, he examined their teeth, ears, prodded their abdomens and gave them distemper shots. All the while Jeannie pressed her lips tightly together to hold it all in—all her sadness, her loss and her loneliness. She and Carrie had been orphaned, too, and left defenseless in this harsh world.

When Jeannie had placed the last kitten back into the box, she turned away, trying to hide the tears that could no longer be held back. Trying to stop them.

"Jeannie, oh, Jeannie," Jake said and within two steps, she found herself in his arms. "Don't cry."

Chapter Five

Jake folded Jeannie into his arms and against him. Jeannie—soft and warm and fragrant, with the subtle scent of lilacs.

"I'm sorry. I'll stop—" But then a sob erupted, ripping the peace of the quiet clinic.

"This is about more than just these poor kittens." His observation slipped out unexpectedly, but he judged it to be true. "What's wrong, Jeannie?" *I can't bear to see you cry. Let me make it right.*

"It's just all the orphans in this sad world. I know how that feels—I was one," she whispered.

Me, too. He'd never put this into words. But he had been orphaned, too. At least, that was how he'd always felt. A lump in his chest, he tugged Jeannie even closer. "I'm here," he said simply.

She rubbed her face against his shirt, her tears moistening the cotton. "My mom…she couldn't take care of us. So Carrie and I ended up in foster care."

"Carrie?" He pressed her closer still. The urge to protect her surged within.

"My little sister." Jeannie chuckled but in a sad minor key. "She's five years younger than I am." She muffled another sob against his shirt. "I ended up losing her, too."

"You lost her?" He lifted her chin with his forefinger. Her dark eyelashes sparkled with tears. Sorrow wrenched him, a sharp, unseen spasm.

She slumped against him. He knew how strong emotions, a crisis could suck out all a person's strength. Concern for her flowing, he guided her toward the two chairs by the door. He urged her into one. Sitting down beside her, he kept one of her hands, so small, in his. "Jeannie, that night at the potluck, your pastor told me that your girls are really your nieces. Is Carrie their mom?"

"That's right." Errant tears still dripped from her eyes. She didn't bother to wipe them away. "Right after high school Carrie moved to Chicago." Jeannie gazed into his eyes, her expression melancholy. "I thought she knew better than to get mixed up in the drug world."

She shook her head, new tears overflowing. "After not contacting me for over a year, she finally appeared at my door in Milwaukee. Just a few days later, I went to the hospital with her. She gave birth to the twins."

In the moment of quiet, a dog recovering in the kennel moaned. This mournful sound blended with their low mood. Jake gave Jeannie's shoulders a gentle squeeze to reassure her.

She wiped her face with her free hand. "Carrie had told me she wasn't using, but…I was so relieved when…there was no trace of drugs in the girls' systems." She shuddered as if rocked by an aftershock.

Jake tucked her closer and laid an arm around her shoulders. "Thank God."

She looked up at him, but her eyes were far away, probably remembering. And suddenly Tommy's face drifted into Jake's mind. If he'd lived, how old would Tommy be now? Sorrow latched on to Jake, an old and painful wrenching of his spirit. He tried to draw breath, but his tight chest pained him.

"Carrie and I brought the girls home to my tiny apartment and we started to make plans. But when the twins were only a few weeks old, Carrie insisted on going back to Chicago to get her things and end it with the man…the man she'd been living with. I begged her not to go." Another sob forced its way from deep within Jeannie. She covered her mouth with a hand.

He coaxed her closer under his arm, rubbing her long, slender back softly. "She didn't come back, did she?"

Jeannie shook her head against him. She trembled, unable to hide her battle against tears. Dragging in air, she straightened up, as if reviving. "I reported her disappearance, but the police never found her."

"She's still missing?"

Jeannie shrugged, a curious little shake that somehow prepared him for what came next. "I'd given up hope. Then over a year later, I got a postcard from her. It said: *I know you'll take care of my girls. Don't worry, I'm fine.* But how can she be fine?"

Jake felt his face twist into a deep grimace. "What did the police say?"

"They couldn't trace who sent the postcard. No return address, just a postmark from a town in the Upper Peninsula of Michigan. They said that it probably meant that she was alive but involved in something illegal. Or in a dangerous relationship she wanted to shield her daughters from."

He voiced that little sound of sympathy that had no name. Why did such a sweet woman have to suffer so?

"If I'd had any money, I'd have tried to hire a private investigator. The police suggested that. But about that time, Milwaukee social services got wind of my taking care of the girls. A social worker came by."

Jeannie gazed at him, eye to serious eye. "Fortunately before leaving Milwaukee, my sister mailed me a notarized letter, giving me legal guardianship of the girls. About that time, I decided to get out of Milwaukee. I wanted a better life for us." Jeannie sighed and then withdrew completely from under his arm.

He missed the contact with her. "I'm glad you did."

"I'm sorry I fell apart like that." She glanced away, wiping her tears. "It was just…in that barn, looking into that woman's eyes. I saw in them what I've felt a few times…like life just brings too much sorrow. I know it's silly to cry about losing a cat—"

"No, it's not," Jake interrupted. *You weren't crying about orphaned kittens.* "I lost a brother, too," he whispered.

Jeannie looked up as if to ask a question. The opening of the rear employees' entrance interrupted them. The pets in the kennels let it be known—loud and strong—they'd heard it, too. "I'm back from lunch!" Sandy called out over the pet chorus.

Turning toward him, Jeannie leaned forward and kissed his chin. "Thanks."

Had she heard him? Startled, he barely had time to respond before she covered the few feet to the box of kittens. "I hope we can find these little ones good homes," she said, setting the box between them. "Should we call Annie back?"

Sandy called out again, "I brought you two subs from the café. Figured you didn't get lunch anywhere. Or lasagna." On the last two words, Sandy's tone turned wry.

It zapped Jake's mind back to the poodle woman and her offer of lunch at her place. He frowned at the memory. How did a gentleman handle such obvious and unwelcome ploys?

Sandy leaned in at the doorway, waving a white paper bag with the aroma of garlic and onion. "Hungry?"

"Yes," Jeannie said. "Let me put these little ones in the kennel and I'll be all over mine."

Sandy led her down the hall toward the rear. Just as Jake entered the hallway, Jeannie turned and mouthed, *Thanks again.*

Thanks? For what? I didn't do anything for you, Jeannie. I just wish I could. And he sure wished Sandy hadn't come back so soon.

For the first time in a very long time, Jake had wanted to talk about Tommy. Jeannie would have understood his lingering sorrow over the loss of an only brother. But she must not have heard his whispered words. Or had she? His cell phone vibrated in his pocket. He pulled it out.

"Hey, Jake, I've got a foster home for those kittens. And I got news for you from the TV station in Rhinelander. They say they'll do an interview with you about our overcrowded situation—"

"Me?" Dismay arched through him. "No way."

"I thought you'd say that." Annie had the nerve to chuckle. "So I offered them Jeannie, her twins and adopted kittens…and you. Will they do it?"

"I'll ask her." *And I'll stay in the background.*

Annie gave him the name and address of the foster home for the kittens. He went in search of Jeannie and found her sitting in the break room, eating her sub.

"How would you like to be on TV?"

Jeannie didn't choke, but she did drop half her sandwich in her lap.

He smiled for the first time that day.

Jake sat in the passenger seat of Jeannie's van, stiff as an icicle. The girls and kittens were behind them. Bummer had insisted on lying on the floor at the twins' feet. Ahead, Annie and the five rescued kittens were on the way in her salt-encrusted SUV.

"Jake," Jeannie said quietly, "you need to loosen up. I feel like you're about to snap like a rubber band. This is just a small TV station. It's not like it's Milwaukee or Chicago or something."

Jake appreciated Jeannie's effort to ease his stage fright. "I don't like speaking in front of people." *Don't like* paled in comparison to his true gut reaction. *I hate speaking in front of people. I'd rather be facing a root canal.*

Jeannie drove up a hillside drive to a building surrounded by a "farm" of huge satellite dishes. Annie had already arrived. She stood inside the doorway with the box of kittens. Jake, Jeannie, the girls and Bummer ran to Annie, who held the door open for them. Then they milled around the receptionist, who pointed them to the coatrack.

The broadcaster, a pleasant-looking young woman in a simple blue pantsuit, came forward greeting them. "I'm Shelley. Let's sit over here." She motioned toward an area of chairs that Jake recognized from watching interviews of local people speaking about community projects and gatherings. "Now, you don't have anything to be nervous about," she said as they were all seated.

Jake wished she hadn't said that. He zoned out then, freezing in place in his chair.

Then the broadcaster rose. "Time to start. I'll join you for our live interview in a few moments."

Live interview. The words gave him an electrical shock of terror. He'd thought it would be taped, so if he said something stupid, it could be edited out. Why had he agreed to this?

Jeannie, Annie and the girls chatted around him, then became silent as the five o'clock news show launched. The critical moment arrived. During a commercial break, Shelley swooped into the chair beside Jake. "Everyone miked?"

Just a few minutes before, another woman had fitted them all with little black bud microphones. So Jake nodded woodenly. *I hate this.*

Suddenly Shelley beamed. "Hi! Today we have the volunteers from our local animal shelter here, Dr. Jake McClure and Annie Slocomb. Dr. McClure, your shelter is experiencing problems. Could you explain the situation?"

Mimi raised her hand. "I can. I can."

Shelley chuckled. "What's your name?"

"I'm Mimi and these are Twinkie and Peanutbutter, the kittens we rescued." At that moment, Bummer perked up and barked; then he began licking the kittens vigorously.

"Good grief," Shelley said.

"Bummer thinks he's their daddy," Cindy explained. "He's just grooming them like a mama cat would."

"Shelley," Annie spoke up, "this is the wonder of kids and animals. Our problem right now is that we have too many animals and not enough children. We no longer have any room for new strays. This winter has been so harsh, I think people are putting off adopting a new pet. But the animals still need us."

"Yes, the shelter is a no-kill shelter," Jeannie said. "I think people should know they need to brave the winter and come to the shelter to adopt."

Jake sat happily silent, letting the females take the lead.

"These kitties need to be adopted," Mimi said, nodding down at the five balls of fur on Annie's lap.

"They are really sweet," Cindy agreed. "But we got two kittens and that's all we can have at our house."

"But other children should ask their parents to bring them to the shelter," Mimi said earnestly. "The animals there all want homes, not staying in cages." She shook her head soulfully.

Shelley chuckled. "This is certainly one of the easiest and most fun interviews I've done in a while. Now if people would like to adopt any of these kittens, what do they have to do?" She focused on Jake.

He cleared his throat. "Drop by the animal shelter. We're open every day but Sunday." Perspiration popped out on his forehead.

"Yes," Annie chimed in, "we're on County K near River Road. We need volunteers, foster homes for animals and most of all, people who can find room for a pet or two in their homes. Pets bring so much love into our lives. Dr. Jake and I have discussed starting a place where disabled or disadvantaged children can interact with so-called unwanted animals. But first we need to get our community supporting the animal shelter. Then we can take it a big step further. Dr. Jake has already offered us his property as the location of this future effort."

Shelley looked startled. "That sounds really interesting. I'd like to have you and Dr. Jake come back sometime soon and tell us more. This sounds like something that would benefit our whole community."

"We'd be happy to come again," Annie replied, "but right now we really need people ready to adopt or foster animals. And we need that to happen *now*."

Shelley gave the contact information for the shelter, thanked them and petted Bummer and then the next commercial freed them from the camera.

"Great idea about the place for animals and disabled children," Shelley said. "I've read about equine therapy for emotionally disturbed children, with NARHA, the North American Riding for the Handicapped Association."

"We're looking to provide something like that here in the future," Annie declared, glancing at Jake.

Jake swallowed. Why had Annie shined light on his secret ambition?

"Great." Shelley hurried back to her desk in front of the cameras. "Keep me posted!"

Still tense, Jake tried to relax. However, Annie's unexpected announcement kept him taut. "Annie," he muttered, "why did you bring that up? I'm not near ready to do anything—"

"If I waited on you, I'd be in my old age before anything actually happened. I know you're too busy with your practice and I'm too busy running the shelter. But by bringing it up here, someone out there may have heard this. And that might be the person who has been wanting to do something similar who will connect with us." Annie shrugged. "How could it hurt?"

"I think it's a wonderful idea," Jeannie added. "I'll do what I can to help."

"See?" Annie grinned. "Gotta run." And Annie gathered up the kittens, petted Bummer and left, whistling.

Jeannie and Jake rounded their tribe up and soon sat back in the van. "I thought that went pretty well," Jeannie said, driving toward the clinic. "Do you really want to turn your acreage into a place for animals and disabled children?"

"Yes, but I'm just too busy now to get it off the ground."

"There's a lot of that going around," Jeannie said ruefully. "Let's pray that someone heard and will pick up the flag and lead the effort."

Jake knew he should agree with every word Jeannie had just said. Nonetheless, an irrational urge to protect his dream reared its nasty head. It was his idea after all. He leaned back and slowly released the tension in his neck and back. *Jeannie's right.* "I can't argue with you about that." But it still didn't sit right. So what was he going to do about it?

In the church basement for the Winter Carnival, Jeannie had parked herself at a crowded table, but alone at one end. She didn't crave company this bleak night. She listened to the faint jangling of the power lines outside, dancing high with the wild wind. Then a violent gust blasted, whistling around the solid red brick church. She rubbed her arms against a phantom chill, then folded them as if protecting herself. Had it started to snow? That could change into a blizzard. Should they have come?

And she wished the girls hadn't invited Jake here tonight. Her chin lowered. Their quiet moment with the kittens had peeled away some self-protective layer, a needed buffer between them. Socializing with him away from work would make guarding herself from getting too close to him even more difficult.

Going to the TV interview had been easier. The girls, the pets and Annie had acted as a buffer. But tonight she might find herself sitting beside Jake. Perhaps at a vulnerable moment. And she might say too much, more than an employee should say to a boss. And still she found herself curious. She wanted to ask him about this idea for bringing unwanted animals and disabled children together. However, he'd seemed upset with Annie for bringing it up. Maybe it was time to step back and let that be, too.

Today, Saturday, had been busier than usual at the clinic.

Maybe Jake had forgotten about the girls' invitation to the Winter Carnival. She hadn't reminded him. Or even if he did remember, this wind might keep him home—dare she hope?

Nonetheless, each time the upstairs side door opened, letting in cold wind, she couldn't stop herself. She glanced over to see who'd just arrived. Still no Jake. However, all around her a cheerful group already crowded the church basement. Buffet tables near the kitchen enticed the hungry with sandwiches, chips and slices of cake for sale. Jeannie sat apart, a silent island amid the lively doings.

Different booths, manned by kids and parents, dotted the perimeter of the large bright room. Nearby was a Go Fish booth, where kids swung a children's fishing pole over a half partition painted to look like the ocean filled with exotic fish. The kids "caught" little carnival prizes. Squeals, giggling and game noises filled Jeannie's ears, lifted one corner of her serious mouth.

Then another rush of cold wind turned her head toward the stairway. Not Jake. That woman who'd brought in the poodle, "Poo," to the clinic had entered. Now Jeannie realized she'd seen the woman here before and that's why she'd seemed familiar. What was her name?…Brooke. Brooke's designer jeans and— perhaps cashmere—sweater clashed with the fleece, flannel and worn denim around her.

A hint of loneliness showed in how the woman looked around for someone to sit with. Jeannie experienced a twinge of sympathy for her. *But please don't make Jake uncomfortable—if he comes.* As Jeannie watched Brooke be welcomed by a couple of women who waved her to sit down with them, her mind and conscience were relieved. Seeking fun in a small town, all kinds of people had ventured out into the harsh winter tonight.

Jeannie had been so busy watching Brooke, she'd missed the door opening again. Jake materialized at the bottom of the stairs. Behind him came Mike, and then Jake's dad appeared right behind him—jostling her peace of mind. Jeannie tried not to let Dan's comments at the Habitat house about her and her girls bubble up. But the hurt roiled up anyway. *When will I learn not to react when people view me in a hurtful, negative way?*

Rising, she purposefully turned her back to them and headed toward the kitchen to help out. She didn't want to be anywhere near Jake. She didn't want to give his dad any reason to issue any more warnings. *I've decided to go it alone for my girls' sake, all right? I haven't set my cap for Jake. And what did it mean to set one's cap?* Silly phrase she didn't even understand.

But Jeannie had underestimated her girls. They popped up before she reached the kitchen door. "Mom! Look! Dr. Jake's here! He brought Bummer!"

Jeannie smiled, hoping to conceal her sensitivity about facing Dan. *But he doesn't think any different than most. Why does everybody always act like I'm out to stalk every eligible male?*

Then she realized her girls were waiting for her to show some response to their announcement. She turned and waved. Jake and his dad were heading right for them. *Oh, wonderful. Time for a quick getaway.* "Hi, Jake," she said over her shoulder, "be sure to sample the buffet."

"I will." Catching up to her, he grinned as if happy to see her. "I thought the girls said there would be hot dogs, but I smell something—"

"That's the sloppy joes, Jake," Ginny chimed in from the nearby buffet table where she stirred the contents of one of many Crock-Pots. "We decided to have both. Hand us a mere four bucks and get a hot meal! Get yourself a plate and fill it up!"

"Great. I'm really hungry." Jake smiled at everyone in that charming boyish way of his that always tugged at Jeannie's heart.

"I'm starving!" Mike rubbed his stomach, teasing the girls. "You didn't eat all the good stuff already, did you?"

As Jeannie followed Ginny toward the kitchen, she glimpsed Dan studying her. Giving him a brave "I'm a confident and inde-pendent woman" smile, she waved to him, too, and escaped into the kitchen. Ginny asked her to refill the potato-chip bowls and set them out onto the food tables—quickly. The buffet line of the hungry had backed up.

When Jeannie carried out the filled potato-chip bowls, she met Jake as he, Dan and Mike went through the line.

"Hey there, good-looking!" Mike called out.

For a puzzled moment, Jeannie thought he'd addressed her. But then she realized he meant Ginny, who blushed like a schoolgirl. Jeannie had heard that expression before, but this had to be the first time she'd ever witnessed it.

"Oh, you," Ginny said, "silly old tease."

"That cuts me to the heart, Ginny." Mike placed a hand over the breast pocket of his plaid flannel shirt.

But Jeannie noticed he was grinning. *How sweet.*

"Good evening, Jeannie," Dan said, sounding grave.

Jeannie looked into his eyes. She lifted her chin. *I have nothing to hide my face about.* "Good evening, Doctor. So glad you were able to come tonight."

He made a gruff sound, something between amusement and irony. "No other game in town. I was getting cabin fever."

She could understand and sympathize with him about that. She softened her voice. "This has been a rough winter." Wind gusts still pounded the church from all sides. She'd become almost deaf to it. She hoped the power had remained on at her mobile home. It wouldn't take much of this cold to freeze her pipes.

Mimi and Cindy crowded close to Dan's elbows. "Hi. After you eat," Mimi said, "you got to come and play some games, Dr. Dan."

"Yeah," Cindy agreed, "we'll show you the good ones."

"The good ones, huh?" Her girls managed to force a grin from him. "Okay." He patted Mimi's head as if she were a puppy and smiled hesitantly at Cindy.

The two girls followed him down the line, chattering away. Undaunted. The man's smile for Cindy encouraged some hope in Jeannie. But would he say something rude to the girls? *Surely not.*

Jake paused in front of her, dipping his hand into the huge bowl for a generous serving of chips. "Your daughters have a way about them," he murmured for her ears only. "Maybe my dad would have done better with daughters."

Jeannie caught this last sentence and wondered what trouble needled Jake and his relationship with his dad. "I'm glad you came." She hadn't wanted to say the words, but they had refused to remain unsaid.

"Me, too. I like your church. It's good to hear laughter, and everyone's so friendly."

At that unscripted moment, Jake and Jeannie turned and glimpsed Brooke approaching the buffet line. The woman pointedly did not make eye contact with them—an awkward moment.

Then the lights blinked out. A few women screamed. Babies cried out in fright.

Instinctively Jeannie reached for Jake. Their hands fumbled in the dark, found each other, and held.

"Everyone!" the pastor's voice boomed over the sound of the wind. "Just a power outage! We have an ample supply of candles and lantern flashlights. Stay where you are while our 'lights-out' workers get them lit and distributed around. We don't want anybody falling." Lighter footsteps still pattered on the linoleum. "Kids!" he ordered. "Freeze!"

Then as if everyone held their breath, silence swathed the hall—except for the sounds of a few people moving into the kitchen, quiet voices, drawers opening, the scraping of matches.

Gripping Jake's hand, Jeannie stepped carefully around the end of the narrow buffet table till she bumped into his side. Standing so still in the pitch-black allowed her to experience him in a new way. He smelled of soap, and pleasantly of dog and horse. He moved his arm, cradling her at his side.

She let herself savor this moment. She recalled the feel of his chin against her lips when she'd kissed him that day they'd rescued the kittens. Tempted to turn and brush his cheek again with her lips, she pressed her lips together. Yet in the darkness, no one could disapprove. *Don't.*

Then a few shadowed figures, carrying lighted pillar candles, filtered out of the kitchen. More and more points of light approached near and nearer, here and there. Finally each table boasted a lantern flashlight or a tall pillar candle or two. Glass hurricane chimneys enclosed each candle, holding the flames steady. Communal relief sighed through the gathering. Jeannie inhaled deeply and let go of Jake's hand.

"The wind must have blown down some lines!" The pastor voiced loudly what they were all thinking. "It shouldn't be long before they come back on. Now that we have our candles and flashlights, let's get back to having fun. *But*—" he said with emphasis "—adults watch the children and the candles. The glass chimneys will keep the flames safe, but kids could knock them over inadvertently. We don't want a fire."

Most nodded, but a few said, "You bet! Will do!"

"Come sit with me, Jeannie," Jake invited.

She knew she should say no.

But Ginny overheard and pushed Jeannie from behind. "Go on. Keep the doctor company."

Jeannie followed Jake to the open end of a table nearby. The people at the table greeted them but then went back to talking among themselves. "I was surprised to see your dad come tonight." Then she realized that she shouldn't have said this and added, "Sorry."

"*I* was surprised to see him come. He always acts as if crossing a church threshold is somehow a betrayal of science. He's different somehow this visit. He told me he's thinking of retiring."

Jeannie took her time digesting this. "That's a big life change."

"Yes, and he seems…tired. He's going to visit some friends in

Madison on Monday. That should cheer him up." Jake lifted his sloppy joe and leaned over his white foam plate to take his first bite. A wise choice—some of the filling dropped onto his chips. "Yum. And clever, too—a sandwich and chip dip in one."

An unbidden smile eased her face.

Candlelight changed the mood of the people in the basement hall. Voices had lowered. Even the children's shouts and squeals weren't as shrill. Did fluorescent light affect behavior? Mood? Jeannie's own spirit lost its prickles. She settled down, just watching Jake eat, enjoy the simple meal.

His eyes glistening in the lowlight, Jake glanced into hers. "I can tell that you overheard my dad last Sunday when we came to work on your house. Overheard the things he said about you and the girls. And me."

Jake's words surprised, but didn't embarrass her. Not in this peaceful happy moment. And the mild, somewhat apologetic way he said the words let her respond easily.

"Yes, I heard. I wish I could tell him that I'm not trying to…" Then she didn't know how to go on. How could she say, *I'm not trying to snare you, Jake?*

Innate honesty stopped her. She was innocent of the intent to entrap; however, not innocent of being attracted to him. She ran her finger in circles on the white paper covering the table.

Jake shook his head. "No, you're not the kind of woman I attract." He waved his head toward Brooke's direction.

His self-disgusted tone stung her. "Oh, Jake, no—"

The pastor's voice rose above the other voices, cutting her off. "You all know why we are here tonight! With their Sunday school money, our kids have pledged this year to support three children living in poverty in various countries around the world. And with tonight's fundraiser, our children will make a special donation to supply the immediate needs of children who are waiting for sponsors."

Jake's hand covered hers as it lay on the table. Suddenly

rebellious toward Dan and others' opinions, she didn't slip hers away.

"We would also like to urge those of you who aren't already sponsors to choose a child tonight to sponsor individually. Our children are going to come around, passing out pages, introducing these children who are seeking sponsors. These children need food, clothing and school fees. Please accept one of these children as yours to help. If you do, then tonight will be a great night indeed!"

Everyone applauded. Mimi and Cindy, along with the other children, began moving through the narrow aisles between tables, passing out flyers. Each sheet showed a photo and information about one child. The twins arrived at their table and offered Jake one. "Dr. Jake, this is a boy who lives in Guatemala," Mimi said. "Would you like to be his sponsor?"

Then Cindy handed one to Jeannie. "We want to sponsor this little girl in Haiti. She's our age. She looks like she's a nice girl. Can we help her?"

Jeannie glanced down at the dark little girl in a faded red cotton dress who was smiling shyly. Jeannie's new better-paying job would make this possible. "Of course we will. Can you read her name?"

"She's Francesse," Cindy said, pronouncing the name *Frances*.

"I think the 'e' at the end sounds like an 'a.' It's a French name. Fran-cess-a."

"And my little boy is named Pablo." Jake reached across to show her his sheet. "From my high school Spanish, that's Paul."

After a quick perusal of Pablo's particulars, Jeannie tried to read Jake's expression. Had he been pressured to accept Pablo? But the low light cast Jake's face in shadow. She realized she didn't have to check his expression—Jake wouldn't turn Pablo down. And then an idea popped into Jeannie's mind, an idea to help the overcrowded animal shelter.

"Dr. Jake, will you come to our house for supper on Friday?" Mimi asked.

Taken completely by surprise, Jeannie gawked at her girls.

"Yeah, we don't got school that afternoon and Aunt Ginny is teaching us how to make her macaroni and cheese," Cindy said, completing the invitation. "So we asked if we could make enough for four."

Jeannie felt herself glow a warm embarrassing red.

"I cannot say 'no' to Ginny's macaroni and cheese." Jake grinned broadly. "What time should I show up?"

Jeannie grappled with how to handle this. The girls were getting out of hand.

"Would you come after Mom gets home from work?" Mimi said.

Jeannie still didn't know what to say. How could she politely rescind the unexpected invitation? She couldn't—or show her displeasure with her girls here and now. She decided to put up the best front she could. "Great. Why don't you bring your dad and Mike, too?" she said, hoping to make this look less like a date by broadening the scope.

"I'll ask them. Mike, for one, can never resist Ginny's mac and cheese." Jake lifted his sloppy joe for another bite.

Mimi frowned. Cindy started to object.

Jeannie shushed her. "You two, go on and spend the rest of your game tickets." Jeannie rose. "I need to help in the kitchen. See you at work on Tuesday, Dr. Jake."

"That's what the girls call me. I'm just Jake to you, remember, Jeannie?"

Again, his tone said so much more than his words. She had hurt him by adding the "Dr." to his name. "Okay. Jake."

She glanced around the room. Across from her in the dim light, Brooke sent her an unreadable look. Yet Jeannie walked into the kitchen, imagining the woman's displeasure scorching her back. *Mimi and Cindy, we are going to have a long talk about this very soon.* She shoved away any guess as to what Jake's father would say now. Or she tried to. But more importantly she needed to do some thinking about her wisp of an idea to help the overcrowded conditions at the animal shelter.

Friday evening arrived. Jeannie glanced around her mobile home. Though it had been a normally busy week, she'd cleaned the main room more carefully than usual. The twins had Ginny's special casserole baking, sending forth a yummy aroma. Jake would arrive any second now. What would he say when he heard her suggestion?

Mike and Dan had declined her invitation. Mike had plans and Dan was visiting other friends. Only Jake was expected to come. Jeannie tried to suppress her fizzing anticipation.

"Mom," Mimi said, "take your hair out of the ponytail." The two girls were scrutinizing her.

"What?"

"Take your hair out of the ponytail. When it's down, it looks prettier," Mimi said.

"Yes," Cindy agreed, "all the girls at school say you got the best hair."

"And the longest," Mimi added.

Jeannie couldn't believe her girls were giving her beauty advice. The distinctive sound of Jake's pickup interrupted her retort.

"Mom," Mimi insisted.

Jeannie turned to go greet Jake at the door. And as she went, she capitulated, pulling the elastic band from her ponytail and shaking out her hair. *All right, I do want to look nice for him. So sue me.*

The frigid temperature urged Jake, with Bummer at his heels, to hurry inside. She greeted him and took his coat and hat. When he turned toward her, she saw that under his coat he sheltered a bouquet of fresh flowers—carnations and daisies and others she didn't have names for. No man had brought her flowers in such a very long time. "Oh," she gasped, dumbstruck.

"Oooh, flowers!" the girls squealed. They claimed them and hurried to the kitchen area to find a vase. Bummer woofed and raced after them.

"Thanks," Jeannie said. "That wasn't necessary, but thanks." Her face warmed with pleasure and confusion, no doubt turning a bright pink.

"It was fun going into the flower shop to pick them out. It's been so cold and white for so long. Everything there was green, moist and warm."

"I know what you mean. The flowers are a little spring in February." Jeannie gestured toward the sofa. "Come, sit down. The macaroni still has a few more minutes to bake. You've had a busy week."

"You've had the same week." He sat down near her on the sofa.

She wondered if he had indeed experienced the same week as she. Every day it became more difficult to keep her distance from this man. And now he'd brought her flowers. *How can I keep this from feeling like more than just coworkers or friends?*

Chapter Six

Being in Jeannie's gentle presence soothed Jake's frazzled nerves from a busy week. The low light in the small room cast the golden sheen of her hair as a halo. And she wore it down tonight—just the way he liked it.

But she looked puzzled.

"Is anything wrong?" he asked, hoping for *No.*

"Oh, it's just being a mom." She shrugged. "I always worry when it gets too quiet in the girls' room." She turned. "Girls! What's going on in there?"

"We're playing with Bummer! He's grooming the kitties," Mimi called back.

Jeannie faced him again. "False alarm." She settled back, half turned toward him, half reclining against the arm of the sofa. "Jake—"

A pounding on the door interrupted her and Annie barged in. "It's cold out there!"

Surprise hit Jake right in the stomach. *I thought it would be just me, Jeannie and the girls.* Of course, he couldn't say that. He bent his mouth into a smile. "Annie, what brings you here?"

Annie was dragging off her jacket and hanging it on a peg by the door. "Jeannie thought she might need me to convince you."

"Convince me?" he asked, stung. He hadn't forgotten how Annie had spouted off on TV about his dream for his grandfather's acreage. What next?

Annie plopped on the sofa next to him. "I don't think you'll take too much persuading—"

Jake held up a restraining hand. "What's going on between you two?"

"I think you'll like it," Annie said, patting his arm in a motherly style. "Tell him, Jeannie."

"I've been thinking and I have a great idea. Or—" Jeannie hesitated "—I think it's a great idea."

"It is," Annie reassured her.

Jake's tension eased. He could trust Jeannie. He leaned back and stretched his legs. "Tell me about it."

"It came to me at the Winter Carnival when the girls asked me to sponsor a child. Why can't we do an Adopt-a-Pet day?" Jeannie asked.

Jake's face scrunched up as he considered this. "You mean go on TV again?" *No way.*

"We might. If they won't do an interview on TV," Jeannie said, "I'm sure the Rhinelander station will include the information in their community notes announcements and on their website."

Before he could say a word in reply, a buzzer went off.

Barking, footsteps. Bummer and the twins pelted from the short hall to the kitchen. Jeannie and Annie got up to help the girls lift the large bowl from the oven.

As if from a long way away, Jake watched as the four of them finished setting the meal onto the ancient built-in U-shaped booth. He knew the source of his odd reaction. The scene reminded him of long-ago suppers with his mom, his younger brother, his grandfather and sometimes his dad. A family supper, how good was that?

"Jake, won't you join us?" Jeannie's voice sounded welcoming.

Awkwardly, he rose and claimed the end of the booth opposite

Jeannie and Annie, side by side with the twins between them in the U. Jeannie bowed her head and the girls recited a simple grace.

Jake fought the pull toward Jeannie, toward the allure of family. Lifting a forkful of the creamy macaroni and cheese casserole, he tried to focus on the scent of it and its rich blend of flavors. "Tell me more about this idea of Adopt-a-Pet."

"Are we going to adopt another pet?" Mimi asked, eyes bright.

"Could we get a dog, too?" Cindy said.

Jeannie shook her head. "No, we need to help other children adopt pets." She looked to Jake. "About a month from now, the girls' school always holds a Winter Pet Parade and the kids can bring their pets to the gym. The principal gives out prizes for the animals—you know, biggest dog, etc. I was wondering if we could persuade the school to let us bring some of the orphaned pets who need homes to the parade and encourage the families without pets to choose one that day."

"That would be great!" Mimi bounced on the bench seat.

Annie ruffled Mimi's hair.

"So what do you think, Jake?" Jeannie asked.

"I think it's got real possibilities. Just as long as I don't have to go on TV again."

Jeannie chuckled. "I think we'll leave TV to these 'hams'—" she winked at the twins "—and Bummer. They'd do a better job at persuading people."

Jake began eating again, relieved and suddenly encouraged.

"If it's a success this year, it might spawn other such events," Annie said while digging her fork into the macaroni. "This is delish, Jeannie." She turned to Jake. "You ought to grab this woman up. A ready-made family and she can cook. What more could a man want?"

Jake looked up, startled. Jeannie looked embarrassed.

"Okay, sorry," Annie said, not looking sorry at all.

Jake made no reply. Jeannie's expression had said it all—she was *not* interested in him.

Later, still deflated, Jake stolidly zipped up his jacket and wrapped his muffler around his neck to keep out the wind. "Thanks again for a great meal." He drew in a deep breath, wishing Annie hadn't come tonight.

"My pleasure." Jeannie didn't meet his eyes.

Why did Annie have to make that stupid remark about what more could a man want? *Jeannie's not the only one with "baggage."* "Come on, Bummer!" he called out. "Time to head home!"

A sudden silence in the girls' room. Jeannie sighed a mom-sigh. "Girls! Please, if we have to go through this every time Dr. Jake brings Bummer over, he won't come anymore."

"O-kay!" the girls chorused with ill grace. Bummer leading them, they appeared, each carrying a kitten. "We're really glad you came," Mimi said, holding up her kitten toward him. Cindy bobbed her head in vigorous agreement.

"You did a great job making my favorite meal," he replied, reaching over to pet each kitten. "Thanks." The urge to kiss Jeannie grabbed him. He resisted. A quick about-face and he opened the door. The cold wind rushed him and Bummer outside; he shut the door behind him.

Marshaling his thoughts away from Jeannie's pale pink lips, he opened the pickup's door. With a little boost, Bummer bounded up into his basket.

Jake keyed the ignition and pushed the button that heated his bench seat. One last glance showed him the twins at the window, waving. He flashed his lights and drove into the cold darkness. He arrived at home and walked with heavy steps into his quiet house. Just then he saw his dad drive up in the old SUV he used during visits.

Soon Dan came in—whistling. Jake had moved into the living room, about to turn on The Weather Channel to see tomorrow's forecast. His dad sat down to watch it, too. Jake studied him from the corner of his eye. Dan glowed. What had he been up to tonight?

This made Jake even more aware of his low mood. He couldn't remember ever feeling this lonely since—since the first night after Sheila left him. Annie's comment about grabbing up Jeannie set his teeth on edge again. Why did people think that a person just forgot the past and started fresh? Annie knew nothing of Jeannie's history, but Annie knew about his. *How could Annie think he'd be ready for marriage?*

Now where did *that* word come from?

While deceptively beautiful snow tumbled down nonstop outside the windows, Jeannie walked around her future home. She'd chosen an open-floor plan. At this stage it was *very* open—just a framework of studs delineated room from room.

Some interior walls would begin to go up today, covering the electrical wires and the plumbing and the outer wall insulation. Thinking of these mundane facts didn't dull her hope of Jake appearing today. He said he might come. Might.

She'd been working on the Adopt-a-Pet idea and she hoped to share her progress with him today. After the TV interview, some families had come to choose a few dogs and kittens. But the overcrowding continued.

She and the girls were getting a new home. She wanted new homes for the animals at the shelter, the strays. As children, she and Carrie had been moved again and again to numerous foster homes and she'd felt like a stray nobody wanted. Maybe that sparked her dislike of seeing the loneliness in all the strays' eyes. Pets needed people and vice versa.

She moved into the room that would belong to the girls and smiled. She imagined making bright, fun curtains for the windows and crocheting new bedspreads. The girls had already chosen the colors for their room—baby blue and daisy yellow. Their verdict on another pink room had been a firm thumbs-down.

The memory of the discussion turned her smile wistful. She'd always made sure her girls knew she loved them and wanted the best for them. *Dear Lord, never let me fail them.*

In the kitchen, Eleanor talked on her cell phone. The front door opened and wind surged inside. Jeannie heard footsteps and male voices. She quelled her instant hope that Jake had come. Resolutely, she moved toward the door to thank whoever had shown up today to work. She didn't recognize the thirty-something man with two teens. The three were busy dusting and shaking off the thick coating of snow from their hoods, faces and shoulders.

Again, strangers volunteering to build her home humbled her. "Hi, thanks for coming. I'm Jeannie Broussard. This is going to be my home."

"Hey." The man took her hand in his large rough one and shook, firm and hard. "Pete Beck. I'm the building trades teacher from the high school. These are two of my students. We're here to help with whatever is needed today."

Jeannie grinned at Pete, who looked like he could build a house single-handed. "Thanks for coming," she said, shaking Pete's and the two teens' hands in turn.

The self-conscious boys ducked their heads and grinned.

"This is their substitute for serving detentions," Pete said dryly, gesturing to the teens to toss their jackets onto a large box.

"Well, I appreciate your help," she told them.

Eleanor snapped her cell phone shut and approached them.

"Detentions, huh?" Her mouth a thin, hard line, she shook hands with Pete. "Okay, we'll get the two of them to work. We're putting up wallboard today. Since you brought them, Beck, do you think they can do a good job?"

"They're young, and hefting sheets of wallboard into place should give them a good workout."

"There are some." Eleanor gestured toward the open area behind her. Sheets of wallboard were stacked there, and near outlets around the room lay cordless drills, charging.

The door opened again and Jake and Dan entered. Snow swirled in around them.

On seeing Jake, Jeannie's heart fluttered, and then at the sight of Dan, it slammed shut. *I will not continue to react to Jake's dad like this. It's childish.* She infused her welcoming smile with enthusiasm. "Thanks for coming, Dan." She hoped she sounded sincere, but after what he'd said the last time, she wasn't truly happy to see him. Had he come just to make sure she wasn't "entrapping" his son? She swallowed down the bitterness on her tongue.

Jake's responding expression dimmed to a shadow of his usual smile. "Hi, Jeannie," he murmured, glancing down.

What was troubling Jake? Jeannie studied what she could see of his face.

"Good day," Dan said, nodding generally to everyone. His frosty expression negated his cordial words. "What's today's agenda?"

Jeannie stepped back from him.

"Pete Beck and his students are going to be doing the wallboard in here." Eleanor eyed Pete. "A local contractor was supposed to come today to supervise wallboarding, but he called to say he was delayed. So I guess God sent you to be our supervisor, Beck. Can you help both crews? Or do your students need constant supervision?"

"They can work alone." Pete turned to Jake, Dan and Jeannie. "How about you? Any experience drywalling?"

"I've done it once before," Jake said. Dan and Jeannie shook their heads no.

"I'll come and help you get started then," Pete offered. "I can give you a few pointers. Make sure you're on the right track and if you need help, you can ask me questions."

"Great," Jeannie said with an attempt at confidence.

Eleanor gave Jeannie a bolstering shoulder squeeze. "I'll stay here and help the guys." She gave the teens a don't-step-out-of-line look. One of them squirmed.

"Jeannie, you help Jake and Dan," Eleanor finished. Soon Jeannie and Dan watched as Jake raised the first sheet in the master bedroom in place and Pete explained how to drill in the wallboard. Jeannie made sure she kept her eyes on Pete. She hadn't wanted to make a fuss about being put with Jake and Dan. Maybe she could slip out later to work with Eleanor.

At the edges of her attention she caught a subtle silent battle going on between Jake and his father, evident in their body language. They appeared to be avoiding, yet rebuffing each other. Was she the source of this tension? Or was it something else this time?

Pete drew Jeannie to the outer wall of the bedroom, leaving Jake and Dan on the other side. Jeannie watched Pete lift one of the sheets of wallboard. She gripped the cordless drill in her hand and began drilling into the studs as instructed. But she kept track of the other two.

"Dad," Jake said, "I'll get the next one."

Sheets of wallboard were stacked in this room, too. Jake hoisted another sheet and hefted it into place against the studs in the outer wall, bracing it there. His dad had begun setting screws and powering them in.

The sound of electrical drills came from down the hall.

Jeannie concentrated on her task, grunting a bit as she drilled in another screw. Jeannie's unease over the father-son breach ratcheted up. The shrill sound of the whirring drills and the vibration in her hand and arm matched her inner tension.

In the kitchen Eleanor switched the radio on to the local country-and-western station. Hank Williams's classic "I'm So Lonesome I Could Cry" warbled amid the drilling. The song made her wonder if Jake and Dan were rubbing each other the wrong way because they just weren't used to being together. Had they become so accustomed to being apart they didn't know how to act when together?

Glancing over her shoulder, she knew she couldn't "connect" a father and a son. She'd been raised in a series of foster homes. Her mother had died in an institution. Her father had vanished from her life. Would she even recognize him on the street? Carrie wouldn't. She'd never met him. If he was alive, did he ever think about his two daughters?

Hank Williams's lonesome voice was interrupted. "Folks, our county has just been included in a severe weather watch. We're expecting temperatures to drop to minus thirty-five tonight. Make sure your pets are brought inside or have a warm, sheltered refuge outside. Dogs and cats can't survive these types of temperatures without our help. Make sure your gas tanks are filled before you drive tonight. And the state police advise residents to go out only if necessary."

Jeannie tensed, letting the drill die in her hand.

"And be sure to check your emergency winter kit in your vehicle. You should carry a shovel, a blanket, a flashlight, flares and food and water. It doesn't say it here, but I'd advise you to make sure your cell phones are charged up. You don't want your cell to fail you just when you might need to call for help." The radio announcer went on with more particulars and repeated advice.

Everyone had stopped to listen. Jeannie immediately thought of the twins. *But they are safe with Ginny.*

"We'll just work a few hours and then all head home!" Eleanor called out. "We should all be safely inside before dark."

Jeannie glanced over her shoulder and her gaze connected with Jake's. The forlorn expression in his eyes had her wanting to fold him into her arms—just as he had done for her the day they'd rescued the kittens. *But I can't. Not here. Not now. Not ever.*

* * *

Jeannie woke up and realized that some time during the night, her girls and the kittens had joined her in bed under her electric blanket. That and the combined body heat had prevented her from waking to the cold. Now she realized her nose was a Popsicle.

She moved the quilt that half covered her head. The icy temperature of the bedroom hit her full in the face. *This can't be good.*

She struggled out of the warm nest, shivering instantly as she moved her feet around, seeking her slippers. Then she whipped on her heavy robe and hurried into the hall to the thermostat. It read forty-nine degrees. Her heart beat—no, no, no.

She raced to the kitchen tap and wrenched on the knob. No water spilled out at her touch. Her mind resisted the truth. She twisted the faucet knob off and then on again. No water. That meant only one thing. The pipes under the mobile home had frozen. But why wasn't the heat on?

She ran down the short hall to the cubbyhole beside the washer and dryer where the furnace huddled. She knelt, peered into the furnace and groaned between her chattering teeth. The pilot light had gone out in the night.

"Dear Lord, of all nights for this to happen." After rising, she found the long matches, knelt down, and then lit the pilot. Proverbially shutting the barn door after the horse had escaped.

The furnace switched on immediately with a blast of lukewarm air. But by now, Jeannie was frozen. She sprinted back to her bed and slid back under the covers. She reached for her cell phone, charging by the bed. In spite of the early hour, she dialed her landlord and gave him the bad news.

"I'm so sorry, Sam. I don't know why the furnace pilot would go out."

"It's because that furnace would make a dinosaur look young," the man replied. "You know I've just been waiting for you to move into your Habitat house. Then I planned to junk your trailer, replace it with a new double-wide and get a new tenant at a higher rate."

His matter-of-fact tone soothed her, but his plans shook her. *I'm not ready to move yet!* "You're not going to fix the pipes then?" she asked, hope teetering on the edge.

"Jeannie, it just isn't a wise investment. Your mobile home is on its last leg. We both know that. Until you came up with the Habitat answer, I was worried about you. All that's changed today is that you're going to have to move out earlier than you thought. I'm sorry."

She pressed a hand over her mouth so he wouldn't hear how hard she was taking this news. "I understand." And she did.

"My insurance will pay a motel room for you until you can find another place. I'll call my brother who owns the Dew Drop Inn on County K and reserve you and the girls a room. He won't mind the kittens either. And your breakfast at the motel café is on me."

"Thanks. Bye," was all she could say. She hung up.

The twins had awakened. "What's wrong, Mom?" Mimi asked, peeking out from the nest of blankets.

"We're going out for breakfast." Pausing, Jeannie choked down all her turmoil and "it's not fair" emotions. No time. Might as well accept what was offered.

She and the girls dressed in record time and packed the kittens into a snug box padded with old hand towels and covered with a doll's blanket. Grateful she had a full tank of gas and a new battery, Jeannie started her van and let it warm some before she bundled her girls outside.

She drove to the small cheery café all done in red and white checks. After she gave their orders, she and the girls went to the washroom to freshen up, washing hands and faces.

When the owner of the café-motel, a stocky man with gray hair, came to their booth, they were eating French toast with warm maple syrup and the café's popular venison sausage. "You're Jeannie, right?" He offered his hand. "I'm Chet."

"Hi," she said. Twinkie and Peanutbutter chose this moment to peep out from under the blanket covering their box.

"I see you brought the whole family." He grinned, his skin crinkling up cheerfully.

Though thankful for his kind tone and friendly smile, Jeannie blinked back the threat of tears. "Yes, I couldn't leave them out in the van. Not at forty-two-below windchill."

He shook his head. "This winter is trying to break us, all right. But I'm not giving in. Sam called me, and I have a nice kitchenette room ready for you, your girls and the kittens." He grinned again.

"Thank you so much. I just feel so disoriented." An understatement.

Chet playfully tapped Mimi's nose. "No school today for you two. Too cold for standing at bus stops."

Mimi and Cindy bounced up and down, chanting, "No school! No school!"

The people around them chuckled while Jeannie hushed them.

"I didn't give school much thought," she said after the twins went back to swirling their French toast through maple syrup. "But I should have expected it."

Chet rose. "If there's anything you need, you just let us know. Sam thinks highly of you. You've never been late with the rent in all the years you lived in that old trailer."

"Your brother has been very good to us. He's always fixed everything and has always been kind."

Chet rose. "Sam doesn't have anything else vacant. I'll spread the word you're looking for something temporary. If you don't find anything, I'll give you a good monthly rate on my kitchenette till your house is done. So don't worry. We won't let you end up on the side of the road."

His understanding and generosity propelled her past her reserve. Tears pooled in her eyes. "Thank you."

"Don't mention it." He patted her on the shoulder and headed toward the cash register to take care of a customer.

Swallowing her tears and still without much appetite, Jeannie forced herself to eat her breakfast. Free food as good as this shouldn't be turned down. Plus, she needed energy to handle this. Pulling out her cell phone, she dialed Ginny to tell her what had happened. Staying here at the motel would force her to drive the twins to and from school. And to Ginny's for after-school care. This would not work out with her clinic work schedule.

"Can we go to Dr. Jake's with you today?" Cindy asked, taking another bite of the thick dripping toast.

Jeannie reached over with a napkin and dabbed some maple syrup off Cindy's cheek. Thank goodness, she worked at the clinic now. Jake's smile glimmered dangerously in her mind. "For the morning."

"Goodie!" Mimi exclaimed.

Jeannie called Ginny and explained the situation. God had provided, but the sensation of being disrupted, ousted and abandoned persisted.

Help me through this, Lord, she prayed.

Chapter Seven

Jake heard the rear door open and the usual welcome from the animals in the kennel. He stepped out of his office. Jeannie had entered and had paused just a few feet from him. Her face tilted downward. Her eyes opened wide, her lower lip trembling till she gripped it with her teeth. She looked so forlorn; she stirred his heart. His caution didn't stop his lips from tingling as if he were about to kiss her. He couldn't keep from going to her. Then Bummer intervened. Rushing between Jake's ankles, the hound greeted the twins with happy woofs. They knelt down to pet him and show him the kittens they'd brought in a box. The air filled with the twins' cooing.

He was grateful that the commotion had interrupted him before he could embarrass Jeannie or him by reaching for her. "The phone has been ringing off the hook." He smiled with an apologetic tilt to his head, ignoring the way her presence sharpened his senses. Or at least trying. "Because of the cold, I think we're going to get a lot of cancellations for routine appointments." He gazed at her, unable to prevent himself from moving toward her. "I take it school has been cancelled."

"We can't go back to live in our house," Mimi said as if broadcasting the live news. She and Cindy still knelt on the floor. "Our pipes froze."

These three short words carried a wallop. Frozen pipes meant disruption, expensive plumbing, a big pain in the neck. His mouth dropped open. "Jeannie." Instinctively and forgetting all else, he reached for her, to draw her close.

She caught his hand in midair and gripped it. "It's been a rough morning."

Her gentle rebuff hit Jake. He hid this, glancing over his shoulder to avoid her eyes. He offered her the only comfort he could. "I just made some fresh coffee. Come get a cup."

"I had two cups at the Dew Drop Inn Café." She let go of his hand. Leaving it cold.

"Hey, you're having a rough day. Indulge yourself. I picked up some of that French vanilla creamer you like."

Her shoulders relaxed, an obvious release of tension. She sighed. A faint smile flitted over her face. "Wonderful." She followed him into the break room that connected to his office.

After waving her to the navy blue sofa, he insisted on waiting on her, pouring her coffee into her personal "I HEART my kittens" mug and adding a generous dollop of the special creamer. Handing it to her, he sat down on the matching navy plaid armchair at an angle to the sofa. "Now tell me about it."

She did and at the end, she said, as if challenging him to disagree, "Everything's going to be all right. This is just...unexpected."

Jake tried to appear sympathetic, not pessimistic. "This winter has been a real...disaster." He reached for her hand. This time she let him take it. "We'll think of something." She squeezed his hand. Their gazes caught and held.

Suddenly aware of the presence of someone else, Jake glanced to the doorway to see Mimi, Cindy and Bummer staring at them. Jake released Jeannie's hand. And not a moment too soon.

The back door banged open. "It's *cold!*" Sandy announced to the universe at large. "What is with this weather?"

Both Jake and Jeannie popped up. Jeannie spilled a few drops of coffee.

Sandy swooshed into the break room. "Coffee. I need *hot* coffee. Emphasis on *hot*." When she greeted them, she smiled knowingly. And then turned away to make more coffee.

Jake knew he was missing something here. Why were the twins still staring at them, grinning? And why was Sandy chuckling under her breath?

The phone rang. Jake walked into his office and picked up. "Dr. McClure speaking."

"I'm ready to chew nails," Annie barked from the other end. "When one of the new volunteers locked up yesterday, she turned the thermostat down too low. Our pipes froze. We don't have any water. And we don't have the funds to fix the pipes!"

Jake reeled with the news. Jeannie's *and* the shelter's pipes had frozen? "This is a bad joke, right?"

"It's bad, but it's no joke."

"We'll need a temporary replacement facility," he said trying to think of possibilities.

"No joke," Annie repeated. "Can you think of any place big enough?"

"Not off the top of my head. I'll have to think about it."

"I'll make some calls and get back to you." She hung up.

Jake walked back into the break room. "You won't believe this." He explained the situation to Sandy and Jeannie. His low spirits sank lower.

"We'll think of something," Jeannie said.

He didn't want to point out that her tone lacked conviction.

"We'll pray!" Mimi and Cindy declared.

After a day of emergency cases and appointments kept by those who braved the harsh weather, Jake found himself unable to resist walking toward Jeannie. How he wished he had a solution for her. "So you're going to the motel tonight?"

Standing with her hands on the back of her steel gray desk

chair, she was stretching her neck and back. "Yes. I've gotten a lot of work done on the spreadsheets and billing today."

So at odds with the mundane topic, her graceful movements riveted him. He tried to switch to showing concern for her situation, not staring at her. "If the twins don't have school again tomorrow," he said, though the tightness in his throat squeezed around each word, "feel free to bring them with you."

"Thanks." She bent her chin forward, no doubt extending her neck muscles. "I heard it's supposed to be a little warmer tomorrow. Perhaps they'll hold school, just not provide bus service." She leaned her head from side to side, creating a tide of long hair flowing over one shoulder and then another. "The district's already stacked up a week of days they'll have to make up in the spring. If this keeps up, the kids will be in school for the Fourth of July."

Her movements mesmerized him. He closed his eyes, leaning against the nearby doorjamb. Jeannie in a kitchenette room at the Dew Drop Inn till spring. That was just wrong.

"I wish we could come up with a place for the shelter animals." She shrugged.

"Me, too. We need running water to be legal."

She clicked off the desk computer and headed toward the rear exit. Bummer trotted hopefully behind her. Jake heard her apologize. "Sorry, Bummer, I can't take you with me tonight."

If Jake could, he'd follow her home, too. Nonetheless, he restrained himself, remaining in the front of the clinic till he heard Jeannie call, "Bye! See you tomorrow!" Then she closed the door.

Abruptly lonely, he proceeded through the office on his way to the rear exit, switching off the lights, making sure the digital thermostat was working right so *his* pipes wouldn't freeze and then preparing to venture out into the relatively balmy minus twenty degrees. Why couldn't he stick to the line he'd drawn between his life and Jeannie's?

Through the early winter darkness, he drove home. Thoughts

of Jeannie, the Dew Drop Inn, and the animal shelter's woes enacted a mob scene in his mind. And regrettably, each moment brought him nearer to the place he now didn't like to be much anymore: home. Dreading home was neither pleasant nor accurate. What he dreaded was another scrape with his father, not home. On the road in front of his house, he stopped and got the mail out of the roadside box. Frozen-board-stiff mail. Now that was cold.

On the way from parking the pickup in the garage to his back door, Jake sorted the mail. One letter for his dad nearly stopped him in his tracks in the snow. The return address was the billing department of University of Madison Hospital. Was it from one of his friends—or had his father been a patient? What would his dad have had done at the hospital? Bummer woofed as if asking why Jake was keeping them out in the cold. Puzzled, inside he unwrapped all his layers, then he walked into the kitchen that smelled of roast beef. Bummer greeted everyone and then walked over to his water dish and dry food bowl. Jake set the mail on the counter where he always did, laying his dad's letter on top.

"Glad you got home on time," Mike said from the sink, where he was peeling a cucumber. "I'm just finishing up the salad. I cooked beef stew. Just felt like a beef stew kinda day."

"I couldn't agree with you more." Jake ducked into the small bathroom off the kitchen and washed his hands. Then he sat at his place at the rectangular table. He inhaled, trying to loosen the strain he couldn't shake.

As his dad entered, Bummer passed him going to the warm hearth in the living room. "How was your day?" He sounded distinctly disgruntled.

Sensitive to the undercurrents, Jake considered his words before he spoke. "Lots of cancellations due to weather."

Dan humphed. "I'm starting to get cabin fever. What do you people do in the winter here?"

Jake wondered if his dad realized how revealing this statement was. After Jake had graduated from high school, his dad had never spent more than the few days around Christmas here. The thought that his dad must really not like being home—with his son—burrowed in like a burr in his sock.

"We manage to keep ourselves entertained," Mike said. "I have a few friends coming over to my place for pinochle tonight. You're welcome to join us."

"Should your friends be driving in this cold?" Jake asked.

"You worry about us like we're your kids or something." Mike set the salad bowl on the table. "Mitch's picking everybody up in his van. He's got a heated attached garage, so he'll just get in his van, drive around to pick up everybody and then park in my garage. He's even got one of those automatic starters. So he just pushes a button. When he leaves, the van's already warmed up." Mike sent him a "So-there!" look.

Jake raised both hands in surrender. "Okay. Okay."

Mike set a large pot of stew in the center of the table with a soup ladle in it and sat down. Jake bowed his head while Mike asked the blessing.

Mike began ladling out the stew. "I heard about what happened to Jeannie and her girls. Ginny called me."

"What's this?" Dan asked, appearing both suspicious and annoyed.

"Her pipes froze last night, so she had to move into a motel," Jake said.

His father grunted. "She should have known better than to turn her heat down too low. What can you expect from people like her?"

Jake ignited white hot. Waves of angry heat billowed from him.

"That's nonsense," Mike snapped. "Her furnace is as old as the hills and the pilot light went out. It's not her fault."

Jake seethed in silence but sensed that Mike could best handle this. *I don't want an out-and-out fight with my dad.*

"I stand corrected," Dan said, somehow managing to sound as if that were a near impossibility.

"Did you hear that the same thing happened to the animal shelter?" Jake asked, trying to divert attention from Jeannie.

"No," Mike said. "What are they going to do with the animals?"

"What happened?" Dan asked. "Did their furnace go out, too?"

"No, some volunteer turned the heat down before she left."

His father looked concerned.

Avoiding further conversation, the three of them dug into the flavorful beef stew, hot yeast rolls and salad. After the meal, Jake told Mike to go on home, he'd wash the dishes.

As soon as the door shut behind Mike, Dan came to the sink. "I'll dry."

Jake longed to refuse his help but of course couldn't. "Okay."

They worked in silence for a time.

"You got a letter from the Madison University Hospital." Jake gestured toward the letter on the counter by the door. And waited to hear what the letter was about.

"Oh, thanks." His father glanced at the envelope. "I had a checkup while I was there. This must be the results of a few routine lab tests."

Jake found that odd. His dad, the typical doctor, had no time for yearly checkups and such. "Oh," Jake finally said. They went on working side by side. Jake thought his dad looked odd, as if something was bothering him.

Then Dan cleared his throat. "I see how you look at her."

Jake knew who his father was speaking about but needed to make him say her name. "Who?"

"That single mom."

His dad's refusing to say Jeannie's name annoyed him. "You mean Jeannie?" Jake asked, shimmering with belligerence.

"Yes. Don't make the mistake of trying to be the prince to her Cinderella."

Jake chewed this insult and tried to swallow it. Was his

dad provoking a fight so he could distance himself further from Jake?

"I'm not in the position to sweep anybody off her feet," Jake said. "And I don't carry a glass slipper around in my pocket." Did his dad have enough sense to drop this?

"She's a nice enough girl," Dan said. "She's just not in our league."

Jake resisted replying, *What league would that be?* Yet now goaded past restraint, he switched to the offensive. "As I recall, you really liked Sheila, who evidently was in our league. We all know how that turned out."

"Sheila was a good wife, just not a good wife for you."

"She remarried two weeks after we divorced, a surgeon in Minneapolis. I think that might lead one to think she had already been shopping for my replacement *before* we filed for divorce." Jake flamed. "But no doubt, she is a good wife for *someone*." Acid spewed up into his throat.

"I didn't realize that." His father's eyes had widened.

Jake scrubbed a dish viciously. "It's not something I'd spread around." *And you weren't even in the state when the divorce was proceeding, so how would you know?*

"You're never going to forgive me, are you?"

Jake knew exactly what his dad meant. Still he didn't answer. *No, I haven't forgiven you.* He began scrubbing the tines of a fork.

Side by side in absolute silence, father and son finished the dishwashing and drying. "I'll be reading upstairs if you need me," Dan said, turning away.

"I'll be in the basement," Jake responded. Bummer appeared. He turned off the kitchen light and descended into the chilly basement with Bummer at his side. He switched on the electric space heater beside his desk, then sat, digging out the grant application and studying it. The grant would bring him the funds to turn his acreage into something good for many kids—if he ever had time to fill out the long application plus write up the rest of the proposal. Bummer rested his chin on Jake's knee. Jake began petting his head out of habit. His dream of transforming the McClure homestead into a place that would honor his mother and his brother's memory needed time. *And I don't have time*.

He bent his head, feeling the sudden impulse to pray more than grace or a fleeting phrase, something he didn't do often. "God, I need help. I feel so…blocked. Jeannie is special and I can't help her. The shelter is on the brink of disaster. Where can the animals stay till spring?" He rubbed his forehead with the flat of his hand, hard. "God, what am I doing wrong?"

Groggy from a restless night, Jake entered the kitchen the next morning. Bummer woofed his "Good morning." Mike was busy at the stove, flipping pancakes. His father sat at the table, sipping coffee.

"Good morning, sleeping beauty," Mike greeted Jake. "How many cakes you want?"

"Two should do it." Jake poured his coffee and took his place. The near argument with his dad at the sink the previous night caused Jake some uneasiness. Could he—*they*—set a more positive tone today?

Within minutes, Mike set a plate stacked with pancakes on the table alongside a pitcher of pure Wisconsin maple syrup and a platter of eggs and bacon.

"Did anyone ever mention the concept of cholesterol to you, Mike?" Dan asked, staring at the breakfast.

"Yeah, I heard of it. My whole life I been eating eggs and bacon or sausage for breakfast. And may I remind you I will be eighty-eight this summer?" Mike smirked. "And my triglycerides are to die for."

Dan shook his head. Mike offered the blessing and Jake snagged his first pancake.

"I got a good idea," Mike announced.

Jake and Dan both turned toward him.

"I'm going to move upstairs into your guest room," Mike said, lifting his coffee mug, "and give Jeannie and her girls my place till she moves into her new house in the spring."

Jake stopped chewing. He swallowed in a hurry. "That's a great idea."

His father's face twisted. "Do you think that's wise?"

"Why isn't it wise?" Mike snapped. "I don't know why you don't like Jeannie. She's a wonderful young woman and a great mom to those girls. You know those twins aren't hers? They belong to her sister who disappeared when they were just newborns."

Dan set down his coffee mug. "I didn't know that."

Jake sneered inside. And then disliked himself for it. How many times had he jumped to wrong conclusions? *I'm not perfect.* This admission eased some of the knot inside him.

"And," Mike continued, "what if the twins *were* hers? Do you think women go around thinking, 'Oh, I hope I'll have a baby and have to raise it all by myself?' In my day, the father and brothers would have coerced a marriage and lots of those were miseries. Or the girl would have been sent off 'to visit an aunt' and the baby would have ended up an orphan, raised as an inconvenience to a cousin or something. Nowadays the girl keeps the baby and does her best. It's not the best way, but it's life."

"Sorry. I'm sorry," Dan hastened to apologize.

Mike was glaring now, his face turning red. "Jeannie's all alone in the world, no family. Everything she's got she's worked hard for. And I plan to help her." Mike jerked his head in a decided nod.

"Me, too," Jake murmured from behind his coffee cup.

"I'll help her move in, okay?" Dan inhaled a deep breath. "I'm very sorry for my attitude about Jeannie."

Jake's mouth opened. His dad didn't do apologies much.

"Okay." Mike relaxed in his chair. "She deserves better than she's had. Ginny will help me persuade her to take my place. Jeannie's so independent that she'll probably refuse."

The truth of this statement smacked Jake. Getting Jeannie to accept this offer was far from a done deal. And then he got *the big idea.* He tamped down the excited look on his face. He wanted to run this big idea by Mike first.

Breakfast finally ended. Jake didn't want to share his idea in front of Dan. But his dad sat at the table, sipping coffee and reading *USA Today,* which he'd picked up in town yesterday. Jake spent a few moments in indecision. He decided to go ahead and tell Mike. His dad wouldn't like what he wanted to do, but too bad. "Are you busy this morning, Mike?"

"Just going to make a loaf of bread in my handy-dandy bread maker."

"I'm due at the clinic in a half hour. But first I want to go out and take a look at the barn. And I want you with me."

"Why?" Mike asked, shutting off the water and drying his hands.

"I want to see if we can use it as a temporary animal shelter." Jake watched for his dad's reaction.

Predictably Dan shook his head and sighed.

Jake forged on. "Do you think it's possible?"

Mike was already heading toward the back hall. "Let's get dressed and go look it over."

Within minutes, Jake and Mike, with Bummer at their heels, entered the barn through a side door and flicked on the lights. The barn was used mostly for the storage of old farm equipment Jake hadn't wanted to part with. He still remembered a time when he'd ridden the tractor with his grandfather.

"Well, we have water pipes to the barn from when we had dairy cattle," Mike commented, scanning the interior. "And as I recall, it was a nice cozy place with cattle inside."

"And we drained those pipes so we can just turn the water back on—"

"First we'd have to get some of the stuff out and fire up the heaters."

"In a winter like this, it will cost a fortune to heat this place," Dan said, coming through the door and shutting it behind him.

"You're always such a team player," Mike remarked, wrinkling his nose. "The animals don't need it toasty warm. And—" he pointed upward "—if we hauled in some bats of insulation and rolled them out on the floor of the loft, it would hold the heat in better."

"What about heat loss through the side walls?" Dan asked.

Jake decided to let Mike handle his dad. His grandfather had left Jake the land, not his father, because he knew that Dan would sell it, not keep it in the family. So Jake would make this decision. *What I decide is what will happen.*

"The original stone foundation extends to the top of the stalls. We can just get some of that non-fiberglass insulation and set it on the stone sill inside to block any drafts." Mike pointed first to one and then the other end of the barn. "We have barn heaters, which run on propane, and we have a separate propane tank for the barn."

Dan looked grumpy but said no more.

Jake decided to reenter the discussion. "We'll need to have someone inspect the plumbing so we know there's no problems— tree roots and such. Then we need to have the propane company come out and check our tank and if it's okay, fill it. If we get those two things done, we can ask volunteers to come and help us make room in the barn and move the animal cages here."

"Sounds right." Mike turned. "Jake, you got to go to work. I'll go make the calls and get the ball rolling."

"Just like that?" Dan asked.

"Just like that," Mike replied. "If Annie's found some other place, no problem. If not, we'll just move ahead. And I'm going to get Ginny to help me talk to Jeannie about my house. Looks like I'll have to get my fixings into the bread maker fast and get on the phone."

"Jake, you realize that if you do this," Dan said in an *I know more than you do* tone, "you'll never get rid of the animals."

"Maybe I don't want to get rid of them," Jake said, suddenly buzzing with anger. "In fact, my dream is to have this barn filled with animals and kids…like Tommy."

At the mention of his late son who had suffered from Down syndrome, Jake's father turned and left the barn. Mike and Jake stood in place, Jake still seething with his unexpected flush of anger.

Mike shook his head. "You two have spent too many years not talking about what happened to your mom and brother. Jake, even if your dad had been here, he couldn't have changed anything. Accidents happen. You're not mad at your dad about the accident. You're mad at him for something else. Figure it out." Mike walked out—leaving Jake alone and bewildered by what he had just said.

Around three in the afternoon, Jeannie pondered the empty waiting room at the clinic. An emergency call hurried Jake out early and Sandy had a dental appointment to keep. The afternoon appointments had petered out.

Today the unusually harsh cold had given way to this winter's "usual" cold, but people still didn't like to be out in the bitter early darkness of afternoon. As soon as the sun started going down after three, everyone planned to be at home if possible. She didn't blame them. *I wish I had a home to go to.*

Jeannie brushed this aside, wondering if Mike had been able to get the barn's plumbing and heating situation checked out. Jake had filled them all in on his plans for a temporary shelter. She hoped everything would work out. As for her, she and the girls were cramped but safe and warm at the Dew Drop Inn. On the way there tonight, Jeannie planned to pick up a few groceries that would work in her restricted kitchen: a dorm fridge, a hot plate, a coffeemaker and a microwave. The twins were back in school and within the hour, she would pick them up.

The clinic door opened and Ginny and Mike walked in.

Jeannie rose. "Hi. Jake's not back from an emergency call."

"We didn't come to see Jake," Mike replied.

"We came to see you," Ginny said with a serious expression.

Jeannie wrinkled her forehead. "What about? I'll do anything I can to help with the animal shelter problem."

Mike approached the counter. "I've got things rolling, though it's going to take time to get the plumbing and heating evaluated. But we came about where you can live till your house is finished."

Hope springing up within, Jeannie moved out from her desk and locked the front door of the clinic. "Let's go sit down in the break room. I'm not expecting any more patients today."

When the three of them were settled in the break room, Jeannie gazed expectantly at them. "Have you found a place for me and the girls?"

"Yes, I'm going to move into Jake's place and let you and the girls take my little house for the rest of the winter," Mike announced.

"Oh, no—" Jeannie raised a hand in objection "—that's too much trouble for you—"

"No, it isn't," Ginny said. "Mike isn't a pack rat. He'll just pack up his clothes and a few books and the place will be ready for you."

"No, really." Jeannie shook her head, the sudden hope shriveling. "I can't allow you to do this. It's too much trouble to put you to."

"We knew you'd take on like this," Mike said. "Now why won't you let me do this for you? It's no big deal."

Before Jeannie could begin her next refusal, the clinic phone rang. She stepped through the connecting door into Jake's office and picked up his phone. "McClure Veterinary—"

"Hello! This is an emergency." The woman caller's urgent voice sounded familiar.

"Dr. McClure is already out on an emergency call. If you give me your situation, location and number, I will have the doctor contact you as soon as possible." Jeannie grabbed a pen and notepad.

"This isn't about an animal. This is Brooke Hyde. Dr. McClure's father has fainted here at my house."

Faces and connections swarmed Jeannie's mind. Brooke? This was the woman who owned the poodle. "Dr. McClure has fainted at your house? Have you called 911?"

"Oh! He's coming to. But I still think his son should come." The woman hung up.

Jeannie returned the receiver to the cradle. "Mike!" she called to the next room. "Dan McClure just fainted at Brooke—" what was her name? "—at Brooke Hyde's place. I'm going to call Jake."

Jeannie dialed Jake's cell. Ginny and Mike appeared beside her. She pressed her lips together in worry. The call went to Jake's voice mail. Hanging up, Jeannie flipped open Jake's patient rolodex on his desk and jotted down Brooke's phone number and address.

She turned to them. "Can you two pick up the girls at school and take Bummer to Jake's? I told Jake I would let Bummer have some time with the girls, so Jake didn't take him along." She started toward the door. "I've got to go to Jake at his emergency call. He'll want to know this." *I hope Brooke has enough sense to call 911 if Dan's condition worsens.*

"We'll take the girls to my place, *where you will be moving soon,*" Mike said. "Call us when you know something."

"I will!" Jeannie jogged to the back entrance, grabbed her coat and was out the door.

Within a few miles, she drove up to a dairy farm and saw

Jake's pickup parked by the tall red barn. She braced herself against the increasing cold in the dimming sunlight. And then she sprinted over the gravel drive packed with snow. She let herself inside the warm barn and paused, listening for voices. Panting, she heard Jake's and hurried down the aisle of stalls to one at the end.

Jake looked up. "Jeannie?"

"Your dad fainted," she gasped, out of breath. She yanked out the paper with Brooke's information. "Here. He fainted at Brooke Hyde's, you know the woman with the French poodle." *The one who hoped to feed you lasagna.* This fact sparked an odd reaction in her. But right now lasagna was beside the point.

"What? Fainted?" Jake held up his hands to show her that he'd been in the midst of doing something physical with the cow, which let out a cow groan or howl or whatever it was called.

"Please call Brooke and hold the phone by my ear so I can talk to her," Jake said.

Jeannie quickly did as he asked. When Brooke answered, Jeannie held the phone up to Jake's ear. She was close enough to hear both sides of the exchange.

Jake: "My office manager said you called. My dad fainted at your place?"

Brooke: "Yes, we were just having coffee. He stood up and passed out."

Jake: "Is he still unconscious?"

Brooke: "No, he's awake now. I just took his car keys away, though. I don't think he should be driving."

Dan: "Here let me talk to my son." Muffled words, then—"I'm fine, Jake. I just passed out. No big deal."

Jake: "Dad, let's not do this macho stuff, okay? You know that fainting means something is wrong."

Dan: "I'm fine."

Jake: "I'm not even answering that idiotic comment. I'm helping a cow with a twisted breech presentation. Stay where you are and I'll come and get you as soon as I'm finished."

Dan's voice was muffled, but he seemed to be arguing with Brooke.

Brooke: "Jake, I won't let Dan leave. Don't worry."

Dan's voice in the background: "I only fainted, for goodness' sake."

Brooke: "Take care of the cow, Jake." Her voice suddenly sounded stern. "Dan, you sit down. I don't want to have to get tough with you." She hung up.

Jeannie accepted the phone and stared at it. She'd never guessed Brooke had that kind of fire in her.

Jake's face had drawn down in deep worried lines. "Can you call Mike? Maybe he should go over there till I'm free."

"Mike and Ginny are picking my girls up at school."

The cow bellowed, as if reminding Jake that she was his main concern at the moment. "I'd better tend to her." Jake turned back to the cow.

Jeannie, who was not even one to watch medical or forensics shows on TV, hurried away from Jake and the cow that was bawling with evident discomfort. Did cows have labor pains? *Poor thing.*

"Jake!" she called over her shoulder. "I'll go get the girls so Mike is free to help you!" Jeannie felt as if she'd been buried in an avalanche. What next?

Jake had driven his dad home, promising Brooke he'd come back for his dad's SUV the next day. Right now, they both sat at the kitchen table with fresh coffee in their mugs, having a speaker-phone conversation with his father's old friend Lewis, his cardiologist in Madison.

Lewis was saying, "You need to come in for more tests, Dan. Afterward, we can figure out exactly what is causing your symptoms. We didn't do a heart catheterization last time. And I have a few more hoops for you to jump through before I make a true diagnosis and we can begin treatment."

Jake listened intently, his jaw set. Why hadn't his dad told him he was ill?

"I just fainted—" Dan objected.

"Jake," Lewis interrupted, "how many times has he told me he *just fainted?* Are you keeping track?"

"I gave up counting. He's like a broken record." Jake sat with his arms folded.

"I'm scheduling Dan for the catheterization and a few more tests ASAP. I'll call as soon as I know the time. Dan, you'll be here overnight. And afterward we'll make sure you don't go fainting on us again anytime soon. Got that?"

"Yeah." Dan sounded anything but happy. "What choice do I have?"

"Exactly. Gotta run," Lewis said. "You'll be hearing from me tomorrow. Jake, I don't want your father alone from now till he's back in my hands."

"Got it. We'll be like Siamese twins."

Chuckling, Lewis hung up. Jake punched the speaker button, cutting the connection. The two men sat glaring at each other in the low light.

Jake knew his dad didn't like the way things were going. *My dad's sick.* The words didn't penetrate. He heard the sound of a car pulling in the drive. Mike.

Soon the older man was banging the back door. "Mom!" Mike called out. "I'm home!"

Mike's teasing egged Jake to grin. He rose to face Mike as he came into the kitchen with Bummer padding along at his side.

"So are you going to live, Dan?" Mike asked.

"He may," Jake said grimly, "if he decides to take care of himself. Remember when he went to Madison *to visit old friends?* Well, the old friends he was visiting were cardiologists—"

"I didn't want to worry you," Dan said. "I thought I'd go and it would be nothing."

Mike sat down and faced him. "Maybe you should start at the beginning and tell us exactly what's going on."

Jake bit his lip to keep from saying the wrong thing.

Dan got up and poured himself another cup of coffee. "When I turned sixty early in January, one of my Colorado friends, a doctor, nagged me into finally having a physical. When he told me I needed to have some further tests done on my heart, I decided I wanted it done in Madison by friends I trusted."

"Heart tests, huh?" Mike commented, sitting down. "Is this serious?"

"I didn't think so, but the test results came in the mail yesterday," Dan said.

"Then he fainted this afternoon," Jake said.

"I know. I was there when that woman with the poodle called the clinic." Mike poured himself a mug of coffee.

Dan looked peeved. "The lab tests showed some cardiac abnormalities, so I called my friend Lewis this morning and he was going to get me back for more tests to be sure. But now I'll be going back sooner and will have a catheterization and a few other tests."

"Sounds like fun," Mike said.

Dan's responding grin trembled slightly. "Yeah, fun."

The tremble hit Jake, switched him from anger at his dad for not confiding in him to the realization that his dad was worried.

Jaw clenched, Jake gripped the handle of his heavy coffee mug. "I'll clear my schedule so I can go with you."

"There's no need," Dan said, not meeting his son's eyes. "I can go by myself."

"No need?" Mike blustered. "You're nuts. Jake will go with you and me, too."

"That's right, Dad," Jake agreed, making certain his voice sounded assured and compassionate.

Dan changed the subject. "So, Mike, is Jeannie going to take up residence in our old farmworker cottage?"

Surprised at this question, Jake tracked his dad's expression from the corner of his eye.

"I nearly had to arm wrestle her." After moving to the sink, Mike began washing his hands. "But she and the girls will move in over the next few days. Tonight I'll pack up my stuff to bring here and then box up the rest of my personal belongings and stow them in the cellar."

"What about the animals moving into our barn?" Jake asked.

"Well," Mike said, turning from the sink, "the plumber's scheduled and so is the propane guy. We'll just have to wait and see. Anybody interested in warmed-up beef stew?"

"I'm starving," Jake said. A question popped in his mind—he resisted asking his father if Brooke had "plied" him with lasagna today. How did the two of them get together?

Focusing on *that* for a moment lessened Jake's pressure. But what made him feel so much better right now was that Jeannie would not be at the Dew Drop Inn much longer.

Jake got busy setting the table and helping Mike get the meal on the table. He tried not to think of all the heart diseases his dad could have and all their complications. Heart disease. Loneliness shot through Jake like an icy syringe. *Dear God, preserve my dad's life. I barely know him. Give us a second chance, okay?*

Chapter Eight

On Friday afternoon after the clinic closed, Jake backed up his pickup so that the rear hatch would open directly in front of Jeannie's mobile home door. He'd come to help her move out of the trailer and into the little house on his property. The day had dawned surprisingly mild and sunny. At twenty degrees above zero, he almost unzipped his jacket. A front from the Louisiana Gulf had flowed up the Mississippi River Valley and brought some warmth with it—even after four in the afternoon.

This contrasted with the cold chill that had settled in his midsection and wouldn't budge. Everything about his dad's heart problems was moving way too fast. No matter what a person's illness or disease might be, it was always heart failure that caused death. How damaged was his dad's heart? And would it disable or sideline his active, type A father?

He pushed these worries down deep inside. He was here to help Jeannie and it was a warm sunny day. He opened the road-salt-encrusted back hatch and then turned to Jeannie's door. His knuckles barely touched the door before Jeannie opened it.

"I saw you backing in. How's your dad today?"

"He's his normal cheery self."

As she drew him inside, Jeannie's smile looked strained. "I

know you're worried, but when we can't do anything, that's when we pray."

I haven't really prayed for a long time, not since Mom died. But that had begun to change.

Jeannie gazed into his eyes.

He tried to look away but could not.

She lightly brushed his cheek with her palm. "Have faith. People will let you down. God won't."

For a moment, he pressed his cheek against her soft palm. When that was no longer enough, he stepped back—before he kissed her.

Jeannie also stepped back, blushing.

"Let's get started then." He forced a broad smile.

"There isn't much. The girls are at Mike's already. Ginny is there to watch them. I could have done it by myself in a few trips with the van." Her voice sounded listless.

Jake tried to navigate the murky currents here. He'd thought he should offer to help her. Didn't she want him to help her move? What could he do now? He couldn't just leave. *And this might have absolutely nothing to do with me. Maybe she just hates having to leave this place where she's lived so long.* He could understand that. Except for college, he'd never lived away from the farm he loved.

"Let's just load up everything that will fit in my truck bed and your van and see how far we get."

"Pretty far," she muttered more to herself, he thought, than to him.

Jake soon found what she meant about not taking long to move. In the girls' bright pink bedroom, he blinked to be sure his eyes weren't failing him. Six neat boxes sat in the stripped, empty-looking room. Just six? "I'll help you break down the beds," he offered. "They should fit in my truck."

"Great. The bunk beds are really the only furniture we'll be taking." Jeannie didn't meet his eyes. "Everything else is built in or came with the mobile home."

He nodded, thinking of the new Habitat house she'd need to furnish this spring. "Let's move these boxes into the living room out of our way," he said, "and then we can break down the beds quick."

Soon they were dismantling the bunk beds and carrying the parts out to his truck bed. He finished up by carrying boxes to the truck and then Jeannie's van. In just over an hour, the boxes had been deposited in the vehicles—with room to spare.

Jeannie wandered through the empty rooms and then joined him at the door. Sensing that she needed a private moment to say farewell to her longtime home, he excused himself. "I'll head right to your new place."

She gripped his arm as he opened the door. "Thanks. I know I'm acting a little weird. It's just that…the girls were only babies when I moved here…" She looked like she wanted to say more, but fell silent.

Her touch gripped him, made him want to pull her into his arms. "No problem," he said, letting her release his arm. He nodded, at a loss for words. Outside, he checked that the pickup doors and rear hatch were shut tight and then drove away. It didn't seem right that a woman and two girls should only own enough to fill up a pickup and a van.

At Mike's place, now Jeannie's home till spring, Jake repeated the backing up to the door. Mike joined him and began helping him unload the bunk beds. The snug white bungalow had a small living/dining room at the front, a kitchen at the rear, one bath, and two bedrooms. Up until his grandfather had retired from farming, a farm hand and his family had always lived there. Then it had been vacant. When Jake started college, Mike had moved in and stayed.

Jake heard Jeannie enter and greet Ginny, who had stayed with the girls. He and Mike were in the spare bedroom, fitting together the bunk beds, and watched avidly by the twins in the doorway.

He and Mike hurried to get the bunk bed frame and mattresses in place. Then they helped Jeannie carry in the boxes and place them in the rooms where they belonged. Again, this took very little time.

As Jake looked around, he saw that the furnishings Mike was leaving for Jeannie looked worn, especially the bed in Mike's room, now Jeannie's. It didn't look like it was going to hold up much longer. And plainly Mike slept in a kind of trough in the middle of the mattress. *I don't like that at all. Jeannie needs her sleep and that bed...*

Jake wanted to linger but got the impression that he'd just be in Jeannie's way. And watching her obvious stress over having to make this unexpected move twisted his stomach into a hefty knot. He and Mike headed for the McClure house just a half mile up the dead end road.

"I'm happy Jeannie finally gave in and accepted my offer," Mike said. "I see now, though, we're going to have to help her get some furniture for her new place when she moves in in a few months. We should look up in the attic. Lots of unused furniture up there."

"That's right. As soon as it warms up some, Jeannie can go through and take what she wants."

Mike gave him an odd sideways look. "We'll have to come up with some clever way to get her to do that. I told you that Jeannie is intending to pay you rent, didn't I?"

"Rent?" Jake nearly stopped his truck. "I don't want any rent from her."

Mike shrugged. "That's what I told her. But she refused to listen."

Jake fumed at his predicament. *I don't want to insult Jeannie, but I won't accept a penny from her.*

Then Jake recalled once more how few possessions Jeannie had. He'd inherited a house, barn and outbuildings filled to the rafters with generations of "stuff." Jeannie evidently hadn't moved to Hope, Wisconsin, with much except a loving heart and two little girls. *How can I help her? Or how can I get her to let me help her?*

That was the question.

Jake stood in his kitchen staring out the window over the sink. Against the late afternoon slate gray sky, snowflakes swirled gently in an unusual lazy wind. Jake gripped the back of the chair in front of him, trying to quell the volcano erupting silently inside him. He, his father and Mike had just arrived home from Madison. Since the tests had taken longer than expected, he and Mike had spent Monday night at a motel near the hospital. From there, he'd called so Jeannie could reschedule his Tuesday appointments.

Usually on Tuesday afternoon, he'd be busy, not standing here thinking darkly. His father's diagnosis had come as a shock— an understatement. As he stood there gripping the chair till his knuckles turned white, a great need swelled inside him. There was only one place he wanted to be.

He turned and obeyed the urge he couldn't ignore. Within minutes he and Bummer drove up to the little house where Jeannie now lived. The fact that the girls would be home from school didn't deter him. He hurried through the cold to the back door and knocked. Bummer scratched at the door.

Through the door, he heard the girls shriek, "Mom, it's Bummer!"

"Sit there on that couch," Jeannie ordered.

He'd rarely heard her use that stern tone of voice.

The door opened and Jeannie looked at him, tears in her eyes.

"What's wrong?" he asked as Bummer bounded into the room and raced to the girls.

Jeannie turned from him, hiding her face.

Oh, Jeannie, why are you crying? "What's happened?" he asked sharply, hanging his jacket on the peg by the door.

"We're sorry, Dr. Jake!" Mimi exclaimed.

"We didn't mean to break it!" Cindy added.

"You two are to go and sit on your beds," Jeannie ordered, "until I tell you to come out."

Downcast, Mimi and Cindy obeyed without a word. Bummer padded after them, woofing quietly as if consoling them.

Jeannie waited for them to go and then motioned for him to follow her.

What had the girls done that had upset her so?

Jeannie preceded Jake into the bedroom and moved to the side.

Jake immediately saw the problem. The old double bed had caved in on itself.

"The girls were supposed to be dusting in here," Jeannie explained, her chin bent down. "I heard the noise and came running."

The contrast between his shock and gloom over his dad's diagnosis and this inconsequential household mishap hit him. He laughed out loud and then tears sprang to his eyes. He sucked them in and tried to hold back his inappropriate mirth.

Jeannie came to him and rested a hand on his arm. "It's your dad, isn't it?"

He wanted to let his father's diagnosis flow out, but was afraid he might break down. He sucked it in. "Later," he murmured. "Let's deal with this catastrophe first."

He knelt down and lifted the bed skirt to survey the damage. "Looks like the slats and bed frame broke."

"I'll pay for it." The agitation had jumped back into Jeannie's voice.

He ducked his head out and rose. "It's just a bed. And an old one, too. The dry air this winter probably finally did the wood in, made it brittle."

"The girls know better—"

"Jeannie," he said, taking her slender hand, "didn't you jump on beds when you were a kid? I did." Then he couldn't help himself. He pulled her into his arms. He buried his face in her sweet lavender-fragrant hair.

Jeannie knew she should pull away, but Jake's chest was so firm. Resting against it gave such comfort. Something within her eased. Then she recalled where Jake had just been and why. What did a silly bed mean compared to a father who might have a life-threatening condition? No wonder he'd reacted as he had to the broken bed.

"How did it go with your dad?" she murmured, her cheek against the soft cotton of his shirt. When he didn't reply, she ventured on, "I don't want to pry but is your dad going to be all right?"

The levee broke in Jake. Emotion threatened to overcome him. "It's bad." For a moment, he couldn't say more.

Jeannie pressed nearer. "I'm sorry," she murmured. "You don't have to tell me."

Her tone was rich with sympathy and he found he could speak again. "My dad was diagnosed with hypertrophic cardiomyopathy."

"What does that mean?" She looked up into his eyes.

He nearly succumbed to her warmth and nearness, nearly bent to claim her lips, so near now. He drew up his resistance. "Hypertrophic cardiomyopathy, HCM, is a condition where the heart muscle becomes thickened."

Her first thoughts were *Poor Jake. Poor Dan.* Jake's dad didn't like her, but she couldn't help feeling compassion for him. "That doesn't sound good."

Her voice curled around Jake's neck, making him even more sensitive to her. "You're right. HCM forces the heart to work harder to pump blood out."

"How long has he had this?" She moved back slightly to look up into his eyes.

Jake shrugged. "We don't know. A person can have it and

not have any symptoms and then collapse and die. HCM is usually the cause when a young athlete dies instantly right after a game."

She rested a tentative hand on his shoulder.

"In my dad's case, an associate finally cajoled him into have his first physical—since medical school, I think. They found evidence of heart abnormalities. That's why he came home for more tests." *Though of course he didn't tell me that.*

She rubbed his shoulder hard and moved closer again. "I'm so sorry."

He leaned his head on top of hers lightly, her hair silken against his cheek. There was something about his father's condition that plagued him too deeply for words. He gently disengaged from her. "Thanks," he whispered.

Jeannie drew away from him and turned to face the bed with him. She wished she could do something for this good man and his father.

"Let's just get the broken bed frame out of here and then we'll go into my barn and find another one," Jake said.

She glanced up at him quizzically. "Barn? You keep beds in your barn?"

He chuckled and it felt good. "In my barn loft and attic, I keep a lot of stuff."

"It's okay. I can just sleep on the mattress and box springs," she said, not wanting to accept more help from him.

"No, and that mattress needs replacing, too."

She drew an envelope out of her pocket and tried to slip it into his. "My rent."

He caught her wrist gently but firmly. "Why can't you accept this as you accept the Habitat house? I don't want any rent. And you need a complete new bed."

"I will pay you rent," Jeannie insisted, holding out the envelope. "And I can buy my own bed. I'll pay you for this wrecked bed, too."

He didn't want to argue with her right now. So he didn't. *But*

I don't want your rent and I will buy you a new mattress set and get a bed frame for you, Jeannie Broussard.

Jeannie didn't want to argue with him now. *But I am paying you rent and you're not giving me a new bed, Jake McClure.*

He read the determination on her face. It triggered a thought which he'd tried to repress till now. Till this moment, he'd refused to let the chance he might have inherited HCM stick in his mind. And an even worse consequence tried to be heard. *No, not now. I need to concentrate on Jeannie and my dad. Not me.*

Jeannie watched the shadows flit over Jake's expressive face. The bed and rent check couldn't be the source of his pain. "Jake?" she whispered.

Glancing at Jeannie, Jake tried to think of something to say to lighten the sober mood they obviously shared. Nothing rushed to his beleaguered mind. Still, these moments with Jeannie had strengthened him. "I'll be fine," he whispered back.

Then across the hall, Bummer began baying.

"What now?" Jeannie asked, heading for the doorway.

Jake followed her, glad Bummer had come to the rescue. He didn't want to blurt out his worries about HCM. No way. Jeannie had enough heaped on her plate already.

Sunday afternoon, a lump still lodged inside Jake's chest. Ever since he'd heard his dad's diagnosis, the heavy lump had settled over his heart and lungs. And the possibility of his having it, too, had only made it heavier. Now he stood in the midst of the barn and tried to drag up some enthusiasm for the temporary shelter, take a deep breath. He had to find a way to push the weight off his heart. A day's hard work should help, he sincerely hoped. Soon volunteers would arrive to help to clear the barn and prepare it for the animals to move in.

The side door opened and Jeannie walked in. "I'm here to help."

Jake stared at her, longing to draw her close, feel her warm breath against his neck. He imagined the comfort of having her softness against him again and shuddered in response.

"You look troubled, Jake. What's wrong?" she asked, coming nearer.

To hide his upset, he turned his back to her. He tried to come up with some way to brush off her question, make light of the situation. But why? Maybe telling Jeannie would lift the weight over his heart. "It's my dad's HCM."

She rubbed his shoulder—her touch feather-light, yet so powerful. "What about his HCM? Have you learned something else?"

Jake grimaced at himself. Why had he been so transparent? He couldn't say: "It's not about him really. It's about me. HCM is usually passed down through families. It's believed to be a result of defects of the genes that control heart muscle growth."

His mind went farther, putting into words what weighed upon him. "I could have this. I could curse a future child to suffer this." His heart lurched and then raced. He twisted away, glancing over his shoulder.

Obviously startled, Jeannie blushed—with what? Embarrassment? *No, Jeannie, this has nothing to do with you.* He nearly reached for her hand.

"Sorry. Just forget I asked." Her contrite voice whispered over his senses.

"No." Another thought, a better thought, came to him. "Come back here. I found a bed frame for you."

"Jake, I already told you. I don't need—"

Happy for the distraction, he took her elbow and pulled her along with him to the rear of the barn. He helped her navigate the dusty center aisle between bales of hay and stored furniture. "Here. What do you think?" He gestured to an ornate iron bed frame painted white.

"Jake, it's an antique!" she exclaimed. "I couldn't—"

Hearing the note of appreciation in her voice, he grinned.

"Yes, you could and you will. We need to get all this stuff out of the way. That's why we're here today."

The side door down below flapped open. Mike called out, "Boy! It's cold out there. Jake, where are you and Jeannie?"

Both Jake and Jeannie turned and headed back to where they started. "I was just showing Jeannie that bed frame we're taking over to her place later."

Mike grinned at them knowingly and winked as if he'd caught them kissing or something. "Sounds like a plan. Bummer is bent out of shape being locked inside the house. He's parked just inside the back door, baying. He knows something's going on."

The moment of intimacy had evaporated. Jake dragged himself into the present conversation. "Bummer will get over being left out. Where do you think we should start, Mike?"

He felt Jeannie slip an envelope into his pocket. He stiffened, guessing that it might be that blasted rent check again. Did he have to deal with that today, too? *I told her I didn't need or want any rent.*

"I think we should move all the spare furniture, every farm implement and machine to the back of the barn." Mike motioned. "Then they'll be out of our way, since we'll be using this side door and the little office there that your grandpa built at this end."

The door opened again. Brooke Hyde walked inside, surprising Jake.

"Hi, Brooke," Jake said, wondering why she'd come. Jeannie waved.

"I'm here because I'm the ditzy volunteer who turned the heat down too low. I didn't realize that the shelter didn't have a basement. And I'd never worked alone." Brooke's tone was light over a current of self-mockery.

"Oh," Jeannie said.

Annie walked in, followed by a group whom Jake recognized as regular shelter volunteers. Annie and Mike took charge. Soon men carried bats of insulation up the old rickety stairs to the loft, and others began moving old tools and farm paraphernalia to the rear of the barn. Then sweeping began.

Jake hustled up the old stairs and helped lay another bat of insulation down. He and the others working with him all wore safety glasses, gloves and white nose-and-mouth masks. Jake stopped to stretch his back muscles. He walked to the end of the loft and looked out a small window. He glimpsed someone walking toward the back door of the house. Brooke. What did she need in there? Jake shrugged. Maybe Mike had sent her in for something.

"Break time!" Annie called out.

He shuffled down the steps to join everyone at the large coffeemaker Annie had brought and filled. She'd also brought several dozen doughnuts. Jake took off his work gloves and sat on one of the many hay bales. Mike always liked to farm a few acres of hay to give to friends or churches for fall decoration and to provide seating at fall outdoor festivities. Sometimes he sold some and gave the money to charity.

Jeannie sat across from Jake. He caught her attention and mouthed: *I told you, no rent.*

She shook her head and mouthed back: *Yes, rent. Stop arguing.*

Jake bit into his doughnut hard. Stubborn woman.

Brooke walked in the side door. "Oh, great. We got here just in time for a coffee break. Do all of you know Jake's dad, Dan?"

Jake swiveled so fast, he splashed a bit of hot coffee onto his jeans.

His dad raised a hand and smiled. "Hi."

Jake blinked. Since they headed back from Madison days ago, he hadn't seen his dad smile. And Brooke had persuaded his dad to come out of the house, something he also hadn't done since they'd arrived home.

His father scanned the room. "You've accomplished a lot this afternoon."

Brooke had poured him a mug of coffee and was handing it

to him. "Pick out a doughnut for me and one for you." She sat down on a hay bale. Dan actually did what she asked and then sat down beside her.

Jake exchanged a meaningful glance with Jeannie, who raised her eyebrows and then smiled. He hoped Brooke was really interested in his dad. That might help. Even as he thought this, a funny sort of scratchy feeling zigzagged through his chest.

He'd never given much thought to the fact that his dad must date women. Again, they'd spent too much time apart. And now his dad had a life-threatening disease and might have to retire from the career that was his life. *And I might have HCM, too.*

Jake drove through the cold, moonless Tuesday night. After two days of work on the barn, he ached all over. Now he'd just delivered a foal at a nearby horse farm, owned by a friend of his dad's. Although he'd been busy handling the difficult delivery, he'd also fended off questions—about his dad's health and also hints about Brooke and Dan becoming a couple. Mentally and physically, Jake ached as if he'd wrestled a shark or maybe something bigger like an irritated whale.

Now he paused in his drive with the motor running. The house was dark except for the back porch light. Had his dad gone to bed already? He glanced at the dashboard clock. It was just past nine o'clock. "Wait here, Bummer." Jake's worry flapped its black wings.

He jumped out, slammed the door behind him and jogged to the garage door. His dad's SUV wasn't inside. Jake parked in the garage and then he hurried inside and went through the house to his dad's room. Nobody home. Where could his dad have gone?

Jake went back to the kitchen and scanned it for a note. He found a small yellow Post-it on the fridge. *Out to supper at the Pavleks. D.*

Though glad to find this, Jake couldn't shake his uneasiness.

The old SUV his dad used had an old battery that might fail. And this cold was bad for Dan's heart, weakened by HCM. The extreme weather alone could tax his heart and trigger a cardiac arrest.

Jake ran outside to check on his outside dogs. Then, shedding his outerwear, he camped in the living room, waiting. He switched on the TV and found a show on Animal Planet about whales.

Finally, after the local ten o'clock news with its depressing weather forecast, Jake heard a vehicle come up the drive. He pressed the TV's Off button and picked up a magazine, trying to act like he was just up reading.

His dad came in, slamming the door against the wind. "You still up?" he called, while noisily scraping snow off his boots and hanging up his coat in the back hall.

"Yeah," Jake replied.

"Thought you needed to get to bed early. You've got clinic hours tomorrow, right?"

"Yeah."

His father appeared in the living room. He halted, propping his hands on his hips. "You didn't stay up because I was out, did you?"

Jake tossed the magazine down and looked intently into his dad's eyes, letting his aggravation build. Why not the direct approach? "Of course that's why I'm still up. It's a treacherous night. That SUV's battery is ancient and you're not a well man. Why wouldn't I stay up to see that you got home safe?"

"You're not my nursemaid."

Jake's jaw hardened. "No, I'm your son." He rose and faced his dad. "And whether you like it or not, I'm going to start acting like one."

"I will not have you treating me like an invalid—"

"I'm not tucking you into bed and spooning up your medicine," Jake snapped. "I said I'm your son and I'm going to act like one. Thanks for leaving me the note. But tomorrow go into town and buy a new battery for the SUV. I don't want you stranded in this kind of weather."

His dad glowered at him and then stalked up the front stairs to his room. "As soon as they decide on my treatment," he called from the second landing, "I'm heading back to Colorado!"

That went well. Not. Jake slumped down, waiting again. He didn't want to run into his dad in their shared upstairs bathroom. *He knows he won't be going back to life as usual. But he's not going to make this even a little easy. Why am I not surprised?*

Jake didn't know how to work all this out, but some way, somehow, he had to bridge the gap between his father and him. His dad couldn't run away from home anymore. They would have to face each other and deal with matters, past and present. Or let them get worse. It was his dad's choice. What would he choose?

Tuesday morning Jake and his dad sat sipping their second cups of coffee. Mike stood at the sink, washing the breakfast dishes. Outside the window, lazy snowflakes fell. Inside, the atmosphere in the kitchen could have been termed "toxic." The delicious breakfast Mike had prepared had been spoiled by his dad's simmering antagonism.

"So, Jake, when are you going to be tested to see if you have HCM?" Dan asked, staring into Jake's eyes tauntingly.

Jake refused to react to his dad's goading. "I've already called and scheduled tests at the clinic in town. They have me scheduled for Friday but will call me if they have a cancellation."

Jake noted that his dad wore dress slacks and a professionally pressed shirt. Why not his usual around-the-house jeans? Jake wanted to ask what his dad's plans were for the day but was afraid that anything he said would be the *wrong thing*. His father's bad mood probably had nothing to do with him. *I'd know how to handle dad's diagnosis and early retirement. I would, if we knew each other better. But we don't—a sad fact.*

"You're all dressed up, Dan," Mike said, obviously trying to change the subject. "Where you off to today?"

"I'm going to the local community college," Dan announced.

Both Mike and Jake faced him. "Oh?" Mike asked in a provocative tone. "Do tell."

"I've been asked to speak to nursing students about working with doctors. The topic is etiquette in the hospital setting."

"Who asked you to do that?" Jake wondered out loud.

"I'm still known here. Have friends," Dan said with a disgruntled frown.

Doing his best to ignore his dad's ill humor, Jake shut his mouth so he wouldn't issue some health cautions. Again, that would be the *wrong thing* to say.

"Not going to tell me I'm too weak to drive myself to the college?" his dad asked.

Jake sipped his lukewarm coffee, not rising to the bait. "You're a grown man and a physician. You know your limits."

"Limits," Dan said the word as if spitting it out of his mouth. Then he looked into Jake's eyes. "I wonder if you'll be dealing with *limits* soon, too."

At the uncalled-for dig, angry heat flushed through Jake. No one liked to be told he had a life-threatening condition. But Jake refused to let his dad take it out on him. *I didn't give you HCM. But you may have given it to me.* Jake leaned forward to reply, but Mike beat him to it.

"That was a nasty thing to say," Mike growled. "It's time you grew up, Dan. You've been 'Mr. Five-Gold-Stars Super Achiever' all your life. But now you're going to have to face being human—like the rest of us."

Bleak silence.

"Sorry," Dan mumbled, hiding behind his coffee cup.

Grateful for Mike's words, Jake masked how his father's words had stung. He hated this tension between them. *It has to end somehow.* "I'm heading to work. Good breakfast, Mike. Dad, hope you do well with your talk."

He walked to the back hall and dressed to face the icy morning. Jeannie's sweet face came to mind. Seeing Jeannie would be a good way to start the day over again with a more positive outlook.

He hoped Mike's harsh but pithy comment would gain some headway in helping his dad cope with reality. They all had to cope with reality daily—humble rural vets and nationally known transplant surgeons, included.

Two evenings later, after opening the door, Jeannie frowned at Jake and Mike, barring the way in. The two men each carried an end of a box spring wrapped in plastic. Cold air rushed in, making her wrap her arms around herself.

"Are you going to let us in or make us freeze here like garden gnomes?" Mike barked.

She gave way, letting them bring in the mattress set. They propped it against the wall beside the dinette table. She wanted to protest but realized the futility of this.

The men obviously read her silence as a good sign. They made three more trips in and out. Finally in the center of her living room sat the white iron antique bed frame Jake had shown her and the new mattress set.

The twins, already in their pajamas, crept out of bed and from the hall archway they watched this happen. She didn't bother telling them to go back to bed. She'd have to settle them down again once this production was done.

"Why don't you rip off the plastic while Jake and I take out the old mattresses?" Mike suggested and then didn't wait for her response.

She did as he requested, churning inside. Of course, they were being kind, but having to accept this stirred up the unhappy past. In silence, she let the two of them set up the new bed. Her chastened girls stood in her bedroom doorway solemnly watching the bed being set up. She joined them there. Once it was done, Mike invited the girls to sit on the bed to see if it was soft enough.

Jake stepped into the hallway toward her. "You're not mad, are you?"

She sighed. How could she be cross? "You don't take 'no' very well, do you?"

He grinned. "I need my office manager to get a good night's sleep. And that old mattress was a recipe for a bad back."

She sighed and shrugged, trying not to take offense at this man's honest kindness. "All right, you took the rent and I'll take the bed." After all, it wasn't charity since a bed had come with the house.

"Great." He looked like he was going to say more.

But Mike came out with the girls, interrupting. "We better get going. These little ones need to get in bed and stay there."

Jeannie nodded, forced to agree, though she longed for a few more moments with Jake. She swallowed this down and walked them to the door. Everyone called out, "Good night!"

Then Jeannie shut the door, herded the girls to their bedroom and then entered her bedroom to put the bedding back on. She found that Mike had already made up the bed and on the quilt sat an envelope. Her rent check back again? *Oh, that man!*

The phone rang. She hurried to answer it. It was Ginny.

"Jeannie, I hope you didn't fuss at those two for bringing you the bed."

"Would it have done any good?" Jeannie let out a long sigh.

"Jeannie," Ginny's voice lowered, "I know it's better to give than receive, but sometimes we have to receive in order to let someone experience the joy of giving."

Jeannie repeated the convoluted sentence in her mind.

"Jeannie? Don't let pride trip you up."

How could she argue with that? "Okay, Ginny, thanks."

"Good night, dear."

Jeannie chuckled to herself. Leave it to Ginny.

* * *

Saturday, the first day of March, came and with it the Big Move of the shelter animals. Jake tried to focus on this and not the tests he'd undergone the day before at the clinic in Rhinelander. Though a vet, he'd had a pretty good grasp of the tests. He thought that the tests had gone well, and he hadn't been able to detect anything troubling. Of course, the lab techs had been noncommittal. They administered the tests; they didn't read and evaluate the results. So this left Jake with a tight band right around his ribs.

Annie must have parked on the street. She came striding up the drive to Jake. "What are you standing out in the cold for? Why aren't you driving over to load up some animals?"

Jake laughed. "Okay, boss!" He saluted.

"And as a bonus, you'll get to see Jeannie. She's in charge of loading up. I'm in charge of unloading."

For once, Annie's innuendo about him and Jeannie didn't rile him. He climbed in his pickup and headed toward the animal shelter a few miles away, unable to stop grinning over the idea of seeing Jeannie. Jeannie was one of those rare people who were centered in the midst any storm. And he felt as if he were in the midst of one now. She always exuded the sense that she was planted on a firm foundation. Jake wondered if this foundation was her obvious faith in God. He'd taken God for granted for years now, as if He were just a distant relative.

On the county road, a driver going in the opposite direction beeped his horn in a friendly greeting. Jake recognized him as another volunteer who'd evidently already loaded up the back of his pickup. Jake beeped in reply and then sped on. When he pulled up to the shelter, Jeannie was supervising the loading of another pickup. She waved and gave him a brilliant smile.

A man could live on that kind of smile for a month. He beamed at her and waited his turn. Finally the truck being loaded headed off and he backed up to the shelter. Then he jumped out and came around to help those ferrying the cages of animals from the shelter into trucks. He and Jeannie had no time to do more than to smile.

When his pickup bed was loaded with a group of loudly unhappy cats, he saluted her and drove toward home. As soon as he left her presence, worries over HCM attacked him. Visions of him clutching his heart and collapsing in his clinic... *Stop that.*

As he backed up his drive to the barn, he noticed a white van with a satellite dish on top. The Rhinelander TV station must have come out to film the animal shelter move. TV again? Jake's jaw clenched. He nearly drove away. But Annie waved wildly toward him. He sucked in air and got out and headed toward her with Bummer at his heels.

"Here's our benefactor, Dr. Jake McClure!" Annie called out, gesturing theatrically toward him. "And his faithful companion, Bummer the basset hound."

Annie, you should join the local theater group, Jake groused silently.

A different TV person shoved a microphone into his face. "Doctor, how does this move affect the needs of the animal shelter? Has there been a significant increase in adoptions?"

"Unfortunately, only a few families came forward after our first interview on your station." He managed to get the words out without stammering.

Annie leaned forward. "That's why one of our volunteers, Ms. Jeannie Broussard, has persuaded the principal at our local elementary school to add an Adopt-a-Pet special to the school's annual Winter Pet Parade."

The interviewer asked for the specifics of day and time, and Annie beamed into the camera. Jake smiled stiffly and counted the seconds till the interview ended. The interviewer thanked them, and then within minutes, the van drove away.

"Great publicity!" Annie enthused. "Glad you showed up right on cue."

Jake gave her a twisted smile and shook his head. "Now can we move the animals inside the barn?"

"Details, details," Annie retorted with unimpaired good cheer.

The Big Move was accomplished before noon. The barn was filled with cages. The cats and dogs let the world know how unhappy they were about the move. Many of the volunteers headed home, but a few came inside the house for coffee and sandwiches that Mike had made with the help of Ginny, Mimi and Cindy.

When Jake sat down at the crowded kitchen table, Mimi handed him an envelope. He looked at it and hoped it wasn't the blasted rent check again. He glanced up at Jeannie.

She leaned over and whispered into his ear, "No, it's not the rent check. You win."

Grinning, he opened the twins' envelope. The note began with *Dear*— Then a blank filled in with what must be Mimi's careful printing: *Dr. Jake, please come to the Pet Parade.* It gave the date and time. Jake smiled and gave Mimi a one-armed hug. "I'll try to make it."

"Bring Bummer," Mimi urged.

Jake chuckled. "I'm sure he'd enjoy it immensely." And he bathed in the glow of Jeannie's smile. "I will, too." Everything was better with Jeannie.

Unable to suppress her bubbling anticipation, Jeannie walked into the twins' school for the Winter Pet Parade. She carried a box with their two kittens. Just inside the school doors, she was welcomed by the principal.

"So glad you could come, Ms. Broussard." He shook her hand. "Parents and pets can go right into the gym. The children will be dismissed to the gym soon."

Jake arrived and the principal turned to him. "Dr. McClure!

Thank you for coming. Why don't you follow this pretty lady into the gym?"

Jake with Bummer—on a leash for once—had barely nodded before the principal turned to greet another parent laden with a pet carrier.

Jeannie had known Jake received a special invitation to come, this one from the principal, along with a request that he bring Bummer, a favorite of the community. But at seeing Jake here, she experienced a twinge of anxiety.

When she handed him the mail earlier today at the clinic, she'd noticed a letter from the lab which must contain the results of Jake's heart tests. Had he opened it?

He walked beside Jeannie on their way into the gym. He leaned close to her ear. "This pet day parade may be a lot of fun. Or result in complete disaster."

Jeannie chuckled, hiding her concern over his health. The worry that he might have HCM nagged her. She hid this behind a bright smile. "The parade's a wonderful idea. Everyone needs a lift from this awful winter. A gymnasium full of kids and pets is bound to do that. Even if it's a disaster, it will be fun." *Have you opened the letter yet?*

"I like that optimism. Let's hope the cats and dogs of Wisconsin have declared a truce for the day." After that, they could not hear nor be heard. The barking and meowing and human voices bounced off the cement-block walls, wood floor and bleachers. Everyone tried to be heard, so nobody could be heard—unless they shouted into someone's poor, noise-numbed ear.

Jeannie was glad her kittens couldn't see the cocker spaniels, schnauzers, poodles and mutts that filled the gym. Most cat owners had tucked their pets into carriers. Even inside these, the cats were spitting and hissing out the cage doors or hunkered down as if this were D-Day. Jeannie looked around for Annie but couldn't see her. She grinned to herself, thinking of the surprise yet to come for Jake. He certainly didn't behave as if he had a clue.

A parent, who wore a baseball cap with a paper taped to it that read "Pet Volunteer," approached Jeannie. "We're going to have the dog's parade first!" she shouted into Jeannie's ear. "Please go to the bleachers over there to wait!"

Tempted to stuff tissue into her ears, Jeannie nodded and followed directions. She sat down, gazing around at all the pets and owners. Dogs and cats made up the majority of pets. But people holding fishbowls, terrariums with turtles and birds in cages added to the cheerful commotion.

Twinkie and Peanutbutter mewed loudly. She peeked under the blanket and reassured them. They did not appear to place much confidence in her guarantees. Jake had moved near the front of the gym and Jeannie realized she needed to put away worries about his test results. In a gymnasium full of animals, she had to stay alert!

With the bleachers on one side now nearly filled with parents and guests, the principal officially entered. And the children, class by class from the youngest on up, followed him into the gym. Jeannie was impressed by the way the teachers kept order. From the raised podium, the principal managed to quiet most of the people and some of the animals. Over the loud speakers, he welcomed them to the Sixth Annual Winter Pet Parade.

Then the parade began with the dogs—the barking dogs. The barking ranged from low "ruffs" and high-pitched "yips" to "booms" that seemed to come all the way from the dogs' tails. The barking enveloped the audience in a delicious cacophony. Adding an occasional "woof" to the mix, Bummer trotted beside Jake.

Scanning the bleachers, Jeannie recognized Ginny and Mike in the audience and then realized that Brooke, in a bright blue active-wear outfit, was marching in the parade with "Poo" in her arms. Then Brooke must have seen her, because she waved. Jeannie waved back at her, wondering how Brooke had been invited to the school event. Jeannie looked around to see if Dan had accompanied her and was surprised to see him just behind

Mike. How had she missed him the first time she scanned the crowd?

While the dogs belonging to students were being applauded and then given prizes, including ones for being the biggest, the smallest and for having the longest tail, Brooke climbed up the bleachers and halted next to Jeannie. She leaned close to her and said, "Hi! My nephew doesn't have a dog, so he asked me to bring Charmeur. Come back and sit with us."

In the midst of excited applause for one of the winners, Jeannie hesitated. But not wanting to be rude, she went with Brooke. Letting Brooke sit beside Dan, Jeannie settled beside Ginny. After considerable commotion during the distribution of ribbons, the dogs left the floor of the gym. The absence of dogs seemed to calm the cats. The gym quieted—relatively speaking.

There was a brief parade of the more unusual pets and another flurry of awards. Then it was time for the final parade, the cats.

Jeannie, with one kitten in each hand, paraded around the gym, waving to her girls. The kittens, who definitely did not like being in a crowd, trembled against Jeannie. She stroked them with her thumbs, silently promising them a special treat for suffering this for their girls.

After Jeannie completed the parade, she headed toward her seat again. But then she noticed her girls moving toward the podium. Jeannie paused, thinking they were going to receive some crazy award for the kittens.

The principal called everyone to order. "Today is supposed to be fun. But also, we have asked someone here in order to give a special honor."

Jeannie beamed. That was why Jake had been invited. The school was going to honor him for his donated services at the animal shelter. She tingled with excitement. Oh, how wonderful. And now she knew why Dan had come, too. Annie must have told him. She nearly bounced on the balls of her feet like her girls often did.

She saw Jake reenter with Bummer. Jake's beaming smile spread good cheer over the gym. Calls of "Hey! Dr. Jake! Hey! Bummer!" ricocheted off the cement-block walls. Bummer trotted proudly at his side.

"Will Ms. Jeannie Broussard join me at the podium?" the principal said.

Jeannie froze in her tracks. Jake was going to receive an award and maybe the girls' kittens. *Not me.*

"Mom! Mom!"

She could hear her girls calling her. But she couldn't move. She couldn't go to the front where everyone would look at her. Walking in a parade with a lot of people and animals, she could do that. But go to the podium? No way.

Then someone came close and took her arm. "I'll walk with you." She glanced up and Dan was there, coaxing her along. He leaned close and murmured in her ear, "Come on. You're holding up the show."

She allowed him to draw her along to the front. Halfway there, her twins ran forward and claimed their kitties. Dan let go of her arm and she followed the girls the rest of the way to the front.

The principal was holding the microphone. He motioned for Jeannie to come closer. The girls led her to him till she stood beside Jake and Bummer, too. What was going on? She was certain Annie had told her that Jake was to receive recognition, not her.

The principal cleared his throat. "Now, Mimi and Cindy's teacher let me know that these two young ladies have quite a story to tell about how they rescued their kittens on a cold winter night. Girls, can you tell us what happened?" He lowered the microphone.

Bummer crowded close to the girls. Mimi put her mouth directly against the microphone. "We were going to the potluck and we found our kitties—Twinkie and Peanutbutter."

"Out in the snow," Cindy interrupted. "And it was cold that night."

Mimi nodded her head in agreement. "So we picked them up and took them inside. And Dr. Jake—"

Cindy took her turn, pressing her lips against the microphone. "Dr. Jake told us how to take care of them."

"But what was real exciting was this!" Mimi exclaimed. She set her kitten on the floor in front of Bummer. Cindy quickly did the same.

Bummer immediately began licking the kittens. They rushed closer to him, mewing. With his chin, he shepherded them under him protectively.

There was a moment of stunned silence. Then shouts, squeals and applause burst forth. The audience loved it.

Her twins bounced on their toes, yelling into the microphone, "Bummer was there and he adopted them! And they think he's their daddy!"

More laughter and clapping. The principal joined in. Jeannie had never felt more proud of her girls. After a few moments, the principal motioned for quiet. The audience calmed down— though a few parakeets squawked and a few cats meowed.

"We want to thank you, Ms. Broussard, for letting the girls adopt these kittens."

Jeannie nodded, hoping this was all that would be required of her.

"I hope," the principal continued, "all you children take a lesson from this. Dogs and cats are not supposed to get along. But look at this dog and these kittens. Bummer, Dr. Jake's basset hound, looked past the little kittens' fur and whiskers and saw instead their need for love and care. This is a lesson in love for all of us."

At that moment, Bummer noted a spot on a kitten that needed grooming and got down to it. This added even more zest to the applause that followed the principal's words.

Once again, the principal raised his hands for silence. "Most of you with pets know Dr. Jake McClure. He is Bummer's faithful companion." The principal grinned. "We all know that

Dr. McClure donates services and supplies to keep our no-kill animal shelter going. Let's have a round of applause for Dr. Jake McClure! And listen to the specifics of the special Adopt-a-Pet Program we're holding today!"

Jeannie beamed. This was Jake's surprise. She couldn't wait for his reaction!

Chapter Nine

Jake stood, stunned. He hadn't been prepared for this. Then small hands pulled his arms, leading him closer to the podium. The principal handed him the microphone and said, "Say a few words to our students, Dr. Jake."

Jake gripped the microphone and could not think of one word to say.

"Jake, why don't you tell them about what you do at the animal shelter?"

Jake recognized Jeannie's voice. He repeated what she'd just said silently and then cleared his throat. "I'm glad that we have a no-kill animal shelter. I'm happy to help out with neutering or spaying dogs and cats so that we slow down our stray-pet population."

Perspiration wet his forehead. He plunged on. "I also vaccinate cats and dogs against distemper and rabies, two deadly diseases that we can prevent. I hope all of you will visit the animal shelter and adopt a rescued animal and/or make a generous donation. If you don't have the funds, please come and volunteer. There is work there for everyone who loves animals. Thank you."

He handed the microphone to the principal, as spent as if he'd just sprinted in a race. He glanced over to see that his father stood behind Jeannie. He prepared himself for a look of disdain from his dad. Nationally known surgeon versus rural vet. However, his dad didn't wear a sneer. He looked as if he was thinking something over.

"You did fine."

At catching Jeannie's words of approval amid the hubbub of the students returning to their classes, Jake experienced a burst of gratitude. He threw his arms around her. "Thanks for telling me what to say," he whispered in her ear. Then he realized that he'd just hugged Jeannie in front of most of the parents in town. He released her and tried to look as if it had just been a friendly gesture.

His eyes met and connected with Brooke's. She stood behind Jeannie. Her gaze told him that she had not been fooled. But in that moment he saw himself plainly. And he recognized his misconception about what kind of woman he thought he attracted and the kind of woman he was attracted to undeniably. *Jeannie isn't anything like Sheila. And if I want to hug Jeannie, I will. If Jeannie wants me to, that is.*

"Congratulations, Son," his father said, appearing beside Jake.

"Thanks, Dad." Jake's throat closed after those two words. He couldn't recall the last time his dad had anything good to say to him. Then he recalled the letter from the lab in Madison in his pocket. The letter suddenly took on weight, hauling his happiness downward.

Jake had trouble focusing on people addressing him. He hadn't opened the letter, putting it off till the end of the day, not wanting it to interfere with his work. He wrenched himself back to face the present.

Catching Jake off guard, Jeannie brushed against him with her kittens in hand. His senses went into hyperdrive. Fortunately, no one expected anything of him. "Here's Annie. Listen," Jeannie said.

Annie had the microphone and was explaining about the overcrowding of the animal shelter, the pipes freezing and the move to Jake's barn. Then she launched into an impassioned plea for the parents whose children did not have a pet to come to each classroom to meet animals who needed families of their own. Listening to Annie's persuasive voice, he almost thought he needed to adopt another pet. *I already have six dogs and three cats. What am I thinking?*

The principal ended the program and invited the families to meet and greet the pets in need of families and then come to the cafeteria for refreshments.

Jeannie smiled up at Jake, drawing him to her irresistibly. "Let's go see if we can 'help' some deserving moms see the advantages of adopting a pet."

He chuckled. "Jeannie, you're something else." *Something great.* He needed her close today. And she gave him just what he needed to open his lab tests—as soon as this event ended.

For once, Jeannie didn't try to distance herself from him. The two of them, plus the girls, their kittens and Bummer, roamed from room to room, watching parents and children getting to know pets. Jake reveled in their closeness.

A few times a parent would nod and a child would jump up and down or hug the parent. Across one of the classrooms, Jake glimpsed the litter of kittens he and Jeannie had rescued. He recalled holding Jeannie for the first time as she wept over these little ones. He kept his arms to himself so he wouldn't reach for her now. But he remembered how soft she'd felt wrapped within his arms.

A family was choosing one of the kittens. Brooke walked up to the family and began a conversation. Soon the mother nodded, and the children chose a second one from the litter. Smiling and chatting, Brooke accompanied them to the door. They left with friendly waves.

Jake motioned for Brooke to come over. "I get the feeling that you talked that woman into taking two instead of one."

"I just told her that the kitten would be better behaved if it had another kitten to keep it company," Brooke replied.

Jake's father entered the room and waved to Brooke. She smiled and joined him.

"Well, those two may appear happier because they have some-one to keep them company, too," Jeannie murmured, watch-ing Dan and Brooke speaking to each other. "Everybody needs love."

Yes, Jeannie, everybody needs love, he thought, holding her gaze for a moment.

Finally, near the crowded school entrance, Jake and Jeannie prepared to go back to help Sandy close up the clinic for the day. Comfortable with Jeannie by his side near the school's entrance, Jake ignored the speculative glances sent their way by people leaving the school. He even felt pride at having someone special like Jeannie at his side.

"Mom! Mom!" The twins caught up with them as they were about to leave. "Can we ask Dr. Jake to come to our house for supper on Friday?"

"Yeah, he did good today and a lot of animals got adopted," Cindy added.

Since Jake stood right beside Jeannie, he wondered how she would handle this. "Sorry, Jake," she murmured for his ears only, "but I must teach them how to behave." The she raised her voice, "Girls, while I would love to have Dr. Jake come for supper on Friday, this is not the way you ask."

"How should we ask?" Mimi tilted her head like a sparrow.

"You should have asked me in private if we had any plans for Friday night and if I'd like to invite Dr. Jake to share a meal with us. That way if we do have other plans, we won't end up like this—in an awkward situation. You have issued an invitation that I might have to take back."

Cindy looked thoughtful. "We can't ask you in private now. Dr. Jake heard us."

"Exactly. Now do you see how this should have been done the polite way?"

The twins nodded, looking solemn.

Jeannie shook her head. Then she turned to Jake. "We don't have any big plans for supper on Friday night and if you don't either, why don't you, Mike and Dan come over to our house?"

He nearly chuckled at the expressions on the twins' faces. They clearly didn't want all three to arrive for supper. Their attempts at matchmaking should have made him uncomfortable, but he only felt happy to be invited, to be wanted. "I'll see what the rest of them say. But I think I'm available. And Bummer, of course."

Jeannie chuckled, grinning at him. "Okay, girls, now go back to your teacher till the bell rings. Mike and Ginny will wait to take you home. Shoo." Jeannie waved them away.

"But is Dr. Jake coming on Friday?" Mimi insisted.

Jeannie shooed them again.

The bright sunlight from the windows of the vestibule high-lighted Jeannie, making him examine her more closely than usual. He found it harder and harder to hold the professional line between him and his pretty, caring office manager. Their lives had become entwined. And he longed to tell her how even the faded denim blouse she wore made her eyes a warmer brown, an inviting and comforting shade.

As usual around Jeannie, he tried to hold back—but what he really wanted to say came out regardless. "I'd hoped you'd known about their invitation in advance and had told them to ask."

"You did?"

"I don't like to feel as if I'd been forced on you." His heart pounded. "If you don't want me to come, just tell me."

A moment of charged silence pulsed between them.

She smiled suddenly. "I guess it's good you accepted, because I want you to come very much."

Jake clamped down on his self-control. Yet ignoring how much he wanted to be with her and the girls had become nearly undeniable. "I needed a lift." *And you always give that to me.* He pulled the envelope with his lab results out of his pocket, opened it and read it.

"I recognize that envelope from this morning's mail. Care to share your test results?" she asked, her tone cautious.

"Yes, it looks like I don't have HCM." Relief radiated from him like warmth from a wood stove.

"Jake!" She threw her arms around him. "I'm so glad."

"I thought you two weren't dating." Annie appeared in the vestibule, half scolding them with a prim and proper expression.

"We're not. Jake's tests came back negative for HCM. I'm just happy."

"Well, I am, too." Annie hugged Jake. "Now will you help me and the other volunteers load up the animals to go back to the shelter?"

As Jeannie and Jake moved to help her, Jake asked, "How many animals were adopted today, Annie?"

"We had six kittens, three puppies and an older female dog adopted. And a few more people were interested but needed to talk to spouses before making a decision."

"Wonderful!" Jeannie exclaimed.

Finally Annie left and Jake and Jeannie were out in the frigid sunshine by her van. "What would you like for supper when you come Friday?" Jeannie asked.

"Maybe you should ask the twins." He grinned. "They may have the menu all planned."

She laughed out loud. "Yes, leave it to my twins."

He let himself gaze at her, drink in the glow of her ivory skin, the way her hair waved slightly around her face. Old, bad reflections of the pain Sheila had caused and the stresses from his dad's illness tried to bob up. He blocked them. *I have supper at Jeannie's to look forward to.* It would give him a dose of Jeannie's peace, what he needed most, wanted most.

On Friday Jeannie tried to keep her anticipation of dinner with Jake under control, yet she couldn't contain her excitement. Her lingering fears of no man being able to accept her girls as his own kept bumping into the reality of what a kind, caring man Jake McClure was. Tonight she wouldn't worry about Jake becoming closer and dearer to her. Tonight, nothing could go wrong.

The telltale sound of Jake's truck pulling up to her back door made the hair on the nape of her neck tingle. She rubbed her neck, trying to subdue this response. One knock and she opened the door.

"Come in." Her voice sounded funny to her own ears.

He grinned and hurried inside. "How's Bummer? Did he behave himself today?

"Of course."

He opened his jacket. And she saw that again under his jacket, he'd sheltered a bouquet of flowers—a mix of cut flowers, yellow, white and pink, with a few red sweetheart roses.

She accepted them, her heart fluttering against her breastbone. "You didn't need to bring flowers again."

"I enjoyed it again."

The list of all this man had set in motion for her benefit streamed through her mind—flashes of her working at the clinic, of his gentle hands examining an animal, of helping her on moving day. She tried to reel in the gratitude and affection they sparked without success. *Jake, you are so good to me, to us.*

Then she noticed something. Why hadn't the girls run out of their room to welcome Jake? "Girls, Dr. Jake's here!"

"We know!" they called back. "We're busy brushing Bummer and the kitties."

"I take it that the girls have spent the day spoiling him rotten?" Jake said, turning from depositing his jacket on the pegs by the door, so unaware of her response to him.

"Yes, they were thrilled to have him spend the day. And since they had it off from school, I think Bummer made the time pass easier for Ginny. And I heard Mike came over and played Crazy Eights with the girls and Ginny this afternoon."

"Mike's quite a gamer, all right."

Gratitude overflowing, Jeannie grasped Jake's forearm. "I can't begin to thank you and Mike for…" She motioned toward the room. She didn't want to break down and hadn't realized that her deeper emotions would turn on her like this.

"Mike's got a big heart."

So do you. Afraid she might make her attraction to him too clear, she turned and walked to the kitchen. She had noticed some dusty vases on the top shelf in the pantry off the kitchen. She stood on tiptoe, getting one down, when the phone rang.

"Jake, would you get that?" she called.

"Sure!"

The ringing stopped and she came back into the kitchen to find Jake standing at the wall phone. His troubled expression brought her to a halt. He waved her to come to him. She hurried forward, vase in one hand and bouquet in the other. "What is it?"

Jake held the phone to her ear. "It's the police."

The words blasted through her composure. She reeled backward.

"Hey." Jake supported her arms so she wouldn't drop the flowers and vase. He guided her to one of the kitchen chairs. Abandoned, the phone swung on its cord against the wall.

"I'm sorry," she gasped, setting the vase and flowers on the table. She half rose, reaching for the dangling phone. Yet she found she couldn't force herself to lift it. She sat back down. "What is it about?"

A voice from the phone could be heard but not the words.

Jake picked up the phone. "Ms. Broussard is here but would rather I hear what this is about." Jake listened and nodded. "Jeannie, just tell the officer that you'd like him to tell me what this is about." He held the phone to her mouth.

She hated this sudden weakness, the descent into the suffering of the past. But previous phone calls from police had caused her too much emotional agony to be taken lightly ever again. She dragged up her courage, her faith that God remained, as always, with her. "Ask him if it's about my sister, Carrie?"

Jake repeated the question to the officer. "No, it's about your house," he told her. He offered her the phone again.

Now her hands worked; she grasped it. "Hello, this is Jeannie Broussard."

"Jeannie, I'm sorry to bother you. But I'm afraid there has been an incident at your home being built at 303 New Friends Street. Can you come to the house? We don't want to break in. We need a key."

"An incident?" she repeated, confused because her unsettling reaction had taken her far from any thought of New Friends Street.

"Yes, we think someone may have entered the premises unlawfully."

She hated police talk, lawyer talk. But this man was just giving her information in the way he had been taught. She couldn't fault him. Except didn't she recognize this voice?

"I have a key and I'll come right away." She hung up as he finished thanking her.

She glanced up at Jake, hovering close in obvious concern. "We need to go to my Habitat house. The police think someone might have gotten in...unlawfully."

"Trespassers?"

She shrugged. She stumbled a bit as she rose. Jake steadied her, cupping her forearms. She looked away. "I thought they might have found my missing sister," she murmured, not meeting his gaze.

He squeezed her arms. "I'll come with you."

She almost accepted. "I shouldn't leave the girls alone. Would you stay with them?"

"I'll call Mike."

"Oh, no, I don't want to bother—"

Jake ignored her protest and dialed his home number. "Hi, Dad. I need to speak to Mike."

Jeannie tried to focus on the reality of what was happening now, not the tide of remembered anguish. *This isn't about Carrie.*

Jake listened for a moment, then said, "Dad, this is an emergency. I need you to come to Mike's house now." Jake hung up and turned to Jeannie. "Mike's out, seeing some pals at the bowling alley. My dad is on his way."

Jeannie wanted to refuse this offer, but she couldn't face this without another human at her side. Though God never left her side, right now she might need a flesh-and-blood shoulder to lean on. She longed to reach for Jake's. She walked to the door instead.

Jake helped Jeannie on with her coat and called the girls to come out with Bummer. "Girls, your mom and I have to go take care of something—"

A knock rapped the door and Jeannie opened it immediately. Dan came inside, his muffler over his mouth. "What's the emergency?"

"Someone may have gotten into my house," Jeannie replied, distinctly uncertain about asking Dan to watch the girls. He'd made it clear that he didn't think much of her and her twins. But tonight, one unexpected wave after another was trying to sweep her feet from under her, carry her away on the overwhelming current. She struggled against it.

"We need you to stay with the girls while we go let the police in to check it out," Jake explained.

"I'm sorry to bother you," Jeannie began.

"No problem. You two go. I'll watch the girls." Dan smiled tentatively. "You go ahead."

Jake ushered Jeannie out to his pickup. Soon they were driving onto New Friends Street. Jeannie had made no attempt at conversation during the drive. Jake cast glances from the corner of his eye toward her. She couldn't reassure him. Rigid horizontal lines, too brittle for idle conversation, immobilized her face.

When he parked behind a police car, she got out and the two

of them hurried over the hard-packed path to the house. In the scant light cast from the street lamp, a police officer waited for them at the side door.

When she arrived at the bottom of the stoop, the policeman greeted her. "Is that you, Jeannie?"

Recognizing Brad's voice swept Jeannie farther into the over-whelming tide. Her strength was being swept away. She fumbled for her key. Brad hadn't changed, still solid, good-looking, with dark curly hair.

"Yes, it's Jeannie." She struggled to act as if seeing him hadn't brought up unhappy memories. "How are you, Brad?"

"Cold, but that's nothing new this winter. I'd heard you were getting one of the Habitat houses. I was glad."

"Thanks." She offered him the key.

"You go ahead and unlock it," Brad murmured.

Jeannie did. Her hands shook and she hoped neither Jake nor Brad noticed. How had the evening changed from a quiet, happy supper with Jake and the girls to this grueling series of attacks on her peace of mind? The police calling her wasn't bad enough? It had to be *Brad?*

Jake followed Jeannie up the steps. He'd heard Jeannie call the policeman—what? Brad? Why was Jeannie on a first-name basis with this cop?

The door open, the policeman, this Brad, stepped inside and flipped the light switch by the door. Jeannie stepped farther in, making room for Jake just inside the door. Jake looked around the unfinished house. Nothing looked suspicious.

Jeannie looked to Brad. "What are we looking for?"

"I'm going to take a walk-through," he said. "I want you two to stay here by the door."

A knock came at the door. Jake took a step closer to Jeannie to protect her. Had the officer called for backup? Should he have kept Jeannie outside?

Brad opened the door. "Hi, are you Marc Chambers?"

"Yes." A tall dark-haired man stepped inside.

Jeannie studied him and then said, "You're my neighbor, or you will be in the spring."

"Yes, my wife Rosa and I thought we saw a light over here last night. But we couldn't see any cars parked nearby and we didn't hear anything."

Brad cleared his throat. "Mr. Chambers called us this evening, prompting me to come out. He said he heard noise tonight like someone fighting."

"Yeah, I heard voices again so I came over. A bunch of kids were hanging around in the back." Marc motioned toward the rear of the house. "When they saw me, they scattered. That's when I called the police. Thought it should be checked out."

"Thank you," Jeannie said.

"Yeah," Jake agreed, resting a hand on her shoulder and noticing that her gaze still avoided Brad's. His protective instincts went on high alert. He'd bet anything that Jeannie was not happy to see this guy Brad here. Why?

The cop cleared his throat as if uncomfortable being here with Jeannie, too. "I'll do the quick walk-through," Brad repeated. "I don't think anybody is here, but just in case, wait here."

The three of them hovered by the door as Brad strode down the hall. They didn't speak, a weird unease held them all in a kind of limbo. After a quick survey of the upstairs and then the basement, Brad motioned them to follow him down the hall. "Somebody's been here all right."

On the drive over, Jake had feared vandalism or at the very least, graffiti. But as they walked down the hall, nothing looked different. Still, he couldn't relax. And the tension between Brad and Jeannie remained constant. Their pointed attempts not to look at each other niggled at Jake. Did they have a history? Or was it just his overactive imagination?

When they reached the back bedroom, they found the evidence of someone other than the volunteers being inside. Empty beer cans and crumpled potato-chip bags lay scattered on the floor. And many footprints and large areas where people must have sat against the walls were plainly visible in the white dry-wall dust on the subfloor.

Brad made a sound of irritation. "That's what I was afraid of. Unoccupied houses attract teen drinking parties." He propped his hands on his belt. "At least they didn't get drunk and wreck anything."

"How did they get in?" Jake asked.

Brad pointed to the window. "I bet we'll find one of these wasn't locked. They probably just slid it open late at night."

Jake glanced at Jeannie. She had a fixed, frozen expression. No doubt strangers trespassing in her home must be unnerving her. On top of whatever lay between her and Brad. And she'd mentioned her missing sister.

Jake pulled Jeannie under his arm. Her shoulders were tight as telephone wire. "This isn't too bad. Just a little mess."

She tried to smile and failed.

"I'm going to notify my department," Brad said. "For the next few weeks, we'll do a walk-around of this property, not just drive by. When are you supposed to be moving in, Jeannie?"

She shrugged. "Sometime in the spring."

Jake squeezed her shoulder, wishing she didn't sound so dead-ened. Being here with this guy Brad, she was withdrawing, suc-cumbing to something, maybe more than one something. He could feel it. Suddenly Jake realized why he recognized the ill ease between Jeannie and Brad. It reminded him of the one time he'd run into his ex unexpectedly. On that occasion, though he'd tried to hide it, he'd felt physically ill. Had Brad and Jeannie been involved and then broken up? He didn't like that guess at all.

"Well, unless you need me, I'm going home," Marc Chambers said. "Why don't you drop by sometime, Jeannie? Rosa would like to get to know you better."

"I will. Soon." Jeannie's smile barely lit her face.

Sticking to Jeannie's side, Jake followed Brad back to the

empty kitchen. Brad called his department to report what he'd found.

As Jake listened, the reality finally sank in—all this fuss, all due to a few kids sneaking away to drink illegally. Nothing bad had happened—it was just unsettling. Yet Jeannie was suffering. Just about seeing Brad? No, this innocent incident dredged up her lost sister. "How much longer will we be here, officer?" Jake asked, a hand on Jeannie's back.

Brad glanced at him and hung up the cell. "Not long. I'm just going to make sure all the windows are locked. That's all."

Jake joined him and checked windows throughout the house. Then Jake and Brad returned to the side door. Jeannie, still not making eye contact with the cop, said, "Thanks, Brad."

"Good to see you again."

Jeannie said nothing, just gave the man a brief, tight, fake smile. Walking behind Jeannie, with a protective hand on her shoulder, Jake headed for the truck and then drove them home. Should he ask her about Brad?

When they pulled up to Mike's, now Jeannie's house, a strange vehicle was parked there alongside Dan's SUV. "I wonder whose car that is," Jake said. What now? *All we wanted was a quiet supper with the girls.*

"I hope your dad didn't need help with the twins," Jeannie said, climbing out and heading for the back door.

Jake hustled to catch up with her. He pushed in right after Jeannie, who'd stopped just inside the door. He nudged her forward gently so he could shut the door behind them.

Dan, Cindy, Mimi—and Brooke—sat in the living room around the coffee table where the Candy Land game had been set out. Bummer woofed in greeting but remained beside Mimi. The kittens were batting around the game markers.

Jake covered his surprise by helping Jeannie off with her coat. Then he turned and said, "Hi, Dad. I see you called for help."

Brooke drew a card and moved her red marker forward. "I

just happened to call Dan on his cell phone and he sounded like he was having more fun than I was having at home alone."

Jake surreptitiously studied his dad, trying to discern anything about his "relationship" with Brooke. Dan looked calm and relaxed. Very different from his customary irritable mood at home. Jake began to breathe easier.

"I appreciate your coming over to help, Dan and Brooke. And I'm expecting you two to stay and eat with us," Jeannie said, looking strained but sounding cordial. "I'm going to check on the oven."

"You don't need to invite us," Brooke said.

"Yes, we can go out for a bite," Dan added.

"No, really, I made enough for an army, just a simple chicken and rice casserole and a salad. Won't be but a few minutes to get it all on the table. Please stay."

Again, she sounded as if she were speaking politely to clients at the clinic instead of guests in her home. But Jake heard the underlying emotional upheaval in Jeannie's tone. Or should he say the dampening of her usual liveliness. He tried to look encouraging and followed Jeannie into the kitchen in the rear.

In the small kitchen he stood in the doorway, unsure of what to say or do. After washing her hands, Jeannie donned oven mitts and lifted a large glass oval dish bubbling with a casserole out of the oven. She gazed down at it. Then she inhaled deeply and began pulling everything together—casserole, hot rolls and the salad. Jake pitched in and helped wherever he could.

As he carried the carafe of decaf coffee to the table, he recalled over the past two years all the too-quiet suppers with just him and Mike. Recently, his dad had joined their exclusive twosome, and then Jeannie and the girls, and now Brooke. This winter had certainly changed a lot in his life, too, and for the better—except for one area, his dad's HCM.

The possibility his dad might have more to face nagged at the back of his mind. He shoved this aside. Jeannie needed his full attention and support now. His dad and Brooke had helped them by taking care of the girls. And both Dan and Brooke were behaving in a friendly fashion. However, his dad could change that with one scathing comment.

Fortunately the simple dining set here had six chairs, so they all fit around the table. Bummer made himself comfortable beside Jake's chair. The kittens rolled and tumbled on the floor nearby. After grace, Jeannie asked everyone to pass her their plate so she could serve the casserole family style. "The dish is too hot to pass," she explained.

"This is a charming bungalow," Brooke murmured. "I was sorry to hear about your pipes freezing."

"It was a blessing in disguise," Mimi chirped.

"That's what Mike told Ginny," Cindy explained. "He likes us living closer and he likes—"

"He likes—" Mimi interrupted, her eyes brimming with excitement "—Ginny!"

Cindy nodded vigorously. "They're going to supper tonight at the bowling alley to watch the bowlers."

"That sounds like fun," Dan said. "I used to bowl when I was in high school."

"I never knew that," Jake said.

"There's a lot about me that you don't know," his father replied.

"I think that's true of all families," Brooke said, accepting her plate from Jeannie. "Children only know their parents as parents, not people."

Mimi and Cindy looked puzzled by this comment.

"This chicken and rice is delicious," Brooke said, turning the conversation to milder matters. "You must give me the recipe."

The casual dinner proceeded with friendly relaxing conversation, interspersed with sudden outbursts of exuberance from the twins. Bummer carried the kittens closer to Jake, one by one. And then the three of them, "Daddy" Bummer, Twinkie and Peanutbutter watched the people eat.

Jake noticed how Brooke's presence soothed his dad. She

managed to sand down the sharp corners of his resentment, the resentment that probably resulted from his diagnosis and enforced early retirement. Jake could have relaxed now except for the fact that he sensed Jeannie was suffering from the aftermath of the call from the police. And that mattered more to him than who Brad might have been to her.

Brooke stood beside Jeannie, drying the dishes. The men had offered to do them, but the twins had asked Dan and Jake to read them their two favorite bedtime stories, "The Three Little Pigs" and "Little Red Riding Hood." The girls insisted that the stories sounded better when a man read the wolf parts. So while Jeannie and Brooke worked side by side in the small kitchen, the girls got into their pajamas and sat in the living room, one on Jake's lap and one on Dan's, listening to the stories.

The evening had drawn to an early close. Jeannie could only be thankful for that. Receiving a police call and facing Brad with Jake beside her had already pushed her nerves over the edge. Dan and Brooke joining them for supper had unexpectedly given her time to collect herself. What a roller-coaster evening. *I'm exhausted.*

Brooke finished drying the final spoon. "Thanks for having us. Your girls are delightful."

Jeannie scrutinized Brooke's face for any hint of irony and found none. "They are unpredictable all right."

Brooke chuckled, then grew somber. "I wish I'd had children. But my ex didn't want us to start a family early. I didn't realize that he intended that I would be his starter wife, not the one he'd have a family with."

Jeannie listened to the bitterness that infused each of Brooke's words. She wondered how old Brooke could be.

As if hearing the unspoken question, Brooke said, "I'm getting to the age where my chances of having a child are dwindling."

So that meant Brooke must be nearing forty. "I wouldn't give up hope," Jeannie said.

Brooke then shook her head and smiled. "I doubt I'd have the energy to be a forty-something with a toddler. A fifty-year-old with a teenager. I see how hard even a young mom has to work to keep up with kids."

"They do push a woman to her limits," Jeannie admitted.

"I heard that your girls are really your nieces. Do you ever hear from your sister?"

A hard ball of grief lodged in Jeannie's throat. Would she ever see Carrie again? Unable to speak, Jeannie shook her head.

"I'm so sorry to bring up something obviously painful. But it's plain that you're a great mom."

"My girls are my treasures here on earth." Jeannie blinked back moisture in her eyes. What an evening—so straightforward at the start, so jumbled now.

Soon the fairy tales were read and the girls had hugged everyone good-night and carried their kittens to bed, followed by Bummer. Dan stood at the front door, helping Brooke with her long white down coat. Jeannie wished she had Brooke's flair for fashion. Her own denim and fleece was comfortable, but every woman wanted to look nice, didn't she?

"I'm going to be giving a small dinner party at the end of this month," Brooke said. "A kind of end-of-winter party. Would you and Jake come?"

Jake looked to her. The fact that Brooke considered her and Jake a couple tangled up her vocal cords.

"Did I say the wrong thing again?" Brooke asked, looking upset at herself.

Jeannie's throat loosened. "No, you didn't. It's just that Jake's my boss and…"

"How about this," Brooke said, "you two can get back to me, okay?"

"Okay," Jeannie said, drawing a shallow breath. "Thanks for understanding."

Finally, the door closed and she and Jake were alone. She drew up her reserves, planning on sending him off with a cheery thanks.

Jake opened his arms. "Come here."

She considered resisting his invitation. Then she did what she had longed to do all evening. She walked to him and rested against his strong chest. "I shouldn't—"

He pulled her closer still, stopping her words against his soft sweatshirt.

She rested against him and found that breathing came easier. His soft kisses on her forehead and hair fell, wordless blessings raining over her. "Jake," she whispered. His physical closeness soothed her, comforted. Yet so many cautions popped up all warning her to stop, to step away.

He tucked her even closer and replied, "Jeannie, sweet Jeannie."

She could have stayed within his tender embrace forever, but Jake urged her to the sofa. He steered her to the cushions and then eased down beside her. However, he never relinquished her hand, staying connected to her.

Then he leaned back and gathered her under his arm. "Rough night."

He didn't say it as a question, just a sympathetic comment.

"You always know when I'm upset," she murmured against his shirt.

"Yes, I seem to have developed a Jeannie radar."

She grew even more solemn. In spite of all her efforts against this happening, she had developed a Jake radar, too.

"Tell me…whatever's bothering you, whatever you want me to know, Jeannie."

She relaxed against him. Part of her wanted to pour out her heart; another part of her sharply warned her not to do that. But who else would ask? Not wishing to burden Ginny, Jeannie had never told her much about Carrie. Jeannie took a deep breath and plunged in. "When we got the call from Brad tonight, it brought everything back from when my sister disappeared." Her stomach churned with each word.

"I guessed that. It's funny, isn't it, how something that no one else would think was upsetting can send us into a tailspin."

She looked up and a smile touched her lips. "That describes it. When you said, 'It's the police,' it was like some big hand grabbed me and shoved me down into a dark pit." Jeannie closed her eyes, warding off tears. *I will not cry.*

Jake kissed her hair again, a benediction.

This gave her courage to bring up something she had worried and wondered about. "Jake, that day in the clinic, the day we rescued that litter of kittens, you said you lost a brother. Then Sandy came and I couldn't say anything, ask about him. I've wanted to ask about him so many times, but was afraid to pry." She held her breath. *Am I prying into something I shouldn't?*

Jake didn't reply.

She shouldn't have asked such a personal question. "You don't need to tell me," she hurried to say. "I shouldn't have asked—"

"It happened almost twenty years ago this month," Jake said in a gruff voice. "My mother and my brother were killed in a snowmobile accident."

Jeannie had no words. She pressed her face against Jake's chest and rested her hand on his shoulder.

"It was one of those freak things. They were on the same snowmobile and for some reason, some reason we'll never know, they hit a tree." His voice churned with emotion. "I wasn't with them. I'd gone to a friend's house for the night."

At the bitterness in his tone, Jeannie lifted her head. She'd been right. Jake did understand how a phone call could devastate someone. She stroked his cheek, wishing she knew how to comfort this good man. Jeannie waited for him to say more. When he didn't, she started to pull away.

"Who's Brad to you?" he asked.

The question startled her. She grimaced. "I guess I didn't do a very good job of acting naturally with him, did I?"

"You were upset. I could tell he knew you, but he didn't talk to you about the girls or—"

"He definitely didn't ask about the girls," she said unable to keep the sardonic twist out of her tone, to deny the bitter taste left on her tongue. "Brad and I dated a few years ago. He knew I was a single mom and said he was okay with it. In the end, he wasn't. That's what ended our...dating." And she hadn't made the same mistake since.

"He didn't like your girls?" Jake sounded disbelieving.

She looked into his eyes. He looked so sincere. She had to believe that Jake liked the twins, but then they weren't dating. Or were they? Brooke thought of them as a couple.

Confused, she pulled away, sitting apart from him. "Yes, he didn't like the girls. Or to be precise, he didn't like *sharing* me with the girls. It became a tug of war and I was in the middle. It wasn't the first time that's happened. But it was the last. That's why I don't date." She hoped he understood that.

But then why had she let him hold her and kiss her? How did he sneak past her barriers? If they did become a couple, would she end up with another tug of war?

Jake nodded politely, but he looked down, and she couldn't read his face. "Do you think you'll ever hear from your sister again?" he asked in a sober voice.

"I don't know." His changing topics suggested she might be right, he was withdrawing from her. Sometimes even the best of men didn't want to deal with children who weren't their own. Being a friend differed from being a boyfriend.

But did friendship include kissing? Jake had kissed her. However, maybe since he hadn't kissed her on the lips, that meant just friendship to him. *But not to me.* A dangerous thought. And what about Brooke's invitation? He'd said nothing about accepting it.

Jeannie sighed. "I'm going to check on the girls."

Jake rose. "I'll go with you and then I should get home. We've got a busy Saturday tomorrow."

Jeannie tried not to feel let down. *I shouldn't have let him hold me.* Why did everything always have to get so complicated?

Chapter Ten

On the next bright but frigid Sunday afternoon, Jeannie entered the local Walmart with the twins to do the week's grocery shopping. Jeannie smiled politely at the greeter, selected a cart and aimed it toward the grocery side of the large store.

With her hand on its side rim, Mimi stopped the cart. "Mom, let's look at clothes first."

Jeannie hadn't planned on buying the girls new clothes today. But why not? "Okay, we'll take a look." After being inside so much because of the weather, maybe the girls just wanted to prolong their outing with a little "window shopping."

Jeannie aimed for the girls' section. But Mimi again abruptly halted her before she reached it. "No, Mom, let's look at clothes for you."

For me? Jeannie studied her daughters' expressions. Mimi had that determined cast to her features, firm jaw and focused gaze. "Clothes?" Jeannie objected. "I don't need any new—"

"Yes, you do," Cindy piped up. "You need some prettier clothes. You're the office manager now."

"And we're going to *own* a house, not just rent," Mimi added.

Jeannie continued to study the twins' faces as she tried to sort out this new development. What were the girls up to? Then

Jeannie glanced down at herself. A faded pair of jeans, warm winter boots, and a fleece shirt under her down jacket—perfect winter Walmart attire.

Then she recalled how few boxes all her clothing had fit in. And when Jake had helped her move, she'd been embarrassed to have to accept help once again. *I want to help others for a change.*

Maybe new clothing would help her let people recognize that though she appreciated their help, she didn't need it anymore. She had needed assistance when the girls were babies, but no more. And what about that dinner party that Brooke had invited them to. The one Jake hadn't mentioned yet. She *would* need something nice for that.

"Let's just look, Mom," Mimi wheedled. "We want you to dress pretty."

Jeannie recalled the stylish way Brooke dressed. The idea of trying to match this tempted her. "Well…"

"Mom, please," Cindy coaxed. "It'll be fun."

Jeannie shrugged in surrender. "All right." New clothes would give her a lift. *I am a woman after all.* She grinned at this. "Maybe I could use a new pair of jeans and a shirt."

Both girls did a little victory dance. That made Jeannie smile again. She did have two good-hearted girls. Mimi led the way into the narrow aisles of the clothing department.

"What size are you, Mom?"

"Size small or a six, but long or tall."

The girls started paging through the hanging racks, scraping hangers. Then they scooped up several pairs of folded jeans from shelves.

"Hold it," Jeannie cautioned. "I said one new pair of jeans and one shirt."

"You need more than that, Mom," Mimi countered with a pout.

"Yeah, you need more than one of each," Cindy agreed.

Jeannie decided not to fight them. "I can only take six items to the fitting room."

"Yeah, but we can bring you more when you finish—"

"I'm not going to be trying on clothing for an hour," she said, pressured, yet a little eager. It would be nice to own something new. She'd been saving every penny for the upcoming mortgage and new furniture for their house. She glanced around at the racks of clothing, tempted to shop for more than she'd agreed to.

A baby-blue oxford shirt caught her eye. "Oh, that's nice." She reached for it, paging through the blue ones till she found her size. She looked at the girls just in time to catch the last second of a conspiratorial exchange of glances. What exactly did the two have in mind?

Soon Jeannie stood in the dressing room. She and the twins had gathered more pairs of slacks and tops for her to start her trying-on session.

"When you got a new outfit on, come out so we can see," Cindy said through the door.

Jeannie sighed. "Okay." Maybe this merely signaled that her girls had matured a bit more. She obediently tried on a pair of khaki slacks and the blue oxford blouse. Both fit. She stepped out for the girls' approval.

The two studied her and then Mimi looked into the cart where the rest of the clothing they'd gathered awaited. "Try this on, Mom." Mimi offered her a darker blue cable-knit cardigan.

Jeannie donned the sweater and modeled the ensemble.

Mimi and Cindy exchanged glances. "Now we need to accessorize."

Jeannie gawked at them. "Accessorize? Where did you hear that?"

"On TV," Mimi explained with a *Don't you know anything, Mom?* expression. "Aunt Ginny sometimes watches QVC."

"And *What Not to Wear*. We like that one best," Cindy said.

Jeannie wanted to laugh but swallowed it. Her girls were

absolutely serious. "So you think I'm in need of a fashion makeover?"

The two nodded, expressions absolutely solemn.

Jeannie had never aspired to being fashionable. But now she had to choke down the fact that her seven-year-olds thought she needed a makeover. Did Jake think the same thing?

Where had that thought come from?

She put both questions out of her mind and stalked back into the dressing room. She recalled her disagreement with Jake about her paying rent on the bungalow they lived in now. Had her neat but worn and serviceable wardrobe made him try to refuse her rent check? A disturbing thought. Did clothes make the woman?

"Mom!" Mimi called to her, bringing her back to the present. "Cindy and me are going to go get you a few accessories. We'll be right back."

Jeannie stared into the claustrophobically close mirror, in danger of bumping her nose against it. *Accessories. What next?*

When she and the girls finally arrived at the checkout, they had selected the week's groceries plus the first outfit Jeannie had tried on. Also a new pair of black jeans, two more blouses—one ivory and one baby pink—and some inexpensive jewelry, a belt and a new purse. Jeannie comforted herself that she hadn't actually spent that much and recalled the Walmart motto—"Save Money, Live Better." But she didn't think anything she'd chosen would be quite right for a dinner party at Brooke's.

"I still think we shoulda got you those high heels," Mimi groused.

"Yeah, pretty women always wear high heels," Cindy joined in.

"Pretty women in Wisconsin wear boots in the winter," Jeannie said dryly.

"You tell 'em, sister," the checker said with a grin.

Jeannie chuckled and got busy placing the food items on

the checkout conveyer. "Now, girls, help me get the cart unloaded."

The twins began setting canned goods on the belt. And on their way outside, they took charge of the bags of new clothing. They grinned and gave each other a high five. Their satisfied expressions made Jeannie suspicious. "What are you two up to?"

They only giggled and ran ahead to the car.

Jeannie shook her head. Although she couldn't help but think how nice it would be to wear some new clothes to the clinic on Tuesday. Would Jake notice?

She backed away from that thought. Her "relationship" with Jake had just sort of developed on its own and had not really been identified. If they went to Brooke's dinner party, would that actually mean they were a "couple"? Would dressing more fashionably make a difference in Dan's eyes? Jeannie tried never to be prideful or think of herself more highly than she ought. But her life had progressed over the past few years. And perhaps her outward appearance should reflect that.

After stowing the groceries in the van and backing out, she drove away. A car nearby pulled out and seemed to follow them all the way home. When Jeannie drove into the drive at the new little house, she watched the car drive farther on, but wondered why. They lived on a dead-end road now. Where could the driver be headed? In a moment, the car was forgotten as the twins raced out with her bags, excited to put away her new clothes.

At the end of a long Tuesday, Jeannie didn't know what to do about Jake's obviously low mood. Bummer looked up at her as if understanding her quandary. She rubbed her forehead, trying to decide what to do, what to say. Maybe she shouldn't pry, but Jake had become very important to her, and she didn't like to see him down.

When she heard the last patient approaching from the examining rooms, she looked up and smiled. A man and his aging German shepherd stopped at the counter to pay. Usually Jake followed his patients to the front, chatting. Not this time. Jeannie accepted the man's payment, exchanged predictions about when spring might arrive. And then as he left, waved goodbye.

She walked out to the waiting area, locked the door, and began straightening magazines. She waited for Jake to come out and do a friendly recap of the day as he usually did. He didn't come.

She didn't relish trying to get him to talk. *But I'm not only his office manager. I'm his friend.* And the only way to find out what was bothering him was to ask him. The recent memory of looking up into Jake's handsome face after he'd kissed her hair flashed in her mind.

The nasty little voice also in her mind taunted: *Right. Friends. Don't lie to yourself. You two are more than friends. At the Pet Parade, half the town witnessed him hugging you. And Brooke invited you as a couple.* He still hadn't discussed that with her either. They must let Brooke know if they weren't coming. It was only polite.

No more putting this off. She marched back to the break room, Bummer trotting behind her. When she found it empty, she realized that Jake had shut himself in his office. Ominous, but it spurred her on. She made a cup of coffee for him and tea for herself and opened the connecting door. She motioned for Bummer to stay and for once he obeyed her, jumping up on the break room sofa. Then she gave her attention to Jake. He sat in his chair behind his desk, just staring.

She halted, studying his expression. *He's far away from here. And not in a good place, either.*

"I brought you coffee," she murmured, approaching him. She set the mug on the blotter in front of him. For a moment, he looked at her as if she were speaking Swahili.

"Coffee," he repeated.

"Yes, coffee," she said, sitting in the chair opposite him. "What's upset you?"

He picked up the mug and stared at her over it, deep worry streaming from his eyes.

She left her tea and moved around the desk. She leaned, half sitting, against it. "Please, Jake, what's wrong?"

He set down the mug and hung his head. He didn't reply, didn't look up.

She thought about pressing him, but decided against that. Not her style. "I'll go finish with the kennel," she excused herself. "Sandy had to leave early."

He held up a hand. "Sorry. I'm trying to decide what to do about something. We'll talk later. Okay?"

"Okay." Jeannie walked with brisk, purposeful steps back to the kennel. Keeping busy often proved the only way to fend off worry and concern. Yet a chill spread through her that had nothing to do with this awful winter that had lingered into March. What was on Jake's mind?

Minutes after Jeannie left him, Jake heard someone pounding on the clinic's back door—fiercely and urgently. He jumped up and began running toward the sound. Jeannie got there first and opened it. A woman rushed in—Mrs. Duffy, holding Pickles, her pug.

Jake raced forward. "What's wrong?"

"Thank goodness, you're still here!" Mrs. Duffy exclaimed. "Pickles is having trouble breathing. Help him!"

Jake lifted Pickles and raced to the nearest exam room. Mrs. Duffy and Jeannie jogged after him. First he turned the dog upside down, which sometimes dislodged foreign objects. "Mrs. Duffy, do you know of anything Pickles might have eaten, something that could have stuck in his throat?"

"I don't know. I was out having lunch and shopping with a friend today. I came home and found him coughing and gagging. He'd stop breathing on and off, too. So I just grabbed him up and drove here as fast as I could."

"You did exactly the right thing." Jake swung the dog right side up again. He set him on the table. Pickles moaned and gasped, wheezed, stopped breathing, then gagged and gasped again.

"Oh, my." Mrs. Duffy began to weep. "Is he going to die?"

"Not if I can help it. Please come here, Mrs. Duffy. I need you to get a good grip on him around his middle." Jake donned latex gloves, reached for his thin penlight, and aimed it down Pickles's gullet. "I see something, kind of orange."

"Oh!" Mrs. Duffy yelped. "My grandson was playing with Pickles yesterday. An orange Nerf ball!"

"Which—no doubt—your grandson forgot to take home with him." Jake reached for a long-handled forceps. He petted Pickles, murmuring to him. "Hold him tight," he told Mrs. Duffy. Then Jake plunged the forceps down Pickles's throat and latched onto the ball. He yanked it out. Pickles promptly vomited onto the examining table.

And Mrs. Duffy burst into tears. "Will he be all right?"

Jake used a wipe to clean off Pickles's jowls and face. Then he lifted the pug from the table and returned him to the embrace of his tearful owner.

Jeannie stepped forward and began to clean up the mess on the examining table. Jake drew closer to Mrs. Duffy. Pickles still gulped air, panting. Jake once again tilted the pug's chin upward and pointed the penlight into his throat. "All clear." He took a deep breath, his heart still thumping.

"Oh, thank you, Doctor," Mrs. Duffy said, still dabbing at tears with a tissue, one-handed. "I'm so happy you were still here."

"Me, too. Pickles is one fine pug." Jake petted the old dog's head.

"Do you need to do anything else?" Mrs. Duffy asked. "And do I need to do anything at home?"

Jake shook his head. "Just let me know if he has any more trouble. I don't think the Nerf ball has caused any swelling or inflammation. It's too soft. Just be careful next time that your grandson takes all his toys home with him."

"I will. I will." Mrs. Duffy lifted her purse from the floor where she'd dropped it.

Jake held up a hand. "I'll send you a bill for an office visit. Just go home and put your feet up and relax."

"Thank you again, Doctor. I will." Mrs. Duffy waddled out of the room. As she walked down the hall toward the door, Jake could hear her gently scolding Pickles about swallowing Nerf balls.

Jeannie let out a sigh of relief. "Wow. That was scary. I thought he was going to stop breathing any moment."

Jake agreed, gazing at her. His heart, too, had raced. And now he knew he shouldn't have put Jeannie off—always better to face things head-on. If Mrs. Duffy had waited, she might have come too late. Plus, he'd rejected Jeannie's overtures of friendship just before.

"I've acted like a jerk today."

She looked up, obviously surprised. "You are never a jerk."

"Yes, I am. I'm letting my dad get me down. I'm sorry. Really."

"You don't owe me an apology. None of us are perfect. What's the problem with your dad?" Jeannie finished cleaning off the table by spraying it with disinfectant.

"Let's go to my office. I need to sit down."

Smiling, Jeannie fell silent and then said in a low serious voice, "The girls and I have been praying for his health."

"Thanks." *My mom used to pray with us. After her death, I shouldn't have stopped.* "Come to my office. I'll tell you and you'll probably make me feel better."

"I'll try." Jeannie walked beside him to his desk. Though there was no one else in the clinic, they shut the door. Jeannie sat in the chair across from him. The only sounds came from the animals recovering in the kennel and even they were subdued.

Bummer scratched at the connecting door. Jeannie rose to

let him in, thinking Jake needed Bummer here, too. The basset hound went to Jake and rested his chin on Jake's knee.

"My dad's symptoms are getting worse." Jake stroked Bummer's ears. "And when I try to get him to call his friend Lewis at Madison, he just blows me off or blows up."

"That's hard. Your dad strikes me as a take-charge kind of guy. He doesn't like being the patient, does he?"

"No." He rubbed his forehead. "I've thought of talking to Brooke." He looked directly into Jeannie's eyes.

She nodded. "Brooke definitely has a good effect on him. But I don't think he'd take medical advice from her, and she might not want to confront him."

"That was my thought, too."

"Maybe you'll just have to let nature take its course. Maybe he'll need a good scare. What are his symptoms?"

"I've caught him rubbing his chest like he was in pain, but when I mentioned it, he denied it." Jake began stroking Bummer's ears again.

Jeannie frowned.

"And a few times he's stood up and then sat down fast. I think he was light-headed and was afraid he'd faint or fall down."

Jeannie shook her head. "He's stubborn all right. I'm not a doctor, but I know those are signs of heart problems."

"So what do I do?"

"There isn't much you can do except observe him and pray he'll see the light. Could he have a heart attack?"

"Yes, he could, and it could be fatal. I'm keeping a supply of nitroglycerin tablets in the house. I'm just afraid I won't be there to put one under his tongue and call 911."

Jeannie sighed deeply. "Maybe you should give Brooke a few of those pills on the Q.T. If he needs one, he probably won't be mad *after the fact* that she had one."

He nodded. "I'm looking forward to her party. I hope it truly will be the end of winter. I usually like winter, but not this year." He shook his head.

Jeannie looked surprised. "Are we going to her party?"

"Are we going to her party?" he repeated, distinctly puzzled.

"You never said anything. I thought you didn't want to be classed as a…as a couple."

"We are a couple, aren't we? I mean though I've never taken you out on a real date." Was she confused or was he? "I mean I've kissed you…"

Jeannie laughed. "Men." She shook her head. "Are we really a couple?" Bummer perked up at her laughter.

He gazed at her face. She looked back at him quizzically. "I guess I shouldn't have assumed that we were going together."

Jeannie sat back in her chair. "Jake, even in this modern age, the man is the one who asks the woman for a date—usually." She fell silent, staring at him.

He finally got it. "Jeannie, would you like to go to Brooke's party with me?"

"Do you want me to say yes?"

"Yes." *I will never understand women.*

"Then I would be happy to go with you as your date."

"Thank you."

Jeannie broke out laughing.

For a moment, he thought she might reach for his hand, but she didn't. She smiled and then left him, saying she needed to do Sandy's end-of-day routine. Suddenly he felt as if he'd swallowed an orange Nerf ball. He'd asked Jeannie for a real date and she'd said "yes." *Yes!*

Jeannie walked into the mall and nearly turned tail home. Jake had let Brooke know they were coming. And then Brooke had called Jeannie to chat a few days ago. And before Jeannie knew it, she and Brooke had planned a shopping trip together. Today, she'd tried to get out of it. Both the girls had bad colds. But Mike had declared that he hadn't caught cold in years and that Jeannie should go on, he'd stay with the twins.

Brooke chuckled. "You look like you've just walked into a dentist's office."

"I haven't been to a mall in quite a while. I usually just shop in Rhinelander."

"Rhinelander has some nice shops downtown, but a mall is like going to a carnival. Loosen up. This is fun. A girl's day out."

"I haven't had many of those," Jeannie admitted.

Brooke gave her a sympathetic look. "I used to have them often, but my husband got custody of our friends. That's one reason I finally moved here—to be near a few college girlfriends. And start over."

Jeannie didn't know what to say to this. "Divorce must be hard."

"It is hard, and especially hard when one party married for life and the other married just till someone better came along."

This ticked Jeannie off. "I don't think you should even say that," she objected hotly. "Just because your ex was fickle didn't mean that he found someone better."

Brooke stopped midstep and stared at Jeannie. "Thank you." She put her hand in the crook of Jeannie's elbow and grinned. "Girl, let's start shopping."

"Just remember I don't have much money to spend," Jeannie cautioned, thinking of Brooke's obviously designer clothes.

"Jeannie, I work for a living, too," Brooke said. "I do medical transcription from home eight to ten hours a day. But my passion is finding bargains. And we're in time for the end, of the end, of the end-of-the-season clearance sales." With this battle cry, Brooke led her into the fray!

Jeannie tried to keep up with Brooke. However, Jeannie ranked clearly an amateur compared to Brooke, plainly in the semiprofessional class. Jeannie lost count of the stores they swept in and out of. Finally, they hit a department store that had a seventy-five-percent-off sale price sale. Brooke paged through the clearance racks at a brisk pace. Soon Jeannie stood in a large dressing room, surrounded by mirrors and two stacks of clothing on hangers.

"I'll sit just outside," Brooke called from the entrance of the fitting rooms. "When you like something, come out and let me see."

In other stores, Jeannie had already tried on so many clothes that Brooke had rejected that she didn't know if she would know what she liked or not. Then from one stack, she chose a pair of brown tweed wool-blend slacks. She had almost left them on the rack. They were marked the wrong size, but they fit Jeannie like they'd been made just for her. Nothing pinched and they weren't too short. She turned before the mirror, trying to see how the slacks fit her from the rear. *I like these.*

She rummaged through the stacks of clothing and found a cream-colored cashmere sweater with a cowl neckline. She looked at the sales tag. Even at seventy-five-percent-off sale price sale, it was pricier than her usual purchases. Bravely she pulled it on and looked into the mirror. *Ahhhh. I have never looked better.* Certain that she must be mistaken, she walked out to Brooke.

"Oh! That's lovely on you." Brooke rose and joined Jeannie as she stood before the three-way mirror at the entrance to the fitting rooms.

"It's the wrong size," Jeannie said for lack of anything better.

"That's why it was waiting here for you." Brooke gazed at Jeannie's reflection. "You are going to buy this outfit."

"Yes, I am." Jeannie beamed at herself. And she bought several more. Brooke kept pointing out how much Jeannie was saving. Jeannie and Brooke walked out with two bulging bags of clothing. "But you didn't get much, Brooke," Jeannie said.

"No problem. I shop all the time. In fact, I cut up my credit cards, had to. Before I moved here, I started shopping to make myself feel better. And all I did was go into credit card debt. I stopped that, however, and have nearly paid everything off."

Jeannie glanced over at Brooke. She was seeing a new side—or two—of this woman whom she thought she'd pegged as snooty. Jeannie had been wrong about Brooke—good news all around.

"Now, we have to hustle." Brooke took her elbow again. "I've made an appointment for us to have manicures and pedicures—"

"Oh, no, I can't afford that."

"The appointments are at the community college with their beauty culture students, at a fraction of the cost. My treat. And then we'll do lunch in their cafeteria. Today the culinary arts students are preparing lunch. Should be yummy."

Brooke steered Jeannie toward the mall door. Something made Jeannie look over her shoulder and she saw—

Jeannie stopped and twisted away.

"What's wrong?" Brooke asked.

Waves of cold shock vibrated through Jeannie. "I thought I saw someone I know."

"Someone important?" Brooke asked, peering around.

"Yes." Jeannie's emotions rioted.

"Then let's see if we can catch up with them. Who is it?"

I thought I saw my sister. Jeannie didn't want to be forced to explain all about Carrie disappearing, didn't want that cloud to descend over this bright day. But she didn't want to lie either, so she told part of the truth. "Some girl I knew in Milwaukee."

"What's she look like?" Brooke was walking quickly and darting glances at the shoppers clogging the mall aisles.

"Dark hair and dark eyes. Very pretty." Cold shock penetrated her every vein, freezing her inside.

Brooke and Jeannie looked around the area, but the woman had vanished.

"I must have been mistaken," Jeannie mumbled. Was that true?

Brooke squeezed her arm. "Come on or we'll be late for our appointments."

Jeannie went along, pasting a smile on her face. Just as they walked out the mall doors, she looked back once more. Could she have seen Carrie, or had she just imagined it? The thought twisted her already unsettled stomach.

Later, Brooke and Jeannie walked into Jeannie's house. Mimi and Cindy came out of their bedroom. Both of them looked tired and flushed.

"How are you two doing?" Jeannie asked, feeling their foreheads. They were slightly warm to the touch. Thoughts of Carrie still jigged at the back of her mind, but concern for her girls overshadowed it, muted it.

"They've been pretty sluggish," Mike said. "But they took their decongestant and drank lemonade. Didn't eat much soup at lunch, though."

"Mom, show us what you bought," Mimi said, plopping down on the sofa.

"I'll let you girls enjoy the fashion show," Mike said, pulling on his jacket and hat at the door.

"Thanks, Mike," Jeannie called as he left with a wave. Brooke sat down on the sofa and talked softly to the girls.

Jeannie showed the twins the clothing she'd purchased and her painted fingernails. Both girls were subdued, but Mimi's more marked lack of enthusiasm worried Jeannie most.

Brooke rose to go. "I'll head home now. See you in a few days." She waved to the girls and Jeannie, zipped up her coat and departed, too.

Jeannie coaxed the girls to the table for a snack and then put them to bed for a nap. Their resistance to the nap lacked real pep, and soon Jeannie covered them up. She left their room with some misgivings.

Her mind went back to that electrifying moment when she'd thought she'd seen Carrie. *Lord, where is she? Is she even alive?*

Am I starting to imagine her because I've prayed for so long without an answer? But if it was Carrie, what would happen now?

Saturday night, the night of Brooke's dinner party, arrived. Jeannie stood in the bathroom, doing her hair. Of course, since this was the last day of March, winter had started complaining and grumbling, stirring up a brisk wind and spitting snow. A bad storm was heading right for Milwaukee, and Jeannie was glad she didn't live there anymore. She had never liked dirty city snow.

The girls were watching *Beauty and the Beast* on DVD in the living room. Cindy had recovered from her cold, but Mimi wasn't up to par yet. Fretting over this, Jeannie gazed at her reflection in the small medicine cabinet mirror. She'd brushed her hair and let it fall to her waist. Her girls had insisted that's how they wanted her to wear it tonight.

Jeannie touched the soft cashmere of the cowl-neck sweater. Ivory made her skin look warmer or glowing…or something. She reached into the cosmetics bag on the sink and took out a pot of tinted lip gloss. She tapped her little finger into it and smoothed it over her lips. She wondered if Jake would kiss her tonight and if this time it would be on the lips.

The thought had no sooner passed through her mind than she was aghast at herself. And then she wasn't aghast. *I want Jake to kiss me.* It felt good admitting it. Her lips tingled as if in anticipation and she smoothed them with a bit more lip gloss. Then she headed out to see how the girls were doing.

"Oh, Mom," Cindy said, bouncing up to hug Jeannie's waist, "you look pretty!"

Jeannie rubbed Cindy's back. Mimi didn't get up from the sofa, but she reached for Jeannie, who went over and put a wrist to Mimi's forehead. Cindy had gone back to school on Wednesday but she'd kept Mimi home the entire week. "Your fever is trying to come back, Mimi."

"I'll be okay," Mimi said, smiling. "You look so pretty, Mom. Dr. Jake is going to be happy you're his date."

Jeannie's heart buzzed with joy. Tonight would be the beginning of a new adventure. *I'm going to let myself take a chance on love again.*

That little mind-messing scolding voice tried to intrude, tried to take away her anticipation, tried to drag her back to the hurt of the other times she'd tried romance. Jeannie refused to listen.

She heard a knock at the door. "Come in!" she called out.

Mike and Ginny hurried inside. "When will this winter give up?" The two of them dusted large wet snowflakes off their heads and shoulders.

"Oh, Jeannie, you look so pretty!" Ginny looked up and exclaimed.

Jeannie just smiled. "You're pretty, too. I've got a large one of those take-and-bake pizzas for you to make for dinner, Ginny. And there's microwave popcorn for snacking."

The phone on the kitchen wall interrupted Jeannie. Ginny and Mike waved her toward the phone and settled down to watch the DVD with the girls.

Jeannie picked up the receiver. "Hi, this is Jeannie."

"Jeannie, this is Carrie."

Chapter Eleven

Jeannie felt as though the floor were coming up to hit her in the face. Her legs trembled. She collapsed into the nearest kitchen chair.

"Jeannie? Are you there?"

"I'm here." Jeannie couldn't think what to say. Her heart pounded and she had to blink away spots of light exploding before her eyes.

"I know it's a shock to hear from me. But I just couldn't wait any longer to contact you."

"Where are you?" Jeannie managed to bring up the words. *Where have you been for seven years?*

"In Wisconsin, nearby. I'm trying to get my life in order. I've only been out for a few weeks."

"Out?" Her sister's words didn't make sense.

"Yes, out of…prison."

Prison—how? Each word Carrie uttered jabbed her like a fist. "But that can't be right. The police would have told me if you were in prison. They couldn't find you in Chicago."

"I wasn't in Chicago. I was in Detroit. Oh, it's a long story. But I was using an assumed name there, and that's the name I went to prison with. I didn't want you to know or anyone to ever know I'd been to prison. I didn't want a felony to follow me or my girls around for the rest of my life. But I realized that you would need and deserved the truth."

Assumed name? Prison? Seven years and only three post-cards? Jeannie's mind had lost its ability to focus. Though she sat still, she felt as if she were being spun around very fast.

"Jeannie?"

Jeannie couldn't speak. Dizzy, so dizzy.

"I know this is a real shock for you. That's why I haven't contacted you before now. I've been watching you, trying to get up the courage to approach you."

"You were at the mall." The words welled up on their own.

"Yes, and I followed you home from Walmart the other day. Jeannie, I know this has really been rough on you. But I'm out now. I'm looking for a job. I'm going to get my life on the right path so I can take care of my girls. Oh, Jeannie, they're so cute. So beautiful. I saw them at Walmart with you. I just want to be a good mom to them. I can't thank you enough for taking care of them for me."

Each word hit Jeannie like a Taser. She couldn't move. She couldn't speak. She couldn't think.

"But I'm ready to be their mom now," her sister said.

At these words, Jeannie hung up the phone. She pressed her hands flat on the table, helping the world to stop spinning.

She looked down at her hands, pressed flat against the table top. What had just happened?

Jake walked into the kitchen. "Jeannie?"

She looked up at him, but didn't speak.

"Jeannie, we should be going now. Brooke's expecting us."

She rose. "Right."

"You look great, but are you feeling okay?"

"Fine. Let's go."

Something was not quite right. He tried to figure out if it was him. Had she decided she didn't want to go? "We don't have to go tonight if you don't want to."

"No, I want to go." She led him out to the living room. Mike was building a fire in the wood stove. Ginny was playing a hand-clapping game with Cindy while Mimi watched.

"Have a good time, Mom!" Cindy said, still concentrating on the rhythm of the game.

"You girls be good." Jeannie walked to the door and lifted her jacket from the coatrack.

Jake took it from her and helped her with it. Outside he helped her into the pickup. And then he got in and drove them to Brooke's. Jeannie said nothing, and Jake didn't want to press her. Brooke rented a condo near the country club golf course. Snow swirled around them as they hurried from the truck to the entryway.

Within minutes, Brooke was greeting them. "So happy you're here."

Jeannie smiled.

"Thanks for having us." Jake looked around at the other guests. Dad and Erv Pavlek, his old high school friend who had gone to University of Wisconsin at Madison with him, had come with his wife. Another couple looked familiar. They greeted Jeannie, and Jake figured out that they knew Jeannie from her church. So far so good.

Brooke went into the small kitchen. Jake followed Jeannie to a love seat, where they sat down. The other two couples made polite conversation, asked them questions, and Jeannie responded with brief but acceptable replies. Something about her suggested a trancelike state. Jake tried to figure out what was going on, but finally gave up.

After a delicious dinner, everyone decided to make it an early evening. Outside the windows, snow fell hard and fast.

Finally, only Jake, Jeannie, Brooke and Dan remained. Brooke stood behind Jeannie and made a gesture with her arms and face that clearly asked Jake: What's wrong?

Jake shook his head. Still, he appreciated the fact that someone else had noticed Jeannie's preoccupation. *I'm not mistaken. What could have happened?*

"Jeannie, thanks for coming," Brooke said, taking her hand.

"Thank you for having us," Jeannie said as if reading a script. "The dinner was delicious."

"You two drive home carefully," Brooke said as Jake followed Jeannie out the door.

Jake waved and then helped Jeannie into the truck. "I think we misjudged Brooke at first," he said, driving onto the main road.

"Yes, she's nice."

Jake tried a few more gambits but could not get Jeannie to do more than agree or disagree in brief sentences. *Did I do something wrong?* He searched his memory for anything that might have triggered this. He came up empty. Should he ask her?

He still hadn't made up his mind by the time they reached the little house. He walked Jeannie through the cascading snowflakes to her door. He had hoped to kiss her good-night, but he couldn't even think of attempting that now.

She turned to him. "Thanks. I had a nice time."

Jake tried to come up with something comforting to say. "Is everything okay?"

Jeannie nodded and then went inside and shut the door.

As Jake drove away, he knew one thing for certain—something was not okay. What had caused Jeannie to go on autopilot for the evening?

Jeannie woke up and tried to remember where she was. And what had awakened her.

"Mom," Cindy said, shaking Jeannie. "Mom, Mimi's sick, real sick."

Jeannie sat up. And looking down, she realized she had gone to bed in her clothes. Daylight glowed at the window.

"Mom, come on." Cindy tugged her hand.

Jeannie let Cindy lead her to the girls' room. Mimi was gasping for breath. When she saw Jeannie, she said, "Mom, it hurts when I breathe." Then she began gagging.

Jeannie rushed forward, grabbed the wastebasket, and helped Mimi throw up into it. She recognized immediately that Mimi had brought up congestion. Jeannie noted traces of blood; worry zipped up her spine.

When Mimi was able to lie back down, Jeannie wiped her mouth and face with a tissue. "Cindy, hurry, get Mimi a glass of water."

Jeannie didn't have to touch Mimi's forehead. Heat radiated from the child. *Oh, Lord, what now?*

Cindy hurried, splashing water from a plastic glass of water. "I ran it till it was really cold."

Jeannie accepted the glass and helped Mimi drink to clean her mouth and throat. "I'm going to get you bundled up. We need to go to Urgent Care." She turned to Cindy. "Get dressed really warm while I help Mimi dress."

Mimi was weak but didn't complain of achiness. That led Jeannie to believe that she didn't have the flu. Pneumonia? The word terrified her. As she helped Mimi put on a sweater and sweatpants over her pajamas, she heard the wind assaulting the little house. They must be getting hit with the fringes of the storm that would be pummeling Milwaukee by now.

Finally, the girls were dressed. Jeannie had wrapped Mimi's face with a scarf and told her to breathe only through her nose. Jeannie opened the door; wind and wet snow rushed inside, nearly bowling them over.

Jeannie shouted, "Hold on to me, Cindy." She swung Mimi up into her arms and bent into the wind. The snow had drifted against her door. She tried to plow through it, but the wind drove her back.

Holding Mimi with one arm and shielding her eyes with the other, Jeannie tried to look ahead to her car. She couldn't see it—just its outline under a mound of snow. She scanned the surrounding area and saw nothing but veils of snow, masking everything she should have been able to see but couldn't.

Cindy was trying to push her way through a drift, nearly as tall as she.

"Cindy, come back. We can't drive there."

"But Mimi's sick."

"It's not safe. Come back." Jeannie led them back inside the few steps. Even the short time outside had layered them with thick wet snow. Jeannie stripped the outerwear from Mimi and propped her on the couch, wrapping her in an afghan. She and Cindy shed their sopping scarves and jackets. Snow had worked its way down into Jeannie's boots.

"What are we going to do?" Cindy asked, her voice trembling with fright.

"We'll call for help." Jeannie went to the kitchen phone and picked up the receiver. No dial tone. She winced as if stung. She instantly tried to switch on the kitchen light. No luck. She hung up the phone and sagged against the wall. Power outage.

She pulled herself together, rushing to her purse, which she'd dropped by the door last night. She yanked out her cell phone and groaned. She hadn't plugged it in last night, and her battery was comatose. *Think. Think. Your girls are depending on you.*

Jeannie looked around the room. A low fire must be burning in the wood stove. That would keep them warm. How long had the power been out? Not that long. Cindy had been able to run water.

Jeannie steadied herself. Mike had stacked wood in the covered lean-to outside the back door, enough to keep them warm for a month if necessary. The well pump was powered by electricity, but she had a few gallon jugs of water set aside for just such an emergency. She had an oil lamp, matches and food. And decongestant to give Mimi. *I won't panic.*

Yesterday's phone call niggled at the back of her mind. But then at the catastrophic pounding of her heart, she shied away from recalling her sister's words. *I have enough to contend with. I'll think about that, later.*

Outside the kitchen door, she gathered an armful of wood, feeling the wind buffeting the lean-to, snow sifting between the cracks. But the wood was still dry. Back inside, she knelt by the wood stove. *Thank you, Mike.* She loaded the wood as he had taught her, added kindling, checked the draft and then lit the new fire, which thrived on the air pouring down the chimney.

She moved Mimi away from the wood stove since a cool room was better for someone coughing and congested. She took the cast-iron kettle that sat on the wood stove, filled it with water and set it back on the stove to make hot tea with honey for Mimi. Then she poured cereal and milk for Cindy and brought it into the living room.

With no TV or radio, the only sound came from the wind, buffeting the house and the wet snow, slapping the windowpanes. Even the kittens fell silent, hovering on the girls' laps. Finally Jeannie spooned the warm tea into Mimi's mouth, knowing that tea was a natural expectorant and the honey would soothe Mimi's throat. *Dear God, help me do everything right.*

Again the phone call tried to force itself to the front of her mind. A wave of panic clenched her stomach. She shook it off. No time for anything but Mimi now. Nothing bad was going to happen to her girls—if she could help it.

The hours dragged on. The noise of the wind and snow knotted the muscles at the back of Jeannie's neck. She read the girls story after story. And when Mimi fell asleep, Cindy sat coloring listlessly in a book near the window. But Jeannie found herself pacing and wishing she had one of those battery-operated weather radios that they were always telling people to buy. About three o'clock in the endless afternoon, Jeannie hovered over Mimi.

Her little girl's breathing had become more and more labored and her fever had spiked. Jeannie didn't need to take her temperature. Mimi's face was flushed red. She woke and could barely draw a breath without going into a coughing spasm. Little Twinkie mewed loudly as if worried, too.

"I have to get help," Jeannie said at last.

"The snow's too deep to drive," Cindy said.

"I can walk to Dr. Jake's house. His father is a doctor. Mimi needs a doctor."

"You'll leave us alone?" Cindy sounded afraid. "What if Mimi gets sicker? I won't know what to do."

Jeannie stooped down to be at eye level. "I can dress warm and follow the fence around to the house. It's not far, less than a half-mile. You stay with your sister. I'll be back with help before you know it."

Cindy looked worried.

"I'll add some logs to the fire and then bundle up." Jeannie did this, and soon she stood ready to open the door. "While I'm gone, watch your sister. Help her."

"I will, Mom." Cindy rushed to Jeannie and hugged her waist. "I'll take care of Mimi. Come back soon."

"I will. Just stay inside where it's warm. Don't go outside—no matter what. You must be brave and keep watch over your sister."

Cindy nodded solemnly and moved to stand by Mimi as if taking up her post. Both of them gazed at her; worry strained their expressions.

Reluctant to leave them, Jeannie forced herself to open the door. Wind gushed inside and wet snow slapped her face. She bent into the wind, pushing herself outside. Navigating the snowdrifts, she headed toward the fence she could barely see. Finally, she gripped the first post of the fence that bordered Jake's property on the roadside. She was already panting.

The memory of Mimi's flushed face and labored breathing made her push on. Snow swirled around her, and soon she couldn't see the little house or even the road, only a few feet away. Though she'd tied her hood tight and wrapped the lower half of her face with her scarf, snow still covered her face. She had to keep wiping the snowflakes from her eyelashes. Only the fence kept her on course. She paused to catch her breath.

The snow surrounded her in its white muffled folds. She gasped for breath and cold filled her lungs. Stark terror splashed through her. She clung to the fence post. Wave after wave of fear crashed over her, more than warranted.

What's happening to me?

The image in her mind yanked her back years and years. Her mother was lying unconscious on the floor of the bedroom. *Mama, don't die. Please don't die. I have to get help.*

She shuddered sharply. And then she snapped back to the present, clinging to the post, still terrified. Jeannie realized she'd viewed the scene from the past as if it were right in front of her, here and now.

But it's not here and now. Mimi is here and now, and she needs me. She pushed the bad memory away and ventured forward, keeping one mitten gripping the fence wire loosely, maintaining constant contact with her guide. Within, she trembled from the force of strong emotion. Outwardly she shivered from the cold, the penetrating cold.

She began to count the fence posts one by one—ten, eleven, twelve. How many would it take to reach Jake? To get to help?

At last, she reached the corner post and turned. Not much farther and she'd come to their drive. A strong gust knocked her from her feet. She flailed in the snow as if drowning. She gasped, rolled over and regained her feet. She wrapped her arms around the fence post again and wiped the snow from her face, gasping.

She struggled on, and then the fence ended. She had made it to Jake's drive. She looked backward but couldn't see the road. How could she make sure not to miss the house, not to get lost in the snow?

The fence post stood to her right. If she walked straight, she would go up the drive. What if she missed the house, invisible in the storm? Normally that thought would be ridiculous. Not today.

She sidestepped once, twice, on and on to her right till the third fence post was right behind her. If she walked straight ahead now, she would hit some part of the house. She stiffened herself to do this.

As much as possible in the driving wind and snow, she made herself put one foot in front of the other. The wind hit her from all sides. She breathed through her nose and bent almost double to protect her eyes, the only part of her exposed to the elements. Moving through the snow drifts was like swimming through thick mud.

Then she stumbled and fell forward. She'd tripped on the first of the front steps. She moved along the step and found the railing. She crawled up the steps, over the porch to the front door. She dragged herself erect and then battled the wind to wrench open the snow-encrusted storm door. She banged the brass knocker on the door. "Jake! Jake!" she yelled.

The door opened and she fell inside.

"Jeannie?"

Strong hands pulled her up. The door slammed behind her. Someone pulled away her sodden scarf and she looked up into Jake's face.

"Jeannie, what's wrong? Why did you come?"

Bummer was barking wildly.

Her heart pounded. Her throat closed. She burst into tears.

Jake trapped her cold face between his warm hands. "What's wrong? What's happened?"

"Mimi," she gasped. "She's much worse. I think it's pneumonia. She's having trouble breathing. High fever. Can your dad come? She needs a doctor."

Jake pulled her farther inside, calling to Bummer to be quiet. Before she could stop him, he dragged off her snow-coated jacket and hung it to drip by the door. Then he led her to the hearth where a healthy fire burned. She huddled by it, warming her numbed hands and feet. Mike, Bummer, and Jake hovered near her.

"Jake." She shivered, stuttering again. "Mimi's really bad. She can hardly breathe. I have to go right back. Can your father go with me?"

Jake nodded for her to look at the sofa. Dan lay there. He tried to sit up. "I'm not in much better shape, Jeannie."

He did look terrible, pale and shaky. She glanced up at Jake.

"What happened?" she asked.

"I passed out again, and my blood pressure is dangerously high," Dan said, sounding disgusted. "If the weather weren't so bad, Jake would have driven me to the E.R. this morning. The county roads are all closed, and we've been warned that not even ambulances are running."

"Earlier I intended to take the girls there, too. But I couldn't even get them to the car. Snow drifts."

Jake motioned toward their bright yellow weather radio on the table beside Dan. "The storm is supposed to last through the night."

All her hopes had been here, getting help here. She sagged against the fireplace. "What can I do then? What if Mimi can't breathe?"

Jake put an arm around her. "I'll come. But I'm a vet. I can't prescribe drugs for or treat humans." Bummer whined as if he knew something was very wrong.

"Tell you what," Mike said. "I parked my snowmobile in the barn the last time I used it. Use that and take Jeannie up behind you."

"That's right," Dan said, sounding encouraging. "I've got my cell. Jake, you can assess Mimi's condition and call me with her symptoms. If she needs me, I'll come. But you go first and see if she's critical."

Jake opened his mouth and then closed it.

"Jeannie," Dan continued earnestly, "I'm taking it for granted that you know that a child with a cough or congestion is better in a cool, but not cold room, right?"

Jeannie nodded. "Yes, I've got the wood stove keeping us warm. But Mimi is across the room, not near it. And I don't have her all bundled up. I am a certified nursing assistant, but I can't do more than I have. She's got a bad fever and her breathing is labored. She's spit up blood traces, too. I understand enough to know those are bad signs."

Dan looked more serious at this. Bummer woofed as if urging action.

"Okay," Dan urged Jake, "go. I know you don't want to have anything to do with a snowmobile. But you remember how to use one. Look at Jeannie. You can't think of making her trudge through a blizzard twice."

Jeannie hung on each word. Jake had to come. He must.

"Just follow the fence line and you'll be fine," Mike said.

"Call me when you get there," Dan said. "Examine the child and tell me what you find. Mike, will you get him my stethoscope from my room. You can listen to her lungs for congestion. It's the same sound in animals or humans. If she needs something, I have some meds in the emergency medical supply I always carry with me."

Jake hesitated.

Dan made as if to stand. "Jake, if you won't go, then I'll have to—"

Jake motioned for his dad to stay on the sofa. "I'm on it. Come on, Jeannie."

Her knees were jelly, but she managed to grip Jake's elbow.

"Get her something dry to wear," Mike said.

Jake led Jeannie through the dining room to the kitchen and the back hall. Bummer trailed after them. Jake handed her one of the extra jackets hanging there along with large mittens and a scarf. Her heartbeat thrumming, she struggled into the outerwear, her fingers and toes still numb.

He quickly dressed himself in a one-piece black-and-white snowmobile suit that looked at bit short on him. "Mike's," he explained.

Even though she wanted to get home, she grabbed his arm. Worry ratcheted her nerves tighter. "I've never ridden a snowmobile."

"Don't worry. I remember how."

"But you haven't ridden for a long time, right?"

"Right. But it's like riding a bicycle. I remember." His tone was grim and Jeannie thought she knew why. But she couldn't let anything interfere with taking care of her girls.

Mike came to them and handed Jake a doubled plastic bag, wrapped tight around something narrow. "I put the stethoscope in this."

Jake nodded. "You go back and stay with Dad. I'll call when I get there."

Mike squeezed Jake's shoulder and turned back, holding onto Bummer's collar so he couldn't follow them.

Jake paused and looked into Jeannie's eyes. "I tied a line between the barn and the back of the house before the blizzard got up to speed. I put my outdoor dogs in the barn with the shelter animals. I needed to be able to get to them. So we can follow that." He opened the door and led her out. Bummer bayed wildly against the wind. The snow surrounded them and shoved them against each other.

She clung to Jake's greater body mass as ballast. He wrapped his arm loosely around her shoulders, shielding her. Ahead, she could see glimpses of the tall red barn flicker between gales of snow.

More and more she leaned into Jake's embrace. Struggling in the wind, assaulted by the heavy wet snow, her strength lagged. She was panting now and sweating under her jacket while her face, feet and hands numbed again with cold.

They reached the barn and Jake drew her inside. She bent forward, her hands braced against her knees, gasping for air. The dogs and cats greeted them loudly. Jake shouted to his dogs to be quiet.

He patted her back and then swung a tarp off a snowmobile. He handed her a helmet and donned one himself. "It's good we're not going far. I only have one face mask. You hide behind me and keep your head low, okay?"

"Right." She'd never ridden a snowmobile, but she could hang on from here to Milwaukee if she had to. She could do whatever it took to get Mimi the help she needed.

Straddling the machine, Jake walked it forward. He reached the door, leaned forward to open it and nosed the machine into the storm. He started the engine and then helped Jeannie straddle the rear seat.

"Hang on tight!" he called over the wind as he remounted the machine. She hugged his waist. They were off!

Jake leaned his head low, seeking the protection of the windshield. He drove down his drive and when he saw the fence post and mailbox, turned sharply, heading toward the little house on the dead end.

They rode at an angle, following the high side of the roadside drainage ditch. The machine ran rough. Jake glanced down at the gas gauge—only a quarter of a tank. He strained his eyes, keeping track of the fence posts, his only reference point in the white world around them.

He slowed, knowing that the fence would turn soon. He didn't want to, couldn't overshoot the fence line. He located the last fence post and hung a left. Not far now. He hated to think of the girls alone in the little house. And of Jeannie braving the blizzard, alone and on foot, to get help.

Again, the fence turned left. He swung wide around the corner, up the drive to the little house. He tucked the vehicle right inside the shelter of the lean-to where Mike usually kept it.

Jeannie leaped off, shouldered by him, and rushed inside. "Cindy! Mimi! I'm back with Dr. Jake!"

He turned off the motor and headed in after her. In the kitchen he stripped off his snowmobile suit and set his helmet on the counter. He hurried into the living room. Jeannie had shed her outerwear on her way to Mimi. She knelt beside the little girl.

Jake ripped open the plastic bags to get the stethoscope. Murmuring soft soothing words to Mimi, he breathed on the metal instrument to warm it and then slid it under the back of her pajama top. "When I press the stethoscope on your skin, take a deep breath for me, okay?"

"Do what he says, Mimi," Jeannie coaxed, sitting on the other side of the child.

Mimi tried to obey, but each time she inhaled, she began coughing. Jeannie murmured and stroked the little girl's arm.

The other twin hovered nearby, holding both kittens and looking near tears. "Is my sister going to be okay?"

Jake persevered and listened to Mimi's lungs. He slipped Jeannie's thermometer under the girl's tongue. And he frowned when finding she had a fever of just over one hundred and two degrees. Not dangerous, but not good. When he finished, he hoped to sound reassuring. But he couldn't evade the truth.

"How is she?" Jeannie asked.

Jake rose. "I think she does have pneumonia. And—"

Mimi began to shake, her teeth chattering. "Mom," she moaned. "I'm so cooold."

Jeannie looked to him, her face drained of color.

"She's having chills, another symptom. I'm going to call my dad."

"Can I give her some more tea with honey?" Jeannie asked.

"Yes, she needs liquids, and the honey will help soothe her throat and quiet her cough."

Jake flipped open his cell phone and speed-dialed his dad's cell.

His father picked up on the first ring. "What did you find?"

"She has a fever of one hundred and two, chills and her lungs are congested." Jake didn't try to lower his voice. The girls needed to learn about illness, and Jeannie needed the facts.

"Then you better come back and get me—"

"Dad, I—"

"Jake, I'm going to give her an antibiotic and an expectorant to break up the congestion. She might not have bacterial pneumonia, but we can't get her to the hospital for a lab test. Even if she has viral pneumonia, an antibiotic will keep her from developing complications. Come and get me. I'll be dressed and standing by the back door." His dad hung up on him.

Jake relayed this to Jeannie. Shrugging on the snowmobile suit in the kitchen, he looked back to see Jeannie and Cindy in the doorway watching him. "I'll be back as soon as I can." His stomach did a figure-eight lurch. His dad shouldn't be out in this harsh weather. Suddenly how much he loved his father flooded him, nearly overflowing into tears. He stepped outside into the gale and swung his leg over the snowmobile. *God, keep us. Keep Mimi and my dad safe. Lay Your healing hands upon them.*

Chapter Twelve

His father was waiting for him just inside the back door. Hearing his master come in, Bummer bayed from the kitchen. Jake recognized the challenging glint in his dad's eye. His dad had dressed warmly and had a muffler wrapped around his face. Through the weave of the muffler, Jake glimpsed a white mask over his mouth. Cold like this would dangerously stress his dad's hearts and lungs. Dan climbed on back and Jake zoomed off, his nerves buzzing. *I hope Mike's gas gauge is accurate. God, get us there and back without any bad consequences.*

Memories of his mom and brother flashed in his mind as he navigated the storm-ravaged landscape. The half mile had never seemed as far before. At last, he turned up Jeannie's drive and zipped into the lean-to. As Dan got off the machine, he staggered.

Jake grabbed his arm and steadied him. Then he swung his leg off the machine and pushed his dad toward the kitchen door. Inside, they stripped off their outerwear. Cindy ran to them and threw her arms around Dan's waist. "You came! Dr. Dan, my sister needs you."

Cindy dragged Jake's dad by the hand into the living room. Jake followed them. Jeannie sat with her arm around Mimi, who reclined against her mom.

"Dr. Dan," Mimi whispered. Jeannie didn't say a word aloud, but her eyes implored Dan for help.

Jake moved to stand behind Jeannie to support her. Adrenaline had his heart on high idle.

His father knelt by the sofa. He pressed his palm to Mimi's forehead. "I'm going to give you some medicine that should make you feel better. First, though, we need to get some moisture in this air."

He looked up. "Jake, go out and get a heavy pan full of snow and put it on the wood stove. We'll let it warm and put some moisture in the air. That will make it easier for this girl to breathe."

Dan rose. "Cindy, please stay with your sister. I have to break up this pill. It's too big, too strong for a little girl."

Jake squeezed Jeannie's shoulder and started for the kitchen to snag a bucket from the pantry.

"Will the medicine taste bad?" Cindy asked, taking her sister's hand. The kittens hovered close by.

"I'll mix it with a little jelly and then it shouldn't be too bad," Dan said, heading toward the kitchen. "Jeannie, I need a set of measuring spoons and Mimi's favorite jelly."

Jake walked outside and returned with a bucket of fresh snow. Jeannie was handing his dad a jar of grape jelly.

"Jeannie, do you have any acetaminophen in the house?" Dan asked.

"Yes. I didn't give it to her because I didn't know if it would help her or make her condition worse."

"As a general rule, acetaminophen is safe for children as long as you follow the dosage. It'll help lower her fever. Aspirin is what you want to avoid because of the possibility of Reye's syndrome. So let's give her the antibiotic and the fever reducer. She should be feeling a bit better soon."

He looked at Jake. "Get that pail on the wood stove. Moist air will help her breathing."

The three of them joined the twins in the living room. Jeannie coaxed Mimi to sit up straighter. She sat down beside her daughter again, letting the child lean against her. Too sick to object, Mimi took her two doses of medicine. Then Jake and his dad sat down across from Jeannie. Cindy climbed onto Jake's lap and lay against him.

Jake studied his father. He appeared spent, and Jake knew he'd crash soon from his own adrenaline high. Dan laid his head back and closed his eyes. Cindy closed hers, too, so Jake rose and carried her to bed and laid her down and covered her. "Will Mimi be all right?" Cindy asked in a scared little voice.

"Yes, you can rest now. My dad won't let anything bad happen to her." Jake leaned over and kissed her forehead.

Then he went to Dan. "Dad." He shook his shoulder gently. "Come and lie down on Jeannie's bed. You'll be more comfortable."

Dan didn't argue. He rose, and with a hand on Jake's shoulder to steady himself, he followed his son into the bedroom. Jake pulled the covers up over the unmade bed and Dan lay down on Jeannie's quilt. Jake found an afghan on the chair and spread it over his dad.

"Jake, I've been carrying nitro tablets for a while. I'm going to finally take one." His dad slipped a tablet from a small bottle and placed the pill under his tongue.

Jake nodded his approval, relief nearly weakening his knees. "Get some rest, Dad. I'm going to stoke the fire."

Dan nodded and closed his eyes.

Back in the small living room, Jake opened the wood stove door and set several new logs in and then shut the door. When he stood, he heard his father's quiet whiffling snore.

Jake staggered to the sofa, drowning in a sudden backwash of emotional exhaustion. "Jeannie, let me carry Mimi to bed."

She looked up. "I'm afraid to let go of her."

Her plaintive tone brought him to his knees. He knelt by her. "You don't have to be afraid. My dad's here. He's given her medicine and he's sleeping on your bed. If he thought she was in critical condition, he would never have left her side."

She nodded and stroked his cheek once. Then she moved Mimi toward him.

Jake lifted Mimi and carried her to her bed and laid her down. Cindy was already napping. Maybe the constant sound of the wind and lashing snow had lulled her to sleep, too. Jeannie covered Mimi with a light blanket and knelt beside the bed, obviously praying.

Jake gazed at Jeannie. With her hair mussed and her clothing rumpled, she had never looked more beautiful to him. Her true beauty lay in the way she bent to kiss Mimi's forehead and the gentle way she patted the very sick child.

"Jeannie, I'm in love with you." Hearing his own words out loud shook him. But he'd only spoken the truth.

She looked at him, her expression full of worry, and he took her hand and helped her up. Her face drawn, she led him from the room. She sat down on the sofa and patted the cushion beside her. "Something bad has happened." Her voice sounded oddly disconnected.

His mind took him back to her preoccupation last night. Brooke's dinner party seemed ages ago. He sank down beside her and lifted her hand to his lap where he cradled it between his. "Tell me."

"Yesterday, no…" She fell silent, her face twisted as if in pain. "What day is it?"

"Sunday."

"That's right." She rubbed her forehead. "I probably sound nuts. But if this is Sunday, then that means it happened just before we went to Brooke's. I remember being at Brooke's, but it was like a dream or something, like I wasn't really there."

"You didn't act like yourself. You were—" He struggled for the right word. "You were on autopilot."

"That's troubling."

"You said something bad happened?" Almost afraid to ask, he kissed her hand and held it close to him. He had to know the truth.

"Carrie called me. I think it sent me into some kind of shock."

He moved closer. "Your sister called?"

She nodded. "Ever since your dad gave Mimi the medicine, it started coming back to me, the reality of what she told me." She pressed her lips together.

He put his arm around her and pulled her close. "I'm here."

She glanced up. "I know. You are very much here." She took a deep breath. "Carrie said she'd been in prison."

"In prison? But why wouldn't the police have told you that?"

"She said she used an assumed name, the one she'd been using in Detroit." Jeannie's voice trembled.

He pulled her even closer, longing to comfort her. "Jeannie, I'm so sorry. That must have been a real shock."

"She…she said she was going to get a job so she could take back the girls. I hung up on her."

"What? Doesn't she realize that she's a stranger to the twins?" Agitation stirred him—charging him up. Jake worked to keep his voice down. "You're the only mom they've ever known."

Jeannie rested her head on his chest. "I don't want to fight my sister for her children, but—"

"You won't fight her unless she won't see reason. She has yet to prove she can be a mom." Outrage, heat, flooded Jake's face and neck. "You've proven you're a great mom." He kissed her hair. "And nobody better say different."

"I want to be happy that Carrie has finally contacted me. But you're right. I can't let her do anything that will harm the girls. If that means fighting her, I'll fight." Jeannie's voice hardened.

Jake turned this over in his mind, sorting it out. His tension eased. He took a breath. "I don't think you'll have to fight her.

You just said she went to prison under an assumed name. She won't want a court case where that can be brought to light. A recently released felon, trying to convince a judge to give her custody of children she's had no contact with since they were babies—I don't think so."

"But maybe after last night, I shouldn't be taking care of the twins either." She lowered her face.

He gripped her chin and turned her face toward him. "What would make you say that?"

A lone tear dripped down her soft cheek. "Well, I went into shock after Carrie called. Maybe I'm not stable either." She tried to turn, but he held on.

"Jake, I never told you this, but our mother, Carrie's and mine, died in an institution. She was deeply depressed most of her life. That's how Carrie and I ended up in foster care. Maybe neither Carrie nor I should be taking care of the twins—"

"Stop speaking nonsense." Jake gripped her chin more firmly. "Your being severely shocked by your sister's totally out of the blue call and her threatening to take the twins from you is normal. And you've recovered already. You're speaking rationally."

He let go of her chin and stroked her cheek, meeting her eyes with honesty. "I recall from my psych classes that a person can experience a trauma shock, which can have the effect you described. It's sort of related to post-traumatic shock disorder but is limited to one event and is usually short-lived. Now I don't want you to say that you aren't one of the best moms I know again." He tucked her closer.

She snuggled into his shoulder. "Oh, Jake, I'm so glad you're here. When I went out into the storm to get you, I had a terrible flashback to the worst night of my life." She shuddered against him.

"I know what that's like." The faces of his mom and Tommy crowded in and he blocked them out. He had to be here for Jeannie, not dwell on his own past. "What happened? Tell me and set yourself free."

"You sound very wise."

"If I do, it's newly developed. Now tell me." He kissed her forehead, wanting to kiss her lips, but knowing that must and could wait.

"Carrie was still a baby and I was just starting kindergarten." Jeannie's voice sounded small and tight. "I think my mom must have overdosed on something, some prescription medicine, maybe. I heard a loud sound, something heavy falling, and went into the bedroom. She was unconscious on the floor. I thought she might have died. We didn't have a phone and we lived in a bad neighborhood, so I wasn't allowed to go outside by myself."

Jake hugged her. *Jeannie, my sweet Jeannie.*

"But I had to get help. I went to the other apartment doors and knocked, calling for help. Nobody was home or would answer. So I ran out on the street and went to the corner drugstore. The man there called the police and an ambulance."

She paused, burrowing closer to him. "We never lived together as a family again. Fortunately, a foster family took both Carrie and me so we weren't split up. But my mother never recovered. Once in a while, a social worker would take us to visit her. But our mom was never better again, never able to face life again."

Jake wrapped his arms around Jeannie tighter. He kissed her hair, her forehead, her eyes and then dipped lower to kiss her lips. "I love you, Jeannie. I want you in my life, now and forever."

"Are you ready for a package deal?" she asked with a wry twist of her lips.

"Wouldn't want it any other way. I love your girls, you know that."

"I do. I'd given up hope, but you do love them. I see it in your eyes and hear it in your voice." She let out a long, deep sigh. "Oh, Jake, I love you, too. I have since that first night we found the kittens. I just couldn't admit it." She turned toward him fully and lifted her mouth for another kiss.

"My sweet Jeannie." Jake bent his chin and pressed his lips to hers.

Finally, they parted and Jeannie sighed a very different sigh from her earlier one. "I've always felt an irrational guilt over not somehow saving my mom. I didn't realize that the guilt was still there in the back of my head. It was. But no more."

Jake's memory took him back. He was a kid again, holding a phone, and a cop was saying, "Your mother and brother have had an accident." Guilt wrapped around his lungs. Jeannie had used the right words: irrational guilt. *I couldn't have changed anything even if I'd been there.*

He tuned back to what Jeannie was saying, "I am not my mother. I'm not Carrie. I'm Jeannie. And I won't let Carrie take my girls from me. It's not that I don't want her in their lives, but she has done nothing to prove that she can be a good mom."

"Except for leaving her girls with you." *A very wise and loving woman.*

Jeannie smiled. She stroked his cheek. "I love you."

He kissed her lightly in reply. "My Jeannie." *My true match.* Joy bubbled up inside him.

She closed her eyes and rested against him. He didn't want to move, didn't want this precious moment to end. The wind lashed the windows, but its frost couldn't touch him. Winter was past in his heart, in both their hearts.

A few hours later, Jake heard movement down the hall. He eased himself from under Jeannie's head. She had fallen deeply asleep and he had moved her head onto his lap. Now he got up and went to see if his dad or the girls needed him. *My girls.* The wonder that he would soon have a family of his own, with a wonderful woman and two great kids, filled him up. He nearly chuckled out loud.

His father stood in the doorway of the girls' bedroom. Jake came up behind him and rested a hand on his dad's back. "How are you feeling?"

His dad jerked slightly in surprise. "Not too good. Not too bad. When this storm ends, we'll call Lewis. He'll want me back in Madison as soon as this weather moves out."

Jake rested a hand on Dan's shoulder and looked past him. Cindy and Mimi were sleeping the peaceful sleep of innocence.

"Looks like we've all enjoyed our long winter's nap," his father said, a smile in his voice.

"I'm going to check the fire. How about a cup of tea?" Jake nearly rubbed the area over his heart. For the first time he could recall, he didn't feel that choked sensation when speaking to his father. He'd shed the past today.

"Sounds good," Dan agreed.

They headed toward the kitchen. Jake stopped, opened the wood stove door and added a few logs. Then gripping the potholder around the handle, he carried the steaming cast-iron kettle to the kitchen.

His father was preparing ham and cheese sandwiches at the counter. "I don't think Jeannie will mind if we help ourselves. And if you look at your watch, you'll see it's nearly seven. My stomach woke me up."

"Make me one, too. In fact, make me two." His appetite roared for food.

Soon Jake joined his dad at the table. He picked up a sandwich. And then he stopped to bow his head for a silent grace and a quick thank-you to God. When he looked up, his dad was eyeing him.

"I haven't seen you do that for years."

"This has been an important day in my life." Jake smiled, knowing that this time he and his dad could just talk, not argue.

"Are you and Jeannie going to get together?"

"Yes, I've proposed and she's accepted." Would his dad stick to his opinion that Jeannie wasn't good for Jake?

Dan finished chewing and lifted his cup of tea. "Bummer will be delighted." He paused. "Proposing takes guts."

His dad's hesitation didn't stir his stomach as usual. Jake lifted his sandwich for another bite. "Not really. Jeannie is an amazing woman, and I'm getting two great daughters in the deal."

His dad studied him. "You sound different."

"I feel different." He took a deep full breath. "It feels good. Dad, we've been separated by more than miles since Mom and Tommy died." Jake chewed, waiting. Would his dad change the subject, say something wounding?

"We have. You've blamed me for not being here. And I've blamed myself."

Jake wondered why, here in the dimly lit room with the sound of wind under their words, they could speak about what had torn them apart for years. "I blamed myself, too." His voice came out gruff.

His dad looked up sharply. "Why?"

Jake shrugged. "Survivor's guilt. I think I thought irrationally that if I'd been there, I could have stopped the accident from happening."

"That's ridiculous. The only difference would have been that you would have witnessed it happening. And that wouldn't have made the loss any easier."

"Harder." Jake drew in an easy breath and took another bite of the sandwich. Ham and cheese had never tasted better.

Dan nodded solemnly, sipping his tea. "Now that's in the past once and for all. Neither of us could have prevented their deaths. And for the record, I loved them both. After it happened, I thought I would die, too, for a while. And coming here was such a reminder of all I'd lost. That's why I stayed away."

Jake rested a hand on his dad's arm. "I know."

Dan pressed a hand over Jake's. "I won't be a coward anymore. And a few days ago when I saw what so many in this community feel about you and your work here, it made me realize that I've missed out on being a part of this community. When I was young, I just wanted to get out into the world. I wanted no part of farming. My dad gave me his blessing, though I'm sure it was hard for him to accept that I wouldn't be taking on the farm." He lifted his sandwich.

"Grandpa never said anything."

Dan grinned. "He wouldn't. From now on, I'm not going to be traveling around speaking and demonstrating surgical procedures. Or skiing downhill in Colorado. That's hard for me to swallow. What will I do?"

Free of the past, free of guilt and resentment, Jake spoke without hesitation. "I've got something you can help with. Something good."

The wind stopped blowing that evening. Jeannie joined Jake looking out the front window. "They'll be able to send the crews out now to get the power lines fixed and the roads plowed," Jake said.

Jeannie wrapped her arms around Jake's chest and rested her head against him. Love for this man expanded within her, warm and full. *I'll always remember this happy day.*

Jake leaned down and kissed the top of her head. "Dad and I will stay till the power goes back on. Mike is home tending our fire so *our* pipes don't freeze this time."

The sound of feet pattered behind them. "Mom! Mimi's hungry."

They turned to see Cindy. Jake bent and swung the girl into his arms. "Then we know she's on the mend. When a sick kitten starts eating again, I know it will get better."

"Were you two hugging?" Cindy asked.

"Yes, we were hugging. I'm going to be your daddy."

Cindy whooped and hugged his neck. Then she leaped from his arms and raced toward her bedroom. "Mimi! Dr. Jake's going to be our daddy!"

Sitting on the couch reading, Dan called out, "And I'm going to be your grandpa!"

Love and joy spurted upward like a geyser within Jeannie's heart. *Thank You, God. Thank You.*

Chapter Thirteen

The April Fools' Day blizzard proved to be that record-breaking winter's grand finale. In the next three weeks of the awakening spring, work on Jeannie's Habitat house sped up. Today Jeannie would move into her new house. She stood in her front yard, surrounded by volunteers carrying in her meager furniture.

Jake had invited her to look in the barn loft and a few stalls for furniture. Since after their upcoming May wedding they would be living in her new house, she would root around there in the coming weeks, adding as needed.

Dan and Mike would live in the McClure family home while Dan helped with the fundraising for Jake's dream. A local plumber had donated his time to fix the burst pipes at the animal shelter, and the animals would soon return home.

Jeannie nearly danced in her driveway on New Friends Street. Her new house, her husband-to-be, how had these miracles happened, and to her? *God is good.*

With a loud crunching of brakes, a furniture van jerked to a stop at the curb. Soon a tall delivery man came forward. "Jeannie Broussard?"

Jeannie waved a hand and everyone stopped what they were doing to watch. She glanced around, wondering why everyone looked expectant.

"Got your new bunk bed bedroom set," the man said.

"What? I didn't order—"

"Yeah, I know." The man cut her off. "I been through this before with that house." He pointed to the Chamberses' house next door.

Rosa Chambers hurried forward. "I can't believe this." She turned to Jeannie. "The same thing happened to me the day I moved in. Somebody sent me a new bedroom set. I've never found out who sent it."

"But—" Jeannie started to object.

"Lady," the delivery man said, sounding put-upon, "all I do is make deliveries, and I got more than just yours today. Now where do I put the furniture? I got to set up the beds, too."

"Don't fight it, Jeannie," Rosa advised. "Just show him which room is the girls' bedroom."

Glancing around, Jeannie realized that she must accept this or be incredibly rude. Probably Jake or Dan had sent it. But they wouldn't have sent Rosa's, would they? "Follow me."

Within a few minutes, the bedroom set for her girls was in place and the two beds were ready for sheets. The delivery men just shrugged away all Jeannie's questions. She watched them drive away and said a silent thank-you to God for the beautiful walnut bedroom set.

A cheerful hubbub filled the rest of the day. Moving in, a potluck with the volunteers and then many, many thank-yous and goodbyes. Finally, only Jeannie, Jake and the twins remained around the kitchen table. At the door ready to leave, Dan and Brooke were petting the kittens and Bummer.

Jeannie's cordless phone sounded. She lifted the receiver. "Hi, this is Jeannie."

"Hi, this is Carrie."

Jeannie's heart lurched against her breastbone. She waved and mouthed goodbye to Brooke and Dan. Then she walked back to her bedroom and shut the door for privacy. "I was wondering why you hadn't called back."

"I've been busy."

Jeannie tried to analyze her sister's voice, but couldn't. She decided to set the tone for this conversation. "Carrie, I went into shock the last time you called. But now that I've had time to think, I need to make it clear to you that my main goal is doing what's best for the twins. You are their birth mother, but I'm the only mother they've ever known. I will not let you come in and disrupt their lives and—"

"You're right," Carrie cut in. "I…I wasn't thinking the last time I called. I was living in a dream world where I'd get a job right away and get a nice place and we could all live together. I've been forced since then to face reality."

"Where are you?"

"I came back to Milwaukee and found our old social worker. She got me into a group home for women who have gotten out of prison or some other bad situation. I'm going to school to get my GED, and then I'm going to work on getting certified as a nursing assistant."

Jeannie's heart stopped pounding. "That sounds good, Carrie. That's what I did. Now I work at a vet clinic as the office manager. I want you to know that Cindy and Mimi know I'm their aunt and that when they were babies, their mom disappeared. So they know the truth. But they call me Mom. It was hard enough that they didn't have a dad. They didn't want to call me Aunt Jeannie when they got old enough to understand."

"I get that. I do." A pause. "Jeannie, do you think I can really get my life together?"

Jeannie listened to Jake and the girls down the hall in the living room. She looked around at her brand-new house. "Yes, I do, Carrie. You need to work at your education and get yourself sorted out. I want you to be in the girls' lives, but not till you're at a better place in your life. You can take time to work on your future. The twins are happy and doing well."

"Thanks to you." Carrie sounded tearful. "I messed up my life. I don't want to do that to my girls."

"Your life doesn't have to stay messed up, Carrie." Jeannie wanted to speak to Carrie about seeking God's will but felt that this wasn't the time. A time would come. "You'll come through this."

Carrie began to weep. "Jeannie, I'm so sorry. I never meant for all this to happen."

Jeannie soothed her sister, wrote down her phone number and promised to call soon. Jeannie hung up and turned at the knock at the door.

Jake halted in the doorway, looking toward her, a question brimming in his expression.

She went to him and wrapped her arms around his chest. She rested her cheek against his soft flannel shirt.

"Is everything all right?" he murmured.

She nodded against him. "Carrie's in a group home in Milwaukee. She's getting her GED."

"She didn't say anything about taking the girls?" Jake asked in a whisper.

"No, she realized she's in no shape to take care of them." Jeannie looked up at him. "She doesn't want to do anything to make them feel insecure."

"Glad to hear it." He kissed her forehead.

"Did you or your dad buy the bedroom set?" She nodded toward the furniture in the room.

"No for both of us. I figured we were either going to move in more family pieces or go shopping together. Do you like it?"

"I love it. What a special gift. I just wish I knew who to thank."

Jake hugged her close. "I need to get going. I have some important stuff to do."

Jeannie lifted her face to him, and he obligingly kissed her. "I'm looking forward to your not having to go home anywhere but here."

"Me, too. A few weeks and I won't have to leave you every night."

Jeannie hugged him and he hugged her back. Her heart threatened to burst with the joy of his touch, of his constant love, of this evidence of God's love for her.

Epilogue

The wedding march was being played on the church organ. In the church foyer, Jeannie slipped her arm into Dan's. Since she had no father, Dan had volunteered to walk her down the aisle. She had gratefully accepted. She'd also accepted Brooke's loan of her wedding dress, a long white sheath. Brooke had even altered it a bit to fit Jeannie's long silhouette by adding a wide ruffle of white satin around the hem.

Ginny and the twins, all three dressed in their Sunday best, waited to head down the aisle. Ginny nudged the girls and they started down the aisle first, clutching their kittens, Twinkie and Peanutbutter, instead of bouquets. They had insisted that the kittens had brought Jeannie and Jake together and should be at the wedding. So Jeannie had gone along with their request.

Then Ginny started down the aisle, carrying a bouquet of red tulips from her garden.

Dan led Jeannie forward. She clutched her bouquet of tulips too, letting the anticipation lift her. Soon the organ struck the signal chords and they began walking toward Jake.

Jake stood at the front of Jeannie's small church, which had recently become his, too. Beside him stood Mike, his best man, and between them sat Bummer, best dog. Bummer was wearing a white bow tie and looked very solemn.

Dan and Jeannie arrived at the front. Dan placed her hand into Jake's and then went to sit beside Brooke. The twins stood on tiptoe to kiss her and then went to sit with Dan and Brooke.

Jeannie looked up into Jake's eyes. Joy such as she had never known rippled through her. She tried not to cry. But she couldn't hold back a few tears, because she knew that Carrie sat on a rear pew. Someday Jeannie hoped that Carrie would be an everyday part of their life. Today Carrie would be introduced to the twins as an old friend from Milwaukee.

Right now as she and Jake looked toward the minister, she made herself focus on this precious moment, a moment she'd thought would never come.

Jake drew her hand up and kissed it. Then the pastor began, "Dearly Beloved, we are gathered together to join this woman and this man in holy matrimony...."

After they had exchanged vows and rings, they turned to face the congregation. The pastor announced: "I present to you, Dr. and Mrs. Jake McClure."

Everyone clapped. Bummer bayed loud and long—sounding joyful, triumphant. And everyone clapped some more and laughed.

Jake took advantage of the moment and kissed his bride again, making her heart soar. All her hopes and dreams for a life of love were now hers. Her heart sang silently, *Praise God from whom all blessings flow.*

* * * * *

Dear Reader,

I hope you enjoyed Jeannie and Jake's story. I love to write stories of how God's love can overcome any sorrow, any past pain. In God, all things are possible—even reconciliation and forgiveness.

So who's sending a new bedroom set to each new Habitat for Humanity homeowner on New Friends Street? You'll have to read the final book in the series, *Building a Family*, to find the answer!

I also want to call to your attention to the Winter Carnival where the Mimi and Cindy "adopted" a little girl in Haiti. There are many charities that make this connection. My husband and I have supported Compassion International for over thirty years.

Drop by my blog http://StrongWomenBraveStories.blogspot.com and find the Compassion icon there. Or go directly to www.compassion.com to learn how you can sponsor a child who desperately needs food and education. Or write to Compassion International, Colorado Springs, CO 80997. Your small monthly support can change a life and impact so many other lives. You won't regret it.

Lyn Cote

P.S. Thanks to Terry and Sheree for naming the kittens on my blog.

QUESTIONS FOR DISCUSSION

1. Have you ever donated your time to something like Habitat for Humanity? If so, what and why?

2. Brooke, or poodle woman, turned out to be much different from how she appeared at first sight. Have you ever met someone whom you didn't like at first but who became a friend later?

3. Dan and Jake had been estranged for many years. Have you ever been estranged from a family member? Were you able to bridge the gap between you?

4. Have you ever lost touch with a family member or friend and wished you could reconnect? Were you able to?

5. Who do you think was Jake's mentor? Who do you think was Jeannie's mentor? Have you had a mentor or been a mentor?

6. Jeannie had tried romance and been disappointed because some men were unable to love her girls as their own. Why do you think some people can love stepchildren and step-parents and others can't?

7. Has there ever been a time in your life when God felt very close and became very real to you? Was it a happy time or a stressful one?

8. If you have a pet, what do you like most about having a pet in your life?

9. Do clothes make the woman?

10. Brooke admitted to getting into credit card debt. What advice would you give a person heading in that direction?

11. Have you ever sustained a shock like Jeannie did when her sister called after disappearing for seven years? How did it affect you?

12. Weather played a major role in this story. Have you ever faced extreme weather of any kind? If so, when and what?

13. Jake asked himself why some fathers and sons rub each other the wrong way. What do you think causes this kind of friction?

14. Who set Dan straight about Jeannie? Have you ever confronted someone in this way?

15. Do you think this story was realistic, true to life? If so, in what way or not?

INSPIRATIONAL

Inspirational romances to warm your heart & soul.

Love Inspired.

TITLES AVAILABLE NEXT MONTH

Available April 26, 2011

AN UNLIKELY MATCH
Chatam House
Arlene James

MIRIAM'S HEART
Hannah's Daughters
Emma Miller

HOME TO STAY
Annie Jones

BIG SKY REUNION
Charlotte Carter

THE FOREST RANGER'S PROMISE
Leigh Bale

INSTANT DADDY
Carol Voss

REQUEST YOUR FREE BOOKS!

2 FREE INSPIRATIONAL NOVELS
PLUS 2
FREE
MYSTERY GIFTS

Love Inspired®

YES! Please send me 2 FREE Love Inspired® novels and my 2 FREE mystery gifts (gifts are worth about $10). After receiving them, if I don't wish to receive any more books, I can return the shipping statement marked "cancel." If I don't cancel, I will receive 6 brand-new novels every month and be billed just $4.24 per book in the U.S. or $4.74 per book in Canada. That's a saving of at least 23% off the cover price. It's quite a bargain! Shipping and handling is just 50¢ per book in the U.S. and 75¢ per book in Canada.* I understand that accepting the 2 free books and gifts places me under no obligation to buy anything. I can always return a shipment and cancel at any time. Even if I never buy another book, the two free books and gifts are mine to keep forever.

105/305 IDN FDA5

Name	(PLEASE PRINT)	

Address		Apt. #

City	State/Prov.	Zip/Postal Code

Signature (if under 18, a parent or guardian must sign)

Mail to the **Reader Service:**
IN U.S.A.: P.O. Box 1867, Buffalo, NY 14240-1867
IN CANADA: P.O. Box 609, Fort Erie, Ontario L2A 5X3

Not valid for current subscribers to Love Inspired books.

**Are you a subscriber to Love Inspired books
and want to receive the larger-print edition?
Call 1-800-873-8635 or visit www.ReaderService.com.**

* Terms and prices subject to change without notice. Prices do not include applicable taxes. Sales tax applicable in N.Y. Canadian residents will be charged applicable taxes. Offer not valid in Quebec. This offer is limited to one order per household. All orders subject to credit approval. Credit or debit balances in a customer's account(s) may be offset by any other outstanding balance owed by or to the customer. Please allow 4 to 6 weeks for delivery. Offer available while quantities last.

Your Privacy—The Reader Service is committed to protecting your privacy. Our Privacy Policy is available online at www.ReaderService.com or upon request from the Reader Service.

We make a portion of our mailing list available to reputable third parties that offer products we believe may interest you. If you prefer that we not exchange your name with third parties, or if you wish to clarify or modify your communication preferences, please visit us at www.ReaderService.com/consumerschoice or write to us at Reader Service Preference Service, P.O. Box 9062, Buffalo, NY 14269. Include your complete name and address.

*Amish widow Hannah Goodloe's son has run away,
and to find him, she needs help—which circus owner
Levi Harmon can provide. If Hannah can convince him.
Read on for a sneak preview of HANNAH'S JOURNEY
by Anna Schmidt, the first book in the*
AMISH BRIDES OF CELERY FIELDS *series.*

"I HAVE REASON TO BELIEVE that my son is on your train," Hannah said. "I have come here to ask that you stop that train until Caleb can be found."

"Mrs. Goodloe, I am sympathetic to your situation, but surely you can understand that I cannot disrupt an entire schedule because you think your son…"

"He is on that train, sir," she repeated. She produced a lined piece of paper from the pocket of her apron and handed it to him. In a large childish script, the note read:

Ma, Don't worry. I'm fine and I know this is all a part of God's plan the way you always said. I'll write once I get settled and I'll send you half my wages by way of general delivery. Please don't cry, okay? It's all going to be all right. Love, Caleb

"There's not one word here that indicates…"

"He plans to send me part of his wages, Mr. Harmon. That means he plans to get a job. When we were on the circus grounds yesterday, I took note of a posted advertisement for a stable worker. My son has been around horses his entire life."

"And on that slimmest of evidence, you have assumed that your son is on the circus train that left town last night?"

She nodded. She waited.

"Mrs. Goodloe, please be reasonable. I have a business to run, several hundred employees who depend upon me, not to mention the hundreds of customers waiting along the way because they have purchased tickets for a performance tonight or tomorrow or the following day."

She said nothing but kept her eyes focused squarely on him.

"I am leaving at seven this evening for my home and summer headquarters in Wisconsin. Tomorrow, I will meet up with the circus train and make the remainder of the journey with them. If your boy is on that train, I will find him."

"Thank you," she said. "You are a good man, Mr. Harmon."

"There's one thing more, Mrs. Goodloe."

Anything, her eyes exclaimed.

"I expect you to come with me."

Don't miss HANNAH'S JOURNEY by Anna Schmidt, available May 2011 from Love Inspired Historical.

Love Inspired HISTORICAL

Save $1.00 when you purchase
2 or more Love Inspired® Historical books.

SAVE $1.00

when you purchase 2 or more Love Inspired® Historical books.

52609783

5 65373 00076 2 (8100)0 11736

LIHCOUPON1